Sto...

10/12

EC 201...

KT-431-247

ALSO BY NEIL GAIMAN AND
AL SARRANTONIO
FROM CLIPPER LARGE PRINT

Stories: Volume 1

Stories

All-New Tales Edited By

Neil Gaiman
and
Al Sarrantonio

Volume 2

W F HOWES LTD

This large print edition published in 2011 by
W F Howes Ltd
Unit 4, Rearsby Business Park, Gaddesby Lane,
Rearsby, Leicester LE7 4YH

1 3 5 7 9 10 8 6 4 2

First published in the United Kingdom in 2010
by Headline Review

A CIP catalogue record for this book is available
from the British Library

ISBN 978 1 40747 310 9

Typeset by Palimpsest Book Production Limited,
Falkirk, Stirlingshire
Printed and bound in Great Britain
by MPG Books Ltd, Bodmin, Cornwall

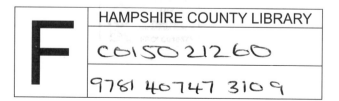

For all the storytellers and tale spinners who entertained the public and kept themselves alive, for Alexandre Dumas and Charles Dickens, for Mark Twain and Baroness Orczy and the rest, and most of all, for Scheherazade, who was the storyteller and the story told.

CONTENTS

Many loving thanks to Jennifer Brehl and Merrilee Heifetz, dual rudders on a long boat, for steering us safely to shore.

INTRODUCTION

JUST FOUR WORDS

Al Sarrantonio and I were discussing anthologies of short stories. He had edited a huge anthology of cutting-edge horror, and another of cutting-edge fantasy, each book, in its way, definitive. And in talking, we realised that we had something in common: that all we cared about, really, were the stories. What we missed, what we wanted to read, were stories that made us care, stories that forced us to turn the page. And yes, we wanted good writing (why be satisfied with less?). But we wanted more than that. We wanted to read stories that used a lightning flash of magic as a way of showing us something we have already seen a thousand times as if we have never seen it before. Truly, we wanted it all.

And slowly, the wish becomes the deed . . .

When I was a child, I pestered my elders for stories. My family would improvise, or read me stories from books. As soon as I was old enough to read, I was one of those children who needed to have a book within reach. I would read a book a day, or more. I wanted stories, and I wanted them always, and I wanted the experience that only fiction could give me: I wanted to be inside them.

Television and cinema were all very well, but these stories happened to other people. The stories I found in books happened inside my head. I was, in some way, there.

It's the magic of fiction: you take the words and you build them into worlds.

As time passed, I became a more discriminating reader (I remember the first time I realised I did not have to finish reading a book; the first time I realised that the way a story was told was getting in the way of the story). But even as I became more discriminating as a reader I started to feel that the thing that kept me reading, the place the magic occurred, the driving force of narrative was sometimes being overlooked. I would read beautiful prose, and I would simply not care.

It came down to four words.

There are the kind of readers who read only nonfiction: who read biographies, perhaps, or travel writing. Readers who read nothing but concrete poetry. There are those who read things that will improve them and their lot, who only read books that tell them how to survive the coming financial crisis, or have confidence in themselves, or play poker, or build beehives. I myself can sometimes be found reading books about beekeeping and, because I write fiction, am always happy to read strange factual things. Whatever we read, we are part of the community of the story.

There are nonreaders, of course. I knew a man in his nineties who, when he learned that I was a writer, admitted to me that he had tried to read a book, once, long before I was born, but he had been unable to see the point of it, and had never tried again. I asked him if he remembered the name of the book, and he told me, in the manner of someone who tried to eat a snail once and did not care for it, and who does not need to remember the breed of the snail, that one was much like another, surely.

Still. Four words.

And I didn't realise it until a couple of days ago, when someone wrote in to my blog:

Dear Neil,

If you could choose a quote – either by you or another author – to be inscribed on the wall of a public library children's area, what would it be?

Thanks!
Lynn

I pondered for a bit. I'd said a lot about books and kids' reading over the years, and other people had said things pithier and wiser than I ever could. And then it hit me, and this is what I wrote:

I'm not sure I'd put a quote up, if it was me, and I had a library wall to deface. I think I'd just remind people of the power of stories, of why they exist in the first place. I'd put up the four words that anyone telling a story wants to hear. The ones that show that it's working, and that pages will be turned:

'. . . and then what happened?'

The four words that children ask, when you pause, telling them a story. The four words you hear at the end of a chapter. The four words, spoken or unspoken, that show you, as a story-teller, that people care.

The joy of fiction, for some of us, is the joy of the imagination, set free from the world and able to imagine.

Talking to Al Sarrantonio I realised that I was not alone in finding myself increasingly frustrated with the boundaries of genre: the idea that categories which existed only to guide people around bookshops now seemed to be dictating the kind of stories that were being written. I love the word *fantasy*, for example, but I love it for the almost infinite room it gives an author to play: an infinite playroom, of a sort, in which the only boundaries are those of the imagination. I do not love it for the idea of commercial fantasy. Commercial fantasy, for good or for ill, tends to drag itself through already existing furrows, furrows dug by J. R. R. Tolkien or Robert E. Howard, leaving a world of stories behind it, excluding so much. There was so much fine fiction, fiction allowing free rein to the imagination of the author, beyond the shelves of genre. That was what we wanted to read.

It seemed to us that the fantastic can be, can do, so much more than its detractors assume: it can illuminate the real, it can distort it, it can mask it, it can hide it. It can show you the world you know in a way that makes you realise you've never looked at it, not *looked* at it. G. K. Chesterton compared fantastic fiction to going on holiday – that the importance of your holiday is the moment you return, and you see the place you live through fresh eyes.

And so the call went out from Mr Sarrantonio and from me, and the stories began to come back to us. Writers rose to the challenge. We learned to expect only the unexpected.

'. . . and then what happened?'

The real magic of this little invocation is that it has inspired hundreds of millions of words, has made people who never imagined themselves as storytellers into tale-tellers who could have given Scheherazade or Dunsany's Joseph Jorkens a run for their money or their whiskey or their lives. We turn the page, and the adventure begins.

There is something waiting for you. So turn the page.

Neil Gaiman
December 2009

LOSER

Chuck Palahniuk

The show still looks exactly like when you were sick with a really high fever and you stayed home to watch TV all day. It's not *Let's Make a Deal*. It's not *Wheel of Fortune*. It's not Monty Hall, or Pat Sajak. It's that other show where the big, loud voice calls your name in the audience, says to 'Come on down, you're the next contestant,' and if you guess the cost of Rice-A-Roni, then you fly round-trip to live for a week in Paris.

It's *that* show. The prize is never anything useful, like okay clothes or music or beer. The prize is always some vacuum cleaner or a washing machine, something you might maybe get excited to win if you were, like, somebody's maid.

It's Rush Week, and the tradition is everybody pledging Zeta Delt all take this big chartered school bus and need to go to some TV studio and watch them tape this game show. Rules say, all the Zeta Delts wear the same red T-shirt with, printed on it, the Greek Zeta Delta Omega deals, silk-screened in black. First, you need to take a little stamp of Hello Kitty, maybe half a stamp, and wait for the flash. It's like this little paper stamp printed with Hello Kitty you suck on and swallow, except it's really blotter acid.

All you do is, the Zeta Delts sit together to make this red patch in the middle of the studio audience and scream and yell to get on TV. These are not the Gamma Grab'a Thighs. They're not the Lambda Rape'a Dates. The Zeta Delts, they're who everybody wants to be.

How the acid will affect you – if you're going to freak out and kill yourself or eat somebody alive – they don't even tell you.

It's traditional.

Ever since you were a little kid with a fever, the contestants they call down to play this game show, the big voice always calls for one guy who's a United States Marine wearing some band uniform with brass buttons. There's always somebody's old grandma wearing a sweatshirt. There's an immigrant from some place where you can't understand half of what he says. There's always some rocket scientist with a big belly and his shirt pocket stuck full of pens.

It's just how you remember it, growing up, only now – all the Zeta Delts start yelling at you. Yelling so hard it scrunches their eyes shut. Everybody's just these red shirts and big, open mouths. All their hands are pushing you out from your seat, shoving you into the aisle. The big voice is saying your name, telling you to come on down. You're the next contestant.

In your mouth, the Hello Kitty tastes like pink bubblegum. It's the Hello Kitty, the popular kind, not the strawberry flavor or the chocolate flavor somebody's brother cooks at night in the General Sciences Building where he works as a janitor. The paper stamp feels caught partway down your throat, except you don't want to gag on TV, not on recorded video with strangers watching, forever.

All the studio audience is turned around to see you stumble down the aisle in your red T-shirt. All the TV cameras zoomed in. Everybody clapping exactly the way you remember it. Those Las Vegas lights, flashing, outlining everything onstage. It's something new, but you've watched it a million-zillion times before, and just on automatic you take the empty desk next to where the United States Marine is standing.

The game show host, who's not Alex Trebek, he waves one arm, and a whole part of the stage starts to move. It's not an earthquake, but one whole wall rolls on invisible wheels, all the lights everywhere flashing on and off, only fast, just blink, blink, blink, except faster than a human mouth could say. This whole big back wall of the stage slides to one side, and from behind it steps out a giant fashion model blazing with about a million-billion sparkles on her tight dress, waving one long, skinny arm to show you a table with eight chairs like you'd see in somebody's dining room on Thanksgiving with a big cooked turkey and yams and everything. Her fashion-model waist, about as big around as somebody's neck. Each of her tits, the size of your head. Those flashing Las Vegas kind of lights blinking all around. The big voice saying who made this table, out of what kind of wood. Saying the suggested retail price it's worth.

To win, the host lifts up this little box. Like a magician, he shows everybody what's underneath – just this whole *thing* of bread in its naturally occurring state, the way bread comes before it's made into anything you can eat like a sandwich or French toast. Just this bread, the whole way your mom might find it at the farm or wherever bread grows.

The table and chairs are totally, easily yours, except you have to guess the price of this big bread.

Behind you, all the Zeta Delts crowd really close together in their T-shirts, making what looks like one giant, red pucker in the middle of the studio audience. Not even looking at you, all their haircuts are just huddled up, making a big, hairy center. It's like forever later when your phone rings, and a Zeta Delt voice says what to bid.

That bread just sitting there the whole time. Covered in a brown crust. The big voice says it's loaded with ten essential vitamins and minerals.

The old game show host, he's looking at you like maybe he's never, ever seen a telephone before. He goes, 'And what do you bid?'

And you go, 'Eight bucks?'

10

From the look on the old grandma's face, it's like maybe they should call some paramedics for her heart attack. Dangling out of one sweatshirt cuff, this crumpled scrap of Kleenex looks like leaked-out stuffing, flapping white, like she's some trashed teddy bear somebody loved too hard.

To cut you off using some brilliant strategy, the United States Marine, the bastard, he says, 'Nine dollars.'

Then to cut him off, the rocket science guy says, 'Ten. Ten dollars.'

It must be some trick question, because the old grandma says, 'One dollar and ninety-nine cents,' and all the music starts, loud, and the lights flash on and off. The host hauls the granny up onto the stage, and she's crying and plays a game where she throws a tennis ball to win a sofa and a pool table. Her grandma face looks just as smashed and wrinkled as that Kleenex she pulls out from her sweatshirt cuff. The big voice calls another granny to take her place, and everything keeps rushing forward.

The next round, you need to guess the price of some potatoes, but like a whole big thing of real, alive potatoes, from before they become food, the way they come from the miners or whoever that dig potatoes in Ireland or Idaho or some other place starting with an *I*. Not even made into potato chips or French fries.

If you guess right, you get some big clock inside a wood box like a Dracula coffin standing on one end, except with these church bells inside the box that ding-ding whatever time it is. Over your phone, your mom calls it a *grandfather clock*. You show it to her on video, and she says it looks cheap.

You're onstage with the TV cameras and lights, all the Zeta Delts call-waiting you, and you cup your phone to your chest and go, 'My mom wants to know, do you have anything nicer I could maybe win?'

You show your mom those potatoes on video, and she asks: Did the old host guy buy them at the A&P or the Safeway?

You speed-dial your dad, and he asks about the income-tax liability.

Probably it's the Hello Kitty, but the face of this big Dracula clock just scowls at you. It's like the secret, hidden eyes; the eyelids open up, and the teeth start to show, and you can hear about a million-billion giant, alive cockroaches crawling around inside the wood box of it. The skin of all the supermodels goes all waxy, smiling with their faces not looking at anything.

You say the price your mom tells you. The United States Marine says one dollar more. The rocket science guy says a dollar higher than him. Only, this round – you win.

All those potatoes open their little eyes.

Except now, you need to guess the price of a whole cow full of milk in a box, the way milk comes in the kitchen fridge. You have to guess the cost of a whole thing of breakfast cereal like you'd find in the kitchen cabinet. After that, a giant deal of pure salt the way it comes from the ocean only in a round box, but more salt than anybody could eat in an entire lifetime. Enough salt, you could rim approximately a million-billion margaritas.

All the Zeta Delts start texting you like crazy. Your inbox is piling up.

Next come these eggs like you'd find at Easter, only plain white and lined up inside some special kind of cardboard case. A whole, complete set of twelve. These really minimalist eggs, pure white . . . so white you could just look at them forever, only right away you need to guess at a big bottle like a yellow shampoo, except it's something gross called cooking oil, you don't know what for, and the next thing is you need to choose the right price of something frozen.

You cup one hand over your eyes to see past the footlights, except all the Zeta Delts are lost in the glare. All you can hear is their screaming different prices of money. Fifty thousand dollars. A million. Ten thousand. Just loony people yelling just numbers.

Like the TV studio is just some dark jungle, and people are just some monkeys just screeching their monkey sounds.

The molars inside your mouth, they're grinding together so hard you can taste the hot metal of your fillings, that silver melting in your back teeth. Meantime, the sweat stains creep down from your armpit to your elbow, all black-red down both sides of your Zeta Delt T-shirt. The flavor of melted silver and pink bubblegum. It's sleep apnea only in the day, and you need to remind yourself to take the next breath . . . take another breath . . . while the supermodels walking on sparkly high heels try pimping the audience a microwave oven, pimping a treadmill while you keep staring to decide if they're really good-looking. They make you spin this doohickey so it rolls around. You have to match a bunch of different pictures so they go together perfect. Like you're some white rat in Principles of Behavioral Psychology 201, they make you guess what can of baked beans costs more than another. All that fuss to win something you sit on to mow your lawn.

Thanks to your mom telling you prices, you win a thing like you'd put in a room covered in easy-care, wipe-clean, stain-resistant vinyl. You win one of those deals people might ride on vacation for a life-time of wholesome fun and family excitement. You win something hand painted with the Old World charm inspired by the recent release of a blockbuster epic motion picture.

It's the same as when you felt sick with a high fever and your little-kid heart would pound and you couldn't catch your breath, just from the idea that somebody might take home an electric organ. No matter how sick you felt, you'd watch this show until your fever broke. All the flashing lights and patio furniture, it seemed to make you feel better. To heal you or to cure you in some way.

It's like forever later, but you win all the way to the Showcase Round.

There, it's just you and the old granny wearing the sweatshirt from before, just somebody's regular grandma, but she's lived through world wars and nuclear bombs, probably she saw all the Kennedys get shot and Abraham Lincoln, and now she's bobbing up and down on her tennis-shoe toes, clapping her granny hands and crowded by supermodels and flashing lights while the big voice makes her the promise of a sports utility vehicle, a wide-screen television, a floor-length fur coat.

And probably it's the acid, but it's like nothing seems to add up.

It's like, if you live a boring-enough life, knowing the price of Rice-A-Roni and hot dog wieners, your big reward is you get to live for a week in some hotel in London? You get to ride on some airplane to Rome. Rome, like, in Italy. You fill your head full of enough ordinary junk, and your payoff is giant supermodels giving you a snowmobile?

If this game show wants to see how smart you really are, they need to ask you how many calories in a regular onion – cheddar cheese bagel. Go ahead, ask you the price of your cell phone minutes any hour of the day. Ask you about the cost of a ticket for going thirty miles over the speed limit. Ask the round-trip fare to Cabo for spring break.

Down to the penny, you can tell them the price of decent seats for the Panic at the Disco reunion tour.

They should ask you the price of a Long Island iced tea. The price of Marcia Sanders's abortion. Ask about your expensive herpes medication you have to take but don't want your folks to know you need. Ask the price of your History of European Art textbook, which cost three hundred bucks – fuck you very much.

Ask what that stamp of Hello Kitty set you back.

The sweatshirt granny bids some regular amount of money for her showcase. Just like always, the numbers of her bid appear in tiny lights, glowing on the front of her contestant desk where she stands.

Here, all the Zeta Delts are yelling. Your phone keeps ringing and ringing.

For your showcase, a supermodel rolls out five hundred pounds of raw beefsteak. The steaks fit inside a barbecue. The barbecue fits onboard a speed boat that fits inside a trailer for towing it that fits a massive fifth-wheel pickup truck that fits inside the garage of a brand-new house in Austin. Austin, like, in Texas.

Meantime, all the Zeta Delts stand up. They get to their feet and step up on their audience seats cheering and waving, not chanting your name, but chanting, 'Zeta Delt!' Chanting, 'Zeta Delt!' Chanting, 'Zeta Delt!' loud enough so it records for the broadcast.

It's probably the acid, but – you're battling some old nobody you've never met, fighting over shit you don't even want.

Probably it's the acid, but – right here and now – fuck declaring a business major. Fuck General Principles of Accounting 301.

Stuck partway down your throat, something makes you gag.

And on purpose, by accident, you bid a million, trillion, gah-zillion dollars – and ninety-nine cents.

And everything shuts down to quiet. Maybe just the little clicking sounds of all those Las Vegas lights blinking on and off, on and off. On and off.

It's like forever later when the game show host gets up too close, standing at your elbow, and he hisses, 'You can't do that.' The host hisses, 'You have to play this game to win . . .'

Up close, his host face looks cracked into a million-billion jagged fragments only glued back together with pink make-up. Like Humpty Dumpty or a jigsaw puzzle. His wrinkles, like the battle scars of playing his same TV game since forever started. All his gray hairs, always combed in the same direction.

The big voice asks – that big, deep voice booming out of nowhere, the voice of some gigantic giant man you can't see – he demands, can you please repeat your bid?

And maybe you don't know what you want out of your life, but you know it's *not* a grandfather clock.

A million, trillion . . . you say. A number too big to fit on the front of your contestant desk. More zeroes than all the bright lights in the game show world. And probably it's the Hello Kitty, but tears slop out both your eyes, and you're crying because for the first time since you were a little kid you don't know what comes next, tears wrecking the front of your red T-shirt, turning the red parts black so the Greek Omega deals don't make any sense.

The voice of one Zeta Delt, alone in all that big, quiet audience, he yells, 'You suck!'

On the little screen of your phone, a text message says, 'Asshole!'

The text? It's from your mom.

The sweatshirt grandma, she's crying because she won. You're sobbing because – you don't know why.

It turns out the granny wins the snowmobiles and the fur coat. She wins the speedboat and the beefsteaks. The table and chairs and sofa. All the prizes of both the showcases, because your bid was way, way too high. She's jumping around, her bright-white false teeth throwing smiles in every direction. The game show host gets everybody started clapping their hands, except the Zeta Delts don't. The family of the old granny climbs up onstage – all the kids and grandkids and great-grandkids of hers – and they wander over to touch the shiny sports utility vehicle, touch the super-models. The granny plants red lipstick kisses all over the fractured pink face of the game show host. She's saying, 'Thank you.' Saying, 'Thank you.' Saying, 'Thank you,' right up to when her granny eyes roll up backward inside her head, and her hand grabs at the sweatshirt where it covers her heart.

SAMANTHA'S DIARY

Diana Wynne Jones

Recorded on BSQ SpeekEasi Series 2/89887BQ and discovered in a skip in London's Regent Street

December 25, 2233

T ired today and having a lazy time. Got back late from Paris last night from Mother's party. My sister is pregnant and couldn't go (besides, she lives in Sweden) and Mother insisted that *one* of her daughters was there to meet our latest stepfather. Not that I did meet him particularly. Mother kept introducing me to a load of men and telling me how rich each of them was: I think she's trying to start me on her own career, which is, basically, marrying for money. Thanks, Mother, but I earn quite enough on the catwalk to be happy as I am. Besides, I'm having a rest from men since I split up with Liam. The gems of Mother's collection were a French philosopher, who followed me around saying '*La vide ce n'est pas le néant,*' (clever French nonsense meaning

'The void is not nothing,' I think), a cross-eyed Colombian film director who kept trying to drape himself over me, and a weird millionaire from goodness knows where with diamante teeth. But there were others. I was wearing my new Stiltskins, which caused me to tower over them. A mistake. They always knew where I was. In the end I got tired of being stalked and left. I just caught the midnight bullet train to London, which did not live up to its name. It was late and crowded out and I had to stand all the way.

My feet are killing me today.

Anyway I have instructed Housebot that I am Not At Home to anyone or anything and hope for a peaceful day. Funny to think that Christmas Day used to be a time when everyone got together and gave each other presents. Shudder. Today we think of it as the most peaceful day of the year. I sit in peace in my all-white living room – a by-product of Mother's career, come to think of it, since my lovely flat was given to me by my last-stepfather-but-one – no, last-but-two now, I forgot.

Oh damn! Someone rang the doorbell and Housebot *answered* it. I know I told it not to.

Did I say we don't give Christmas presents now? Talk about famous last words. Housebot trundled back in here with a *tree* of all things balanced on its flat top. Impossible to tell what *kind* of tree, as it has no leaves, no label to say who sent it, nothing but a small wicker cage tied to a branch with a fairly large brown bird in it. The damn bird pecked

21

me when I let it out. It was not happy. It has gone to earth under the small sofa and left droppings on the carpet as it ran.

I thought Christmas trees were supposed to be green. I made Housebot put the thing outside on the patio, beside the pool, where it sits looking bare. The bird is hungry. It has been trying to eat the carpet. I went on the Net to see what kind of bird it is. After an hour of trying, I got a visual that suggests the creature is a partridge. A game bird apparently. Am I supposed to *eat* it? I know they used to eat birds at Christmas in the old days. Yuk. I got on the Net again for partridge food. 'Sorry, dear customer, but there will be no deliveries until the start of the Sales on December 27, when our full range of luxury avian foods will again be available at bargain prices.' Yes, but what do I do *now*?

Oh hooray. Housebot has solved the problem by producing a bowl of tinned sweet corn. I shoved it under the sofa and the creature stopped its noise.

Do trees need feeding?

December 26, 2233

I do not believe this! *Another* tree has arrived with *another* partridge in a cage tied to it. This time I went haring to the front door to make them take it away again, or at least make whoever was delivering it tell me where the things were coming from. But all the man did was shove a birdcage into my hands with two pretty white pigeons in it and go away. The van he drove off in was un-labelled. I raged at Housebot for opening the door, but that does no good. Housebot only has sixty sentences in its repertoire and just kept saying, 'Madam, you have a delivery,' until I turned its voice off.

We have had a partridge fight under the sofa.

I took the pigeon cage outside onto the patio and opened it. But *will* those birds fly away! I seem to be stuck with them too. At least they will eat porridge oats. The partridges won't. We have run out of tinned sweet corn.

I give up. I'm going to spend the rest of the day watching old movies.

Liam called. I asked him if he had had the nerve to send me four birds and two trees. He said, 'What are you talking about? I only rang to see if you'd still got my wristwatch.' I hung up on him. Oaf.

December 27, 2233

The sales start today! I was late getting off to them because of the beastly bird food. When I brought up Avian Foodstuffs, I found to my disgust that the smallest amount they deliver is in twenty-kilo bags. Where would I put all that birdseed? I turned the computer off and went out to the corner shop. It was still closed. I had to walk all the way to

Carnaby Street before I found anything open and then all the way back carrying ten tins of sweet corn. I had promised to meet Carla and Sabrina in Harrods for coffee and I was so late that I missed them.

Not a good day. *And* I couldn't find a single thing I wanted in the Sales.

I came home – my Stiltskins were killing me – to find, dumped in the middle of my living room, yet another tree with a partridge tied to it, a second cage of two white pigeons and a large coop with three different birds in it. It took me a while to place these last, until I remembered a picture book my second stepfather had given me when I was small. Under H for Hen there was a bird something like these, except that one was round and brown and gentle looking. Not these. Hens they may be, but they have mean witchy faces, ugly speckled feathers and a floppy red bit on top that makes them look like some kind of alien. When I got home, they were engaged in trying to peck one another naked. The room was full of ugly little feathers. I shrieked at Housebot and then made it take the lot out onto the patio, where I made haste to let the beastly hens out. They ran around cackling and pecking the partridges, the potted plants and the three trees. They were obviously hungry. I sighed and got on to Avian Foodstuffs again. Problems there. Food for which kind of bird? they queried. Hens, I tapped in. Pigeons. Partridges. They have just delivered three twenty-kilo sacks.

They are labelled differently, but they look suspiciously the same inside to me. I know because I opened all three and scattered a heap from each around the patio – and another heap indoors because I have had to rescue the partridges. They all eat all kinds.

Exhausted after this. I phoned Carla and Sabrina. Sabrina was useless. She had just found some Stiltskins half price in pink and couldn't think of anything else except should she buy them. 'Toss a coin,' I told her. Carla was at least sympathetic. 'Help!' I told her. 'I'm being stalked by a nutter that keeps sending me birds.'

'Are you sure it isn't one of Liam's practical jokes?' Carla asked. Shrewd point. He probably rang with that nonsense about his watch just to make sure I was home. 'And haven't you told your Housebot thingy not to let any of this livestock in?' Carla said.

'I have, I *have*!' I cried out. 'But the darn thing takes not the blindest bit of notice!'

'Reprogramme it,' Carla advised. 'It must have slipped a cog or something.'

Or Liam reprogrammed it, I thought. So I spent an hour with the manual, pushing buttons, by which time I was so livid that I rang Liam. Got his answering service. Typical! I left an abusive message – which he probably won't hear because of Housebot trying to clean up feathers and making the howling noise it does when it chokes – but it relieved my feelings anyway.

December 28, 2233

I spent a glorious morning at the Sales and came back with six bags of Wonderful Bargains, to find I have four parrots now. *Plus* one more partridge (and tree), two more pigeons and three more of those unspeakable hens. Housebot has ignored my attempt at programming as if I'd never tried. The patio is now a small forest full of droppings. The pigeons sit on the trees and the hens rush about below. Indoors are four scuttling partridges and four of those large rings on sticks where parrots are supposed to perch, not that they do. The red one has taken a liking to my bedroom. The green one flies about all the time, shouting swearwords, and the multicoloured two perch anywhere so long as it isn't their official perches. *I* have put those in the closet because Housebot stops whenever it runs into one. I have ordered a twenty-kilo sack of Avian Feed (parrots), which is actually different from the others and which the parrots mostly consume from saucers on the kitchen table. I walk about giving a mad laugh from time to time. I am inured. I am resigned.

No I am NOT!

Someone has taught those damn parrots to shout, 'Samantha! I *love* you!' They do it all the time now.

I put on my most austerely beautiful clothes and my Stiltskins and stormed round to Liam's flat. He looked terrible. He was in his nightclothes.

He hadn't shaved or combed his curls and I think he was drunk. His flat was just as terrible. I saw it because as soon as he opened the door I marched in with Liam backing in front of me, shouting at the top of my voice. I admit that the nightclothes made me angrier still because it was obvious to me he had a woman in there. But he hadn't actually. He was just lying about. He said. 'Just shut up and tell me what you're yelling about.' So I did. And he laughed. This made me furious. I yelled, 'You are stalking me with *birds*!' and to my great surprise I burst into tears.

To my further surprise, Liam was almost nice about it. He said, 'Now look, Sammy, have you any idea how much parrots cost?' I hadn't. He told me. It was a lot. 'And before you get suspicious that I know,' he said, 'I only know because I did an article on them last month. Right? Since when did I have enough money for four parrots? And I don't even know where you buy hens, let alone partridges. So it's somebody else doing this to you, not me. He has to be a rich practical joker, and he has to know how to get at your Housebot to make it ignore your orders and let these birds in. So think about all the rich men you know and then go and yell at the likely ones. Not me.'

I gave in. 'So I've walked all this way for nothing,' I said. 'And my feet hurt.'

'That's because you wear such silly shoes,' he said.

'I'll have you know,' I said, 'that these are the very latest Stiltskins. They cost me thousands.'

He laughed, to my further indignation, and told me, 'Then go home in a taxi.'

While I was waiting for the taxi, Liam put his arm round me – in an absentminded way, as if he had forgotten we weren't still together – and said, 'Poor Sammy. I've had a thought. What kind of trees are they?'

'How should I know?' I said. 'They haven't any *leaves*.'

'That is a problem,' Liam said. 'Can you do me a favour and let me know if what your stalker sends next is something quite valuable?'

'I might,' I said, and then the taxi came. I don't like these latest taxis. A mechanical tab comes out of the meter that says TIP and it's always huge. But it was probably worth it to know that Liam hasn't been doing this to me.

December 29, 2233

Whatever idea Liam had, he was *quite right*! The usual tree and avians started arriving, one more partridge, more hens, more pigeons and four more parrots, noisy ones. I left Housebot, who had traitorously let them in, to deal with the damn creatures – although I have to feed the things because I can't get Housebot to get it through its circuitry that living things have to eat: Housebot simply goes round clearing up the piles of birdseed

28

unless I order it to stop. Anyway, I left it shunting coops and the latest tree onto the patio and set off for the Sales. I was halfway down the steps outside when a courier arrived and made me sign for a smallish package.

Someone's sent me a *book* now! I thought disgustedly as I went back indoors. I nearly didn't open it, but, because of what Liam had said, I thought I might as well. What are valuable books? I thought as I tore off wrapping. Antique Bibles? First editions of *Winnie the Pooh*? But it wasn't a book. A book-size jewel case fell on the floor. I picked that up quickly before Housebot could clear it away. I gasped a bit when I opened it. There were five rings in it, all of them very flashy and valuable looking. One bulged with diamonds – or what looked like diamonds – and the rest looked like sapphires, emeralds and equally valuable stones, all in gold settings. And there was a note on top, not in real handwriting, if you see what I mean, but in that kind of round, careful writing that shop assistants use when you ask them to include a message. It said: 'From your ardent admirer. Marry me.'

'*Blowed* if I will!' I said aloud.

The rings are all too small. I think that proves it wasn't Liam. He once bought me an engagement ring, after all, and he knows that my fingers are rather wide at the base. Unless he's being very cunning, of course. Whoever sent the rings seems to have very flashy taste. They all reminded me so much of the kind of glass-and-plastic rings that people give you when you are a little girl that I took the whole case of them with me when I went out to the Sales and had them checked out by a jeweller. And they are real. I could buy five more pairs of Stiltskins if I sold them. Well!

I meant to tell Liam, but I met Carla in Oxford Street and I forgot. When I told her, she wanted to know if I was thinking of marrying the unknown stalker. 'No way!' I told her. 'My mother probably would, though.'

December 30, 2233

Oh my God! I have six geese now. As well as another tree, another partridge, further pigeons, more hens and four extra parrots (making twelve of them and bedlam). I couldn't believe these geese. I got to the door just as a whole team of men finished handing them indoors. The last one rode in on top of Housebot. They are *big* birds and not friendly. At least they are too large to attack the partridges under the sofa, but five of them went out onto the patio and started subduing the hens at once. The shrieks and cackling out there actually drowned out the yells from the parrots. But one goose stayed indoors and seems to have gone broody on the sofa cushions. She stretched out a long, angry neck and tried to peck me when I made an effort to persuade her to join the rest outside. So there she sits, large, boat shaped and white, with her yellow beak swivelling about to make sure I don't disturb her and her shoe-button eyes glaring unnervingly.

The only good thing about this morning was that the same courier turned up with another parcel of rings. He is a nice young man. He seems awed by me. He said hesitantly while I was signing for the delivery, 'Excuse me, miss, but aren't you on that media clothes show? *Catwalk*?' I said yes, I was, but we weren't filming at the moment. He sort of staggered away, thoroughly impressed.

The rings today are all antique fancy gold. With the same message as yesterday. Liam couldn't have afforded any of this, even if he mortgaged his flat, his pay and his soul. I forgive him.

And I supposed I should feed the geese. I got on to Avian Foodstuffs again and they sent round a waterproof sack of slimy green nibbles. The geese don't seem to care for them. They ate all the hen food instead. The hens protested and got gone for again. To shut them all up, I tipped out one whole sack of hen food in the corner of the patio and this just caused another furious battle. Then it rained and the geese all came indoors. The beam that opens and shuts the sliding doors to the patio is set low so that Housebot can get out there to clean the pool, and it turns out to be just goose height.

I then discovered that geese are the most incontinent creatures in the universe. My living space is now covered with lumps of excrement, and the geese waddle through it, tramping it about with their large triangular feet. You interfere with them at your peril. I cracked and phoned Liam.

He said, 'Don't call me. Your phone is probably bugged, if your Housebot is. Meet me at the café on the corner.'

How unwelcoming can you get? To make it worse, that cafe is the one where we always used to meet when we were together. But I ground my teeth, got into rainwear and went.

He was sitting outside in the rain. He looks rather good in rainwear. He had even got me the right kind of coffee. He said, 'What is it now? Geese?'

I was flabbergasted. 'How did you know?'

'And five gold rings yesterday and today?' he said.

'Yes, but all too small,' I said.

'Ah,' he said, looking pleased with himself. 'Then you have an admirer who is not only rich but mindlessly romantic. He is sending you items from an old song – it used to be very popular two hundred years ago – called '"The Twelve Days of Christmas."'

'Then whoever he is, he hasn't *notion* how angry he's making me!' I said.

'The idiot thinks he's wooing you,' Liam said. 'He probably belongs to one of those societies where they trail about in medieval clothes, or armour and so forth. But he's also up to date enough to tamper with your Housebot and probably bug your phone.

So think of any of the rich men you know who fits this description and then you'll have him. Come on. Think.'

I had been trying to think. But you try thinking with a row of parrots sitting on the rail of your bed and the rest swooping about shouting that they love you. I had made no progress. I sat and watched raindrops plop into my coffee and thought hard. I do know a lot of rich men. You do, in my trade. But they were all mostly media men and those are *not* romantic. A more cynical lot you can't imagine. Unless I had annoyed one of them of course . . . And most of the clothes designers are gay.

'Oh,' said Liam. 'My other conjecture is that he's thoroughly unattractive. I suspect he's used to having to pay a lot to get women interested. Rather pathetic really.'

I instantly thought of the truly unattractive set of fellows Mother had introduced me to on Christmas Eve. 'That's *it*!' I cried out. 'Bless you, Liam! I'll phone Mother this evening.'

'I don't think it's your mother doing it,' he said.

'No, no,' I said and explained. He agreed that I might be on the right track and we talked it over for a while. Then he said, 'By the way, the trees will be pear trees,' and handed me a list. 'So you'll know what to expect next,' he told me and got up and left. Just like that.

I was too angry to look at the list. I wish I had.

December 31, 2233, New Year's Eve

I'm going to three parties today, so I'm getting out of my bird-infested flat as soon as I can. But I did ring Mother. I raved at her rather. She may have thought I was insane at first, but when I calmed down and described the geese – by the way, the one on the sofa had laid an egg when I got back – she began to see I might be having real trouble. She said, in the cautious, respectful way she always talks about money, 'Well, you *might* be talking about Franz Dodeca, I suppose. Not that he would do a thing like that, of course. He owns Multiphones and SpeekEasi and Household Robotics and he's a multimillionaire and he's naturally very much respected.'

'Which is he?' I asked. 'Of the freaks you introduced to me.'

'Not *freaks*, darling,' she said reproachfully. 'He was the one with the charming diamante teeth.'

I thought grimly of this Dodeca, a short fat man in an unbecoming pin-striped suit. A pale freckled creature, I recalled, with thin reddish hair scraped back over his freckled scalp. He kept baring those dreadful glittering teeth at me in creepy smiles. And this idiot owns my diary, my phone and my Housebot! I hoped he swallowed one of his teeth and choked. 'Tell him,' I said to Mother, 'to stop sending me *birds*. Tell him he hasn't got a chance. Tell him he's destroyed his already nonexistent chances by stalking me this way. Tell him no and *go away*!'

Mother demurred. I could tell she was reluctant to pass up the chance of all that money in the family. But after I had told her at least ten times that there was absolutely *no chance* of my marrying this idiot, even if he owned the *universe*, she said, 'Well, darling, I'll phone him and try to put it tactfully.'

If she did phone dear Franz, she has had no effect. The swans arrived this morning, seven of them. Along with six more geese, et cetera, et cetera. At least I got five more gold rings. They came with a note of dreadful pleading, signed, 'Your eternally loving Franz,' which looked odd in round shop-assistant writing. I suppose Mother must have phoned the man, since he seems to know that his cover is now blown. But it doesn't seem to have stopped him.

The swans had obviously been drugged. The delivery crew carried them in big drooping armfuls, through the living room and onto the patio, where they carefully wedged them into the pool. The geese waddled in after. There are now twelve of them and they're laying eggs everywhere. As if it wasn't enough to be overrun with hens – also laying – and a new set of green screaming parrots. The swans were just waking up when I left. Housebot tried to make me an omelette before I went and I nearly threw up.

Thank heavens! Even the Dodeca millions can't make anyone in this country work on New Year's Day. No further birds arrived. Nothing came. Relief! Or it would be if the swans didn't fight the geese all the time. And I realised when I got in around four this morning that the place smells. Horribly. Of bird droppings, rotting seeds and old feathers. Housebot can't keep up with the cleaning.

I shall have to stop wearing my Stiltskins. My feet are killing me after last night. One of my big toes has gone kind of twisted. I have very hazy memories of the fun, though I do recall that I ran into Liam at the Markhams' fireworks party and, besides jeering at my Stiltskins, he wanted to know if I'd consulted his list yet. I said I didn't want to know. I told him about dear Franz too – I think. He was, I dimly remember, insistent that I throw away my phone and scrap Housebot. The man has no *idea*!

But this memory has made me realise that I will almost certainly get more swans and more geese tomorrow. I can't rely on Mother to stop them. There is no more room in the patio pool. But it has occurred to me that the big house next door, which belongs to my last-stepfather-but-two, has a large garden with an ornamental as-it-were lake in it. I shall phone Stepdaddy Five. As far as I know, he's still in a hut in Bali, recovering from having been married to Mother.

I got through to him eventually. He was, as ever, sweet about it all. 'Isn't that just like your mother!' he said. 'I know Franz Dodeca slightly. He's a total obsessive, too rich for his own good. Come here to Bali and I'll undertake to keep him off you.'

Well, I couldn't do that. It strikes me as incest. Instead I asked him to lend me the garden of his house next door. He agreed like a shot and gave me the entry code at once. But he warned me that his caretaker gardener might not be pleased. He said he would phone this Mr Wilkinson and explain. 'And keep me posted,' he said. 'Nothing happens here in Bali. It suits me, but I like a hit of distant action from time to time.'

January 2, 2234

Just as well I made that arrangement with Stepdaddy Five. They brought yesterday's swans et cetera today, plus today's lot, making fourteen inert, heavy floppy swans and twelve more geese. I showed the lot through Stepdaddy Five's front door and out to the lake in his garden. The geese seemed to like it there. When the trees and the pigeons and the hens came, I showed them out there too. But the parrots had to stay with me because they were not hardy enough, they said. At least I got ten more gold rings.

We are getting seriously short of bird food. I went round to the corner shop, but they don't open till tomorrow. Avian Foodstuffs are on holiday for the week. Again.

I don't believe this! The swans were not all. I was just about to cross the road from the corner shop when I saw, trudging and bawling down the street, a whole herd of cows. Eight of them anyway. They were being driven by eight young women who, to do them justice, were looking a bit self-conscious about it. People in cars and on the pavements were stopping to stare. Some folk had followed them from Piccadilly, apparently. You don't often see cows in London these days.

My stomach felt queer. I knew they were for me. And they were. Honestly, how can this Dodeca even imagine I might want eight cows? Cows are not in the least romantic. Their noses run and they drop cowpats all the time as they walk. They dropped more cowpats through Stepdaddy Five's nice hallway as I showed the lot of them out into his garden. I said to the girls, 'If you want to stay, this house has fourteen bedrooms and there's a pizza takeaway down the road. Feel free.' I was feeling more than a little light-headed by then. The parrots don't help.

Now it's got worse. Mr Wilkinson arrived half an hour after the cows and bawled me out for allowing a herd of cows to trample his lawn. I said I would get rid of them as soon as I could. I was going to phone Mother and extract this Dodeca's phone number from her and then phone him and tell him to come and take his livestock *away*.

And see how *he* liked it. Before I could, though, a severe woman with a mighty bosom turned up on the doorstep, saying she was from the Bird Protection Trust and that my neighbours across the street had reported me for cruelty to birds. They had, she said, counted one hundred and seven various birds being delivered to my flat – *busybodies!* – where they were certainly overcrowded. I was to release them to better quarters, she said, or be liable for prosecution.

After Mr Wilkinson, she was the *last straw*. I told her to get the hell out.

January 3, 2234

No, the last straw was today. I did phone Mother last night and she did, after a lot of squirming, give me Dodeca's private number. The trouble was that I didn't know what to *say*, and all these parrots make it so difficult to *think* – not to speak of yet another swan versus goose fight erupting every five minutes. My God those birds can be vicious! Then I sat on an egg when I started to phone Dodeca and gave up. I said I'd do it today.

Today started with those cowgirls coming round here whining and whingeing. There were beds but no sheets or blankets next door, they said, and it was not what they were used to. And where did they put the twenty gallons of milk? I said pour it away, why not? And they said it was a waste. Anyway, I got rid of them in the end, but only by

39

ordering a stack of sheets and blankets online, which cost a bomb.

Then the bird deliveries began. By then we were almost out of bird feed, so I ushered this lot, swans included, into Stepdaddy Five's garden and raced off to the corner shop. They only had canary food, so I bought all they had of that. I was staggering towards my flat with it when I saw an entirely new sort of van drawing up and Housebot, that traitor, blandly opening my front door to it. The men in it began unloading and putting together a large number of frameworks. I crossed the road and asked them what the hell they were doing.

They said, 'Out of the way, miss. We have to get all these into this flat here.'

I said, 'But what are they?'

'Trampolines, miss,' they said.

This caused me to bolt into my flat and race about scattering canary food and looking for that list Liam gave me. I found it just as they manoeuvred the first trampoline in. There were supposed to be nine of them. How they thought they were going to fit them in I have no idea. As I opened the list, one of the men got attacked by the broody goose on the sofa and they all went outside to let it settle down. Liam had written, 'Ninth day: Nine lords a-leaping; Tenth day: Ten ladies dancing; Eleventh day: Eleven pipers piping . . .'

I didn't read any more. I gave a wild wail and raced into my bedroom, where all the parrots seemed to have congregated, and to shrieks of 'I *love* you, Samantha,' I packed all the parcels of rings into my handbag for safety and raced out again to the nearest public phone, praying it wouldn't have been vandalised.

It wasn't. I got through to Liam. 'What is it now?' he said grumpily.

'Liam,' I said, 'I've got nine trampolines now. Is it really true that I'm going to get ballet dancers and skirling Scotsmen next?'

'Pretty certainly,' he said, 'if you got milkmaids yesterday. Did you?'

'Yes,' I said. 'Liam, I have had enough.'

'What do you expect me to do about it?' he said.

'Marry me,' I said. 'Take me away from all this.'

There was a dreadful, long silence. I thought he had hung up on me. I wouldn't have blamed him. But at length he said, 'Only if you can assure me that I'm not just an escape for you.'

I assured him, hand on heart. I told him that the mere thought of Franz Dodeca had made me realise that Liam was the only man for me. 'Otherwise I'd get on a plane and go to my sister in Sweden,' I said. 'Or maybe to Bali, to Stepdaddy Five.'

'All right,' he said. 'Are you coming round here at once?'

'Quite soon,' I said. 'I have to fix Dodeca first.' We then exchanged a surprising number of endearments before I rang off and raced back to my flat for what I sincerely hope was the last time.

I got back just as a minibus drove up and

unloaded half a dozen fit-looking young men in scarlet robes and coronets and three more middle-aged ones, who looked equally fit. Most of them were carrying bottles of champagne and clearly looking forward to some fun. They all poured into my flat ahead of me. I had to sidle among them and past the men squeezing the last trampoline in and past several enraged geese and terrified partridges to get to my phone – a phone dear Franz was certainly bugging. While I punched in his number, the chaps all climbed on the trampolines and began solemnly bouncing up and down. One of the geese accidentally joined them. I had to put my hand over one ear to detect that I had got Dodeca's answering service. Good.

'Franz, dear,' I said after the beep. 'I'm so grateful for all the things you've been sending me. You've really gone to my heart. Why don't you come here and join me in my flat? Come soon. And then we'll see.' And I rang off, with the delightful thought of dear Franz arriving and the traitor Housebot letting him in among all this.

More than all this it would be, I discovered as I left. Another herd of cows was coming down the street, lowing and cowpatting as it came. From the other direction, I could see the big lady from the Birds Protection, or whatever it was, advancing. She seemed to have a policeman with her. And Mr Wilkinson was just storming out of Stepdaddy Five's front door. I ran the other way, past the herd of cows. And who should I see but the nice courier lad just getting out of his van with a fifth parcel of rings.

I stopped him. 'You know me, don't you?' I said. 'Can I sign for them now and save you coming to my door?' He innocently did let me and I raced away with the parcel. 'I've brought you a dowry!' I said to Liam as I arrived –

'No, Liam, don't! I haven't finished yet!'

A male voice: 'Don't be stupid, Sam. You know he'll be listening in. Do you want him to know where we are? I'm going to throw this away before you tell him any more.'

The diary ends here.

LAND OF THE LOST

Stewart O'Nan

She was a cashier at a Bilo in Perry whose marriage had long since broken up. Soon after that her two boys moved out of the house, leaving Ollie, her German shepherd, as her sole companion. From the beginning she followed the case in the paper and on TV, absorbing it like a mystery, discussing it with her co-workers and customers – so much so that her manager had to ask her to stop. Early on she visited the Web site and left messages of support in the guest book, from one mother to another, but after James Wade confessed that he'd buried the girl somewhere west of Kingsville, she began keeping a file. At night when she couldn't sleep she sat up in bed and went over the transcripts and the mother's map, convincing herself it was possible. She couldn't believe a feeling so strong could be mistaken.

She didn't tell anyone what she was doing – she wasn't stupid. The first time was the hardest because she felt foolish. In the privacy of her garage, while Ollie looked on, she stocked the trunk of her car with a shovel, a spade, a dry-cell flashlight and a pair of work gloves. She opened

44

the door and he leaped into the backseat, capering from window to window, frantic just to be going somewhere.

'All right, calm down,' she said. 'It's not play-time.'

Searching on foot took longer than she thought. They came across nothing more sinister than a rotting seagull, but she wasn't disappointed. Bushwhacking through the overgrown no-man's-land behind the commercial strip on Route 302 was an adventure, and looking gave her a sense of accomplishment. They could cross this location off and move on to the next one.

Later she added more serious gear like bolt cutters and a lightweight graphite walking stick recommended by professionals, whose Web sites she treated like the Bible. She religiously docu-mented everything, taking videos of any ground they disturbed, writing up her field notes as soon as they got home.

As fall came on she rearranged her shifts, working nights so she could take advantage of the daylight. In a couple of weeks the ground would be frozen and she'd have to shut down until spring. It was then, when she was feeling rushed, that she discovered a U-Store-It outside Mentor with a stockade fence and a dirt road running through the pines behind it. Across the raw lumber, kids had sprayed their illegible fluorescent-red names.

She walked Ollie along the fence until he stopped, sniffing at a weedy mound. She pulled him away twice, and both times he came back to the same spot. 'Good boy,' she said, giving him a treat, and looped his leash around a tree.

She prodded the mound with her walking stick. The dirt was sandy and loose, and she went back to her car for the shovel.

She dug her first hole deep, then shallow ones every three feet. She was out of shape, and had to dip her head and wipe her face on her shoulder. It was cool out, and when she stopped for a drink of water the sweat on her neck made her shiver. By the time she reached the middle of the fence, the sky was starting to get dark. At the four corners of the self-storage, high floodlights popped on, buzzing and drawing bugs, throwing weird shadows. She checked her cell phone – it was almost five. She needed to go home and get ready for work. Rather than leave the site unguarded overnight she decided to call the FBI.

They told her it was too late in the day. They'd send someone out to talk to her tomorrow.

When she complained to her older son, he asked how long she'd been doing this.

The agent they sent asked the same question. He looked over her binders and the picture of the girl on the mantel and the big map tacked up in the kitchen.

'I'm just trying to help,' she said. 'If it was one of my kids, I'd want everybody to pitch in.'

'I would too,' the agent said soothingly, as if it was common sense.

The next day they took her out to the site in an unmarked Suburban to watch a backhoe dig a trench along the fence line. Agents in windbreakers and latex gloves sifted the dirt through metal screens, then spread it on tarps for the dogs. A project like this would have taken her weeks, and she was glad she'd called. She imagined the girl's mother hearing the news. She didn't care about getting the credit. It was enough to know the girl was finally home.

They found nothing. Just dirt. Worms. It had all been a coincidence. As the agent said, there was graffiti on everything these days.

Meaning she was crazy.

Dropping her off, he thanked her. 'I know your heart was in the right place.'

Was it? She could admit that at least part of the reason she was searching for a stranger's daughter was that no one else needed her. Just Ollie.

She promised her sons to take a break after that. She took down the map and stored the picture in a drawer and watched the last weeks of fall pass.

Honoring her pledge was easier in the winter. She used the time to rethink her strategy and stockpile supplies. Some sites recommended a pitchfork to turn the soil, others a pickax. On paper, again and again, she rearranged her trunk, as if she were traveling cross-country. She enrolled Ollie in an online course for sniffer dogs, practicing with scented rags in the backyard. He didn't

47

always get them right away, and stood looking at her as if she might give him a hint.

'Do you want to pass or not?' she asked. 'Or am I just wasting my time?'

She kept an eye on the Web site, and cruised the chat groups for news. She was afraid one day the page would come up and say she'd been found, but month after month, nothing changed. It had been two and a half years. Besides the family, she might be the only person looking for her.

In March the ground thawed and she tacked up the map. She'd turned her older boy's room into a command center, emptying his desk and filling the drawers with her notebooks. On a brand-new corkboard she posted her schedule. Four days a week she'd search, weather permitting. She'd been too impatient in the fall, letting her emotions get the best of her. She'd actually expected to find the girl her first time out, as if she were psychic. She needed to be calm and methodical. If she was going to succeed, it would be because she knew how to work.

Ollie just liked riding in the car and going for walks. He had his certificate, but the death scent made him sneeze. The smells that interested him came from other dogs, and he immediately covered them with his own, lifting his leg and making her wait. As spring turned to summer the only thing he'd discovered was a bee's nest, provoking a swarm and earning him a bump on the nose. He would have stayed and tried to fight them if she hadn't dragged him away.

She made the mistake of telling her younger son, who told her older son, who called and said he thought they agreed she was going to stop.

'I don't see why you're so upset,' she said.

'I'm worried about you. Do you understand why?'

'No.'

'That's why,' he said.

After that, every time he called, he made a point of asking how the search was going.

She refused to lie.

'The same,' she said.

'What does that mean?'

It meant she was ranging farther and farther west, devoting whole weeks to a single exit off the interstate, tromping the buggy jungles behind truck stops and fireworks outlets, breaking ground by every stockade fence she came across, graffitied or not. Her knees creaked, her arms ached, and then at work she had to lean over the conveyor and lift a gallon of milk into someone's cart, and she thought maybe he was right. She was too old to be doing this.

There was always the possibility James Wade had been lying. As her map filled with pins, she tried not to let it bother her.

In August, jumping a drainage ditch, she twisted her ankle and missed three weeks, ruining her schedule and giving her son a new excuse to badger her. To catch up she went out five days a week, but felt like she was rushing, cutting corners.

The weather was mild, Indian summer lingering deep into October. If it held up (and the Weather Channel said there was a chance), she'd have a shot at finishing.

One bright afternoon she was outside Fairport Harbor, behind a Ryder truck center, when Ollie stopped and lay down in a shallow trough filled with pine duff. He rested his head on his paws and flattened his ears back as if he were being punished. It wasn't anything she'd taught him.

'Come on, get up.' She whistled and clapped, and still he didn't budge. She had to coax him away with a treat and tie him to a tree, and even then he hunkered down, cowering.

The Ryder place wasn't a self-storage, and the fence, though heavily tagged, was chain link with green plastic slats, but she went to get the video camera anyway.

The trough was tub shaped, around five feet long, and sunk a few inches below the ground around it. She brushed away the leaves and pine needles and laid the pitchfork beside it for scale, narrating as she panned along the fence. 'November third, 2008, 1:27 P.M.'

When she'd gotten enough coverage, she set down the camera and took up the pitchfork. She dug into the very center of the trough, jabbing the prongs through the crust, pushing it deeper with her foot, pulling back on the handle so the ground cracked and broke around the times. She stuck it in again, levering open a hole.

Behind her Ollie whined.

'Shush,' she said.

The third time she dug down and yanked back, the pitchfork snagged on a swath of fabric.

It was discolored with mud and stank of mildew, but was unmistakably a piece of green nylon, a wisp of white batting poking from a hole.

She set aside the pitchfork, tossed away her gloves and tugged at the piece, pulling another couple inches through the dirt. It was the shell of a sleeping bag, she could see the thick seam of the zipper. With a finger she wiped at the crumbling mud, revealing rusty teeth.

Thank God, she thought. What would Brian say now?

As long as she'd waited for this moment, she didn't want to see what was inside. The thing to do was stop and call someone, but after last year, she couldn't. She knelt beside the hole, digging it free with her bare hands. This time she would make sure. Then everyone would know she wasn't crazy.

LEIF IN THE WIND

Gene Wolfe

'He's been out there,' Ena said, 'for an hour and fifty-two minutes. It took him twenty-eight to nail that plate back down. I've been trying to get him to come back in ever since.'

Brennan rubbed his chin. It was a big one, and required quite a bit of rubbing. 'He answers you? He replies?'

'Sometimes. Not always.'

'But he's conscious?'

'I think so.'

'Fugue state?'

Ena shrugged.

'Talk to him.'

'I'll try.' Ena's gesture switched on the mike. 'This is Ena again, Leif. Brennan is here with me now. What are you doing?'

'Watching the sunrise, Ena. The planetary shadow is fading. Fading Fading . . . This sun appears behind the horizon curve, just peeping out past it now. I can feel the first breezes of its solar wind.'

Brennan tried to make his voice soft. 'You can't possibly feel a solar wind, Leif. You're suited up.'

'I feel it.'

Ena said, 'Please come back, Leif. We've completed the survey, done everything we were supposed to do, and—'

Brennan interrupted her. 'The job's finished, Leif. There's no life down there. We have rock samples, cores, the works. Habitable planet, no life. Seed it and there could be colonies here in two hundred years. Maybe less.'

Leif said nothing.

Ena said, 'I've never begged a man for anything—'

'Birds. I see birds.'

Brennan snorted. 'You don't see birds, damnit! There aren't any, and if there were, you couldn't see them from up here.'

Ena said, 'Think of me, Leif – if you won't think of yourself, at least think of me. The trip home will take fifteen more years. What if Brennan dies?'

Silence.

'Walt died. So did Barbara and Alaia. Brennan could die, too. I'd try to take the ship home all by myself, and I'd go insane. I couldn't bear it. You know what the tests showed – nobody could.' She paused, waiting. 'Think of me if you won't think of yourself.'

Leif exclaimed, 'You should see these birds! The detail! The colors! The combs and crests and wattles!'

Brennan said, 'You're dreaming them, Leif.'

'I couldn't dream anything like this. It isn't in

me. It isn't in anybody. They're so big, and they get smaller as they come closer. Smaller and smaller, like jewels.'

Ena looked at Brennan, expecting him to reply, and saw that he was suiting up. She switched off her mike. 'Are you going out there after him?'

'If I have to, yes.'

'I know you could outwrestle him, but can you catch him?'

'I'll have to.'

She switched her mike back on. 'Leif, I'm offering everything I've got. I'll be your slave if you'll just come back.' She gulped, and wondered whether her mike had picked it up. 'I'll do your details, all of them, and mine, too. We'll be heroes when we get home, and I'll give you a bath first, and clean and press your uniform. I'll shine your boots and polish your brass. You said I was beautiful once, remember? Wouldn't you like a beautiful slave?'

Brennan muttered, 'Did he really?'

'I'll – sleep with you like you wanted, Leif. You can do whatever you like with me, and I'll do whatever you tell me to. Please?'

Leif said, 'They're nesting in me, all the beautiful birds. Perching on nerve fibers, sipping from tiny veins, Ena. Fluttering and singing. This is how a tree feels in summer.'

Wearily, Ena switched off her mike. 'He doesn't care about me.'

'He doesn't care about us,' Brennan told her. 'Not now he doesn't.'

Leif said, 'The wind murmurs in my branches, and the birds nest there.' He sounded rapturous. Ena's screen showed a silver starfish, arms wide, legs spread, face invisible behind the glare of sunlight on his visor. Slowly, the starfish revolved, rolling like a wheel.

She heard the airlock open. 'You're going after him?'

Brennan stepped into the airlock. 'Wish me luck.'

'I do,' she said. The airlock closed, and she added, 'I wish you both luck. I hope you don't kill each other.'

Still later: 'Most of all I wish me luck.'

Was there nothing she could do but sit and watch? She unsnapped her belt, floated up, and pushed off.

Walt should have looked just as she remembered him from last time – so quickly frozen that no big crystals had formed, eyes shut, and very, very dead.

He did not. Dead, yes, but still *there*. So quickly frozen, she thought, that his soul had not had time to leave his body. Brennan thought it might be possible to reanimate him back on earth, and Brennan might be right.

Walt's eyes were not completely shut. Surely they had been before?

Surely. But Walt was peeking out like one who feigns sleep.

'I may sleep with Leif if Brennan brings him back. I'll have to sleep with Brennan. You're dead,

Walt.' Ena paused. 'You're dead for now, anyway. I won't be cheating on you.'

From behind a plastic shield as clear as air, Walt watched her in silence.

'You understand, don't you?' She began to close the lid. 'Besides, I – we're not all that different from you, we women.'

She returned to the bridge, floating along ovoid black corridors that should have echoed but did not. It had been wrong to silence them, she thought. The sound absorption was too good, it worked too well. Ghosts whispered in the black corridors now, Alaia's ghost and Barbara's.

Walt's ghost.

On her screen, Brennan had a line around Leif's waist and was playing it out behind him as he returned to the ship. Brightly lit by rising Beta Andromedae, the slack orange line traced fantastic loops and whorls against the still-dark planet they orbited. Ena switched on her mike. 'Did he give you any trouble, Brennan?'

'Not a bit.'

Changing viewpoints, she watched Brennan enter the airlock, turn, and begin hauling Leif in. No resistance, but . . . She inserted a sedative cap in the injector. Leif, she told herself, was not particularly strong. And pushed aside the knowledge that all psychotics were.

Inside, he removed his helmet without assistance. His expression was rapt, his eyes elsewhere. The neck was one of the best places.

Leif relaxed, swaying, and Brennan said, 'That was probably a good idea.'

'It can't hurt.' Ena was opening Leif's suit.

'I'm full of birds,' Leif told her.

'I see.'

'They're nesting in me. Have I mentioned that?'

Absently, she nodded.

'We are their trees. That's why there are no trees down there. We trees have just arrived.' Leif paused. 'I would like to sit down.'

'No reason not to,' Brennan told him. 'Step out of the boots and I'll put you in a chair.

When Leif did not move, Brennan lifted him out, the magnetic boot soles holding them to the deck. When Brennan had Leif in his console seat, Ena belted him in.

The first jump covered four thousandths of one light-year; recharging for the next would take thirty-six hours.

'Are we going home?' Leif asked. He sounded sleepy, and had not touched the buckle that held him in his seat.

Brennan said, 'Right.' He was refolding Leif's suit.

'You'll have to walk in the spinner,' Ena told Leif, 'just like Brennan and me. Just like you did on the trip out. Can you do it?'

Leif seemed not to have heard her.

'Two hours a day,' Brennan said. 'If you don't, your legs will break when we get home.'

Ena was inspired. 'Your limbs, Leif. That's your arms and your legs. You know what happens when limbs break.'

Leif stared at her. 'The nests fall down.'

'Exactly!'

'I'm going into the spinner now.' Leif released his buckle. 'Three hours. Three hours every day for me. I won't forget.'

When Leif had gone, Brennan chuckled, wrapped Ena in his arms, and kissed her. When they parted, he whispered, 'You were always the smartest woman on board.'

They were recharging for the fourth jump when Ena heard the first bird, its clear trills carried through the ventilation system. A twenty-minute search found it in Specimen Storage number 3, where it had nested among her neatly labeled sacks of rocks.

It was somewhat larger than a crow, and was not (she decided) exactly as a bird should be. That sinuous neck, armored in diamond scales, might have belonged to a snake; the sides of its long, curved beak were toothed like the blades of saws. It spread its wings when she approached, threatening her with retractile claws that sprouted from their forward edges.

'I don't want to hurt you,' Ena said softly. 'Really, I don't. You're very, very valuable to all three of us. You're an alien life-form, you see.' It was difficult to remain calm.

The bird rattled its feathers – a warning buzz, loud and abrupt.

She kicked off from a specimen bag, backing away. 'I'm going to bring you something to eat. I don't know what you'll like, so I'll try several things.' Could it eat their food?

Brennan was checking the recharge readings. 'Pile's running good,' he told her. 'Next jump should be right on schedule.'

'Leif's birds are real.' She had drifted over to her console.

'Are you kidding me?'

Seeing his skepticism, she nodded. 'Sure. But don't you hear that noise? Listen. I think it's coming through the vents.'

After a moment he left his seat and kicked off, stopping aft vent. Ena smiled to herself.

'That's a bearing getting ready to fail. Probably one of the fans. I'll see to it.'

As he shot out into the corridor, she called, 'Good luck!'

She was checking the pile herself when Leif wandered in. 'Do you need me?'

'Not really.' She smiled. 'The best thing you could do right now is to shower and put on a clean uniform. Will you do that? For me?'

Leif nodded.

'Thank you! I really appreciate it. Put the one you're wearing in the laundry, and I'll see to it. Don't forget to empty the pockets.'

'There's nothing in there.' Leif seemed to wait for her to speak. 'All right, I'll empty them anyway.'

It was almost time for the jump when Brennan returned. 'There's a bird on the ship!'

'No shit?' Ena feigned surprise.

He grabbed at a handy conduit and swung to a stop, panting. 'Sweetheart, you ought to see it! It's taller than I am.'

'If you're going to sniff solvents,' Ena said icily, 'I don't want you to call me sweetheart. Cut it out. Cut it out right now. This is the only warning you'll get.'

'It's down on H Deck. Come on, I'll show you.'

'One of us has to stay on the bridge, and since you've been sniffing, it had better be me.'

'Leif can do it.'

'Leif isn't around, and God only knows what he'd do if he were alone here.'

'It's real. Do I have to take a picture?'

Feeling almost sorry for him, she shook her head. 'No. No, you don't, Brennan. Catch it and throw it off the ship. It'll be out in space somewhere, and I can pick it up in my viewer.'

'Don't you understand what this means?'

'Yes. It means that Leif can infect others with his hallucinations. Or else you've been sniffing. I like the second one better.'

'I'm going to catch it,' Brennan told her. 'Catch it and confine it. Then I'm going to show it to you. Don't jump without me. You're not qualified.'

'You mean I don't have the paper. By this time I know how to do it as well as you do.'

'Don't jump!'

Then he was gone. Ena smiled to herself as she tried to track him through the surveillance cameras. When FULL CHARGE appeared on her upper-left screen, she jumped.

A day and more passed before Brennan returned. Ena slept on the bridge, tethered to a hatch handle and hanging weightless among 552 instruments. Leif wandered in and volunteered to bring her food and water. She was using the surveillance cameras to search for Brennan when Brennan touched her shoulder.

'You jumped – I felt it.' He was trying hard to look severe, but could only look haggard and triumphant.

'Sure,' Ena said. 'I knew you would. I jumped, and that's why the pile's burning and power's flickering. I don't know what that vibration is, but it darned near—'

'Very funny.' Brennan belted himself into his console seat. He studied the screen, clicked twice, and studied it again.

'Did you catch the bird?'

'I did.' Brennan nodded. 'I got a number three cargo net and rigged it up to close when the bird tried to get through. When it was ready, I drove the bird in front of me with a welding torch.'

'Where is it now?'

He sighed. 'Empty ration locker, or I hope it is. It may still be tangled in the net. I don't know.'

'We can't keep it there for fifteen years.'

'Right. We'll let it out, v-tape it, kill it, v-tape it some more, strip the bones and save them.' Under his breath he added, 'If it has bones.'

Ena said, 'Tissue specimens, too. Maybe we should freeze the head.'

'Yeah.'

'There's something you're not telling me.'

'It tried . . . Tricks. You wouldn't believe me.'

'You didn't believe *me* when I told you Leif's birds were real.'

Brennan straightened up. 'I'm still not sure you were right. Maybe I caught a delusion. You want to fetch the 'corder?'

'Somebody's supposed to stay on the bridge.'

'Leif. I'll get him.'

This time she offered no objection.

The green food lockers were on C Deck. Brennan caught the handle of one in Aisle 10. 'This is it. I'm going to level with you, sweetheart. I don't think it's still in here, but this is where I put it. I threw it in and locked the door.' He took the key from his pocket, a strip of plastic no larger than a paper clip.

Ena sighed. 'Walt was supposed to have those. Keep us from eating too much.'

'Walt's dead.'

She nodded. 'So now I can eat all I want.'

'With three gone, it won't matter. Don't worry about it.'

'So I ought to eat too much. Bored people always eat too much.'

Watching her, Brennan nodded. 'That was why Walt kept the keys.'

'But I don't. I don't eat enough. I keep driving myself to eat. Or try to, anyway. All my uniforms are loose.' She paused. 'Aren't you going to open it?'

'In a minute, maybe. Boredom makes people eat – you're right about that. Depression keeps them from eating. Get somebody depressed enough, and she'll starve herself to death. You tried to bribe Leif with sex. I heard you.'

Slowly Ena nodded.

'I'm not going to say I don't want sex. It would be a lie, and you'd know it was a lie. Every man wants sex, but that's not the only thing I want. I want you to love me. I want you to love me the way you loved Walt. Okay, I want it for my own selfish reasons. Hell yes, I do. But I want it for your sake, too.'

Brennan paused. 'For a second there you were trying to smile. I wish you'd made it.'

She said, 'So do I.'

'When I kissed you, up on the bridge, you kissed back.'

She nodded.

'So there's hope for us.'

'"Hope is the thing with feathers."' Ena waited

for Brennan to speak. When he did not, she added, 'That's Emily Dickinson.'

'Yeah, I know.' Brennan pulled himself toward the food locker. 'You want me to show you the bird and quit talking about all this, because it bothers you. I've got it. Only it might help you, too, so I've got to keep it up. You think I don't miss Barbara? You think I don't wake up when the cabin's dark, wondering if she's asleep? I need you almost as much as you need me. You don't have to believe that.'

'What I believe doesn't matter.'

'The hell it doesn't! I need you, and that's why I'll never quit. You'll see, and Ena . . .'

'What?'

'We'll get back home alive. Both of us.'

She kissed him, and it was like – yet not quite like – their kiss on the bridge.

'I don't think the bird's still in here,' Brennan said rather later. 'Not really. It was too tricky for that.'

'We didn't think they could nest in Leif either.'

'Yeah. What the hell are they? Devils? They can't be angels.'

Ena said, 'I don't think we've got the word. Or the concept either. We'll have to develop them.'

'Maybe. If we can.'

Brennan opened the locker, and something smaller than a bee flew out.

'It got out,' he said. 'Some way it got out. Where the hell did it go?'

'"They get smaller as they come closer."'

'What's that supposed to mean?'

'What it says, perhaps. Leif said it before you pulled him in.'

Brennan rubbed his jaw. Rather to her surprise, Ena discovered that she enjoyed watching him rub his jaw.

'Mine didn't get smaller when I was chasing it.'

Ena nodded. 'It wasn't coming closer. You were, or you were trying to.'

They jumped.

'Sonofabitch! Did you feel that?'

'Yes.' She discovered that she was holding his arm, and let go. 'Yes, I did. It was Leif, up on the bridge.'

'Sure. Had to be.' Brennan glanced at his watch. 'He went the minute recharge was complete.'

She nodded. 'Now we'll have to see in which direction.'

They held a trial the next day, a kangaroo court with Leif tied into his seat. 'I'm the prosecutor,' Brennan explained. Brennan no longer sounded, or looked, angry, but his voice was deadly serious. 'You're the defendant and the counsel for the defense, too. Ena's the judge. She and I think that will be fair. What you think doesn't matter. I'm going to put the case against you. You'll be given an opportunity to rebut it. Ena will decide on your penalty.'

'If any,' Ena said.

'She'll decide your penalty, if there is one. Do you understand?'

'I didn't want to hurt any of you,' Leif said. He might have been talking to himself. 'I just wanted to go back. Fuel's forty-seven percent surplus. Food's—'

Brennan raised his fist and looked at Ena.

She shook her head. 'We used to be friends, Leif. I'd like us to be friends again. Like us to be friends right now.'

'All right.'

'Good. This is a trial. I am your judge. Do you understand that?'

'I'm not stupid. I just want to go back.'

'I know. Brennan?'

'He sabotaged our mission. Not by some accident. Not even by inattention. He did it deliberately. He brought his damned birds in. We don't know how many there are, but there's a lot. You and I will have to round them up and kill them. It may take years, and we may never catch them all.'

Leif started to speak, but Brennan silenced him. 'He negated our last jump, and he'll be a danger to us, and to the mission, for the next fifteen years. Say that we let him live. We'll have to lock him up and feed him, just you and me, on top of all our other duties. We'll have to make sure he stays locked up, because we can't trust him out for a minute. One of us will have to walk with him in the spinner, and that will have to be me, because he might jump you. If—'

'I might jump you, too,' Leif said.

'Sure.' Brennan grinned. 'Want to try?'

'He will try,' Ena said thoughtfully. 'He might even succeed, if he catches you off guard. Now stop arguing with him.'

She pointed to Leif. 'You're to be quiet until it's your turn to talk. We'll tape your mouth if we have to.'

Brennan cleared his throat. 'You're right. I don't think he'd succeed, but he'll try. Sooner or later, he'll try to jump me. If he does succeed, the mission is shot. Finished. Ruined. Six lives and billions of dollars, all wasted.'

Ena nodded.

'That's not the only danger. This ship wasn't built as a prison. No matter where we lock him up, he'll have years to try to figure some way out. I've never wanted to kill anybody, and God knows I don't want to kill Leif. We're going to have to do it just the same. Can we keep him sedated for fifteen years? Have you got enough dope for that?'

Ena shook her head.

'For one year?'

'We might keep him lightly sedated for a year or more. Not for two.'

'How do you know lightly would be enough?'

'I don't,' Ena said.

Brennan sighed. 'Okay, you've got my case. Can he be killed, legally? I don't know and you don't either, but we both doubt it. So I'm not asking you to kill him or even help me to. I'll do it alone. I'll stick him in the airlock without a suit, and we'll write it up in the log. Maybe they'll try me for murder when we get home. Maybe they won't. I'll take my chances. Now let's hear Leif.'

'I didn't endanger the mission,' Leif began. 'I've explained that already. There's plenty of food and plenty of fuel. The air plant's running fine. What I tried to do would have delayed the ship's return to earth by a few days. No more than that. You two are perfectly capable of taking the ship back. If you were to die, it's perfectly capable of taking itself back. The six of us were put on board to take care of emergencies, and because we'd be needed once the ship got to Beta Andromedae. We've done all that, or at least we've done it as well as three people could, taking pix, measuring the magnetic field, mapping, and all the rest of it.'

'You finished?' Brennan asked.

'No. You blame me for bringing the birds. If what you say were correct – it's not, but if it were – I'd deserve a medal. Neither of you found alien life. Not a speck. Not a trace. I found it, and returned to the ship with live specimens. You won't concede a thing, I know. But if your accusation were correct, that would be the fact and I would be a hero.'

Ena said, 'You say it's not.'

'I do. The birds came into me while I was suited up, out in space. I told you they were there.'

Reluctantly, Ena nodded.

'I didn't want to come back onto the ship, infected as I was. Brennan forced me to. If bringing my birds onto the ship was a crime, Brennan is the criminal. Not me.'

'You're the one who sabotaged our mission,' Brennan said.

Ena raised her hand. 'We've heard the accusation and Leif's defense. I don't want to get into it again.'

Leif said, 'You promised me a chance to defend myself. I have one more thing to say. It will take less than a minute. May I do it?'

She nodded. 'Go ahead.'

'Brennan threatens me with death. Surely you can see that I wanted to return to Beta Andromedae so that I could die there. I'll suit up and go out again. You need only let me do it. Put a K beside my name in the log, and note that I was a suicide. It will be true, and if either of you is accused of my murder a veriscope reading will prove your innocence.'

Ena smiled. 'Brennan?'

'I'm willing if you are.'

'I'm not. Not as it stands. You'll have to do us a service first, Leif. Go through the ship and collect the birds. All of them. Get them back inside you. They went in once, and I think they'll go in again if you approach them right. Do it, and we'll go back as you ask and put you out.'

He had spread himself like a starfish, and the birds had flown. All of them – or nearly all. Now he blew like a dry leaf in the solar wind, revolving like a cartwheel.

His air was running out. His body would die; and that which would not die would be free at last, free to rove the universe and beyond.

Death waited beside him, warm and dark and friendly, and Leif could hardly wait.

In her cabin, Ena smiled to herself as she shook the small brown bottle. She had caught the faint fragrance of Brennan's aftershave when he relieved her on the bridge. He could not possibly have brought enough to last for half the voyage; thus he had hoarded some and was using it now.

The odor haunted her, delightful and unidentifiable. What aftershave had Walt used, what cologne? She had known those things once, but they were gone and only the memory of Brennan's faint fragrance remained. Russian leather? Spice? Neither seemed correct.

Turning the bottle over in her hand, she reread the label she had read so often since finding the bottle in a food locker: VANILLA EXTRACT.

She would smell like a cookie.

Opening the bottle, she applied the thin brown liquid it contained to five strategic spots.

Brennan would welcome her return. They would kiss, and she would unbutton his shirt. And then –

She interrupted the daydream to listen. A bird sang in her right wrist.

UNWELL

Carolyn Parkhurst

I was feeling a bit unwell, so I called Yvonne to come and sit with me. I believe that sisters have a responsibility to look out for one another, even though that doesn't seem to be a popular view with everybody these days. I think that if more people would take their family responsibilities more seriously, then the world wouldn't be in the kind of trouble . . . But the phone was ringing.

'Hello,' said Yvonne.

'Yvonne, I need you to come over this afternoon. I'm not well.'

I heard her sigh on the other end; I don't believe she even tried to mask it. 'Is it really important, Arlette? I've got a million wedding things to do.'

'Oh, the wedding. Is that coming up soon?'

'It's Saturday, Arlette, and you know it.'

'Well, I hope I'll be able to make it. I've been feeling weak all day, and I'm not at all sure I'll be myself by Saturday.'

'Arlette, please don't start . . .'

'Well, it's hardly my fault if I'm ill. But perhaps if I had a little help . . .'

There was a long silence. I could just see her on the other end, wearing that outlandish engagement ring on her finger. A woman her age. 'All right,' she said. 'I'll get Arthur to do some of my errands for me. I'll be over in half an hour.'

We hung up, and I leaned back against my bed pillows, well pleased.

The fact is, this should by all rights be my wedding. Yvonne and I met Arthur at the same time, and it was clear from the beginning that I was the one he was interested in. It used to be, in biblical times, and I believe some other notable points in history, that if there were two unmarried sisters, the younger one wasn't allowed to be married before the elder. It was illegal. If the younger sister tried to break the rules and run off and get married anyway, they'd put her to death. I should tell that to Yvonne. They'd cut her head right off. It was just the way it was.

We met Arthur on a seniors' cruise that Yvonne took me on in honor of my seventieth birthday. It was her idea, and not a very good one, I must say – the room was cramped, the food was terrible, and most of the other passengers were pathetic old bores. When Yvonne gave me the tickets, she had said, 'Who knows? Maybe we'll meet a couple of nice widowers,' but there were three women for every man, and what men there were were bald, toothless and demented. I actually saw one of them trying to eat soup with his fingers. So when Arthur walked into the dining room, tall and unstooped, with his full head of silver hair gleaming in the light from the nautical-themed chandeliers, all the old biddies in the room seemed to sit up a little straighter. And when he sat down next to me, I thought, Watch me. I am going to charm the pants off this man. So I started up a conversation about current events – test him, I thought, see if he's still in possession of a fully functioning mind – and he seemed to be able to talk about something more than what kind of medication he was taking, which automatically made him a better dining companion than anyone else at the table. He and I chatted and laughed all through the meal, and Yvonne just sort of melted into the upholstery, as usual. It's always been that way; there's a softness to her, a sleepiness, that I can't stand. If it weren't for me, the world would have eaten her up long ago.

So Yvonne sat quietly and picked her way through her prime rib – no appetite on that girl, never has been – while I began laying the ground-work for my grand seduction. Things were going quite well, and I was sure I had him in my pocket. Arthur and Arlette, my mind kept singing, Arthur and Arlette. I was ecstatic, and God knows I deserve some happiness. Yvonne knows how lonely I've been since my Stephen passed away. She doesn't mind being alone; she's used to it. But I was made to be married, and in my mind I already had the church decorated, the flowers arranged artfully on the tables.

And then at the end of the meal, something odd happened. Arthur rose from his seat, helped me out of my chair and said, looking right at me, 'Might I interest you in a walk in the moonlight, Yvonne?'

I felt a little prick of acid in my stomach, and my whole body tightened. I saw Yvonne raise her head hopefully, but I shot her a look. 'Well,' I said to Arthur tartly, 'I'd be a lot more interested if you tried calling me by the right name.'

For an instant, Arthur's face turned cool as he flicked his eyes between me and Yvonne. Then he widened his eyes in a gentlemanly show of shock and proceeded to fall all over himself apologizing. 'I'm so sorry,' he said. 'I must have misheard the introductions. So Yvonne is your sister?'

'That's right,' I said. I drew my wrap around me, closing myself up. It'd take a little more wooing to make up for a flub like that.

'Please forgive me,' he said. And then, as if this had anything to do with anything, 'You two look so much alike.'

Well, that was a fatal misstep on his part. Our whole lives, Yvonne and I have been told we look like twins, but I don't see it myself. I don't see it at all. True, we're only thirteen months apart – and oh! how often I've wished I could go back and recapture the glory of those precious thirteen months when it was only me! – and we have similar coloring, but my features are much more graceful. Any person who thinks that comparing me to Yvonne is a compliment has a lot to learn. And the lessons might as well begin as soon as possible.

'Sorry,' I said, my voice as icy as the wretched frozen swan sculpture defiling the buffet. 'But I'm feeling a bit tired this evening, and I think I'll pass on your kind invitation.' And I swept off to bed, my dowdy sister in tow.

My plan was to keep Arthur at arm's length for another half day or so, and then gradually let him win me over again through much hard work and flattery. But at breakfast the next morning, I could see I'd made a tactical error. Arthur ignored me completely and began doting on Yvonne as if she were some rare bird he'd been hoping to spot for years. By mid-morning, they were heading to the on-board casino together; by late afternoon, they'd signed up for a ballroom dancing lesson. And I was left sitting on my deck chair, stewing in my fury, watching the waves pass me by.

Truth be told, this is not the first time Yvonne and I have found ourselves in a situation like this. When I first met my late husband Stephen – I was twenty-one at the time, and Yvonne was twenty – he was already dating Yvonne. She and I were both working in our father's bakery, which I thought was a pleasant enough thing to do while I was waiting to find a husband. But it wasn't enough for Yvonne, and she'd started

76

taking classes at a local college. She wanted to become a librarian – like you need to go to school to learn how to say 'shhh.' Well, none of us knew anything about it till later, but apparently there was a young man who rode the bus at the same time as Yvonne, and the two of them used to look at each other over the tops of their books as they rode. And one or the other of them would smile a little, and then they'd get all embarrassed and look away. Quite a romance, wasn't it, all that reading and looking away – *Casablanca* it was not. Finally, after a year of this – *yes*, it took a full year for one of those ninnies to make a move – the young man moved over to sit next to Yvonne and say hello. They became inseparable after that, riding the bus together and talking about books. The young man's name was Stephen, and he was a poet. At least, that's what he said; the truth was, he was an accountant with ambitions to be a poet.

Anyway, she brought him home one night to have dinner with Mother and Father and me, and you could have knocked me over with a feather. Here I'd been flirting with every man who came into the bakery, while mousy little Yvonne bent her head over her books, and she'd found a man all by herself.

So Yvonne brings this man home, this shy, gawky man who spent a year trying to get up the courage to say hello, and we all sat in the parlor and looked at him. And I'll tell you, he was handsome. He had these big eyes, like a doe, and his legs were so long, they stretched way out to the center of the room. But I watched him and Yvonne watching each other, two little mice peeping out of their holes, and I thought this boy needs a woman who will turn him into something. Someone lively and bold, not timid like Yvonne. I looked at their future together, and I saw a lifetime of quiet nights, sitting side by side, waiting to see which one of them would gather the courage to say, 'Would you like milk in your tea?' Reading books together – that's exactly the kind of thing they would have done. It made me want to yawn. This Stephen, he needed a woman who could teach him how to have fun, a woman who wasn't afraid to speak her mind. Stephen and I were meant to be together, I could see it right away. Didn't we deserve some happiness? And what would Yvonne do with a man like that, anyway? Yvonne had her studies, her solitary pursuits. She was always happiest on her own. And so, for the sake of us all, I set out to save Stephen from Yvonne.

It was harder than I expected. He had become quite enamored of her, for reasons I never could quite imagine. I tried all the more subtle forms of flirtation – never were more gloves dropped in a young man's path, never were a young lady's shoulders more often proclaimed to be chilly – but they went right over his head. And then one day, I got a little help from fate. The three of us were supposed to go to a nearby lake together for a picnic – by this point, I'd insinuated myself into most of Stephen and Yvonne's activities – but Yvonne got sick and couldn't go. Stephen was all ready to cancel the whole thing, but I put on a sad face and told him I'd spent all morning in the kitchen, cooking up my special deviled eggs, and why couldn't the two of us have a nice day? And Yvonne, predictably, took my side and told us to go and have a good time. Really, that woman never knows when to stand up for herself. So Stephen and I went to the lake ourselves, and I made sure we found a nice, secluded spot. We spent the afternoon sitting in the shade of a lovely weeping willow tree, and we just had a wonderful time, talking and laughing. Later, Yvonne would ask me how I could do such a thing to her, but at the time, it didn't feel like Yvonne had anything to do with it at all. We were falling in love, that's all there is to it. I'd sneaked some of Father's whiskey into the picnic basket, and neither Stephen nor I was much of a drinker, so we both got a bit tipsy, and when a sudden thunderstorm forced us to take shelter in the backseat of his car, we just did what came naturally. Our love was a force of nature, I always said.

Of course, there were tears and accusations, but a month later, when I told Stephen I was pregnant, it just seemed like it would be for the best if the two of us got married. And by the time I realized that I'd gotten my dates confused and I wasn't pregnant at all, we were already back from our honeymoon.

For a while, Yvonne kept herself away from our door, and she and Stephen seemed a bit awkward whenever they were near each other, but I made it clear that I wouldn't have the two of them tiptoeing around over some little doomed infatuation, and they got the picture pretty quick.

Stephen and I had a good marriage. At first, he wasn't the kind of husband I'd hoped he would be, but with my guidance, he began to take shape. I got him to give up his poetry and his reading, and all the other silly things he liked to fill his time with, and to concentrate on his career instead. Within a few years, he'd risen through the ranks of his firm, and we had enough money to make a nice life for ourselves. Stephen lost the boyishness and softness he'd had when I married him, and it pleased me to see the hard edges he developed in their place. We tried for a while to have children, but we never could – some problem with my uterus that I'm sure you don't want to hear about – and if I'm being honest with myself, I think it's probably just as well. I'm not really the maternal type.

It was a few years after we got married that Mother gave me the Christmas ornaments. Mother had quite an artistic eye, and her Christmas tree was always breathtaking. Over the years, she'd amassed a beautiful collection of ornaments, some of them quite valuable, and I know Yvonne had always hoped they'd pass to her someday. I think she was quite hurt that Mother chose to give them to me, but it was fast becoming clear that her role was going to be that of maiden aunt, hovering at the edges of our family Christmases, and it just wouldn't have made any sense for her to have them. Mother was a practical woman, and she saw this as well as I did. She knew it was the way of the world, and there was nothing you or I could do about it. But Yvonne never could see things that were plain to everybody else, and I know she took it as a slight. Honestly, it's forty-five years later, and I don't think she's gotten over it yet.

That first Christmas we had the ornaments, I had a big party for the whole family. I made a beautiful ham dinner, and we all sat beneath my perfect Christmas tree and opened gifts. Stephen played the piano – now there was one hobby I approved of – and we sang carols late into the night. After everyone left, Yvonne offered to stay late and clean up a little, since I'd done all the work of the party, and I agreed to her kind offer. I went up to bed, leaving Yvonne in the kitchen and Stephen still sitting at the piano, picking out tunes.

It must have been two hours later when I woke up and discovered that Stephen wasn't in bed with me. The lights were still on downstairs, and I crept down to the living room. Stephen and Yvonne were sitting on the couch together. They had their arms around each other, and they were looking deep into each other's eyes, their foreheads touching. She was stroking the back of his neck and speaking to him in a low voice. In the instant before the floorboards creaked and they looked up and saw me, I heard her say two words to him. I heard her say, 'Leave her.'

Then, like I said, there was the business of the floorboards, and the two of them snapped their heads around like they'd been caught stealing, which, in a way, they had.

'Get out of my house,' I roared, and for a minute I wasn't sure which of them I was talking to. They just sat there, frozen. I plucked one of the ornaments from the tree, a little white porcelain angel, and threw it at them with the newfound strength of a woman betrayed. It hit the wall over their heads and landed on the floor, chipping one of its wings, but it didn't break. It was made of harder stuff than I'd thought.

Stephen didn't leave me, of course. What a thought. Say what you will about him, he took his responsibilities seriously. I think he knew he had it pretty good with me. Really, not so much changed after that; I got a new fur coat out of it, and a trump card to play in every argument we ever had. And when Yvonne came around, sniffling and saying her sorries, I welcomed her back with open arms. Friends close, enemies closer. But I made sure that she and Stephen never had a single minute alone together, not a single moment in thirty years. When Stephen was lying in his hospital bed, two hours away from dying, he asked

me if he could have a few minutes to say good-
bye to her alone, and you know what I said? No.
I said no. Simple as that.

It was the pictures that got me thinking. I don't
know if you've ever been on a cruise – if you
haven't, don't waste your money – but one of the
many irksome things they do is take endless pictures
of you and then try to sell you prints. There's a
whole hallway dedicated to displaying these
souvenir masterpieces, and you have to go through
and pick your face out of the crowd. It's quite
depressing, actually, the sameness of all the
photos. Here's the whole herd of cattle, walking
up the gangplank; here they are stuffed into their
ill-fitting evening wear, posing next to the poor
captain, who has to hear the same jokes over and
over again – 'If you're here, who's driving the ship?'
And it turns out you're just like the rest of them,
smiling for the camera and trying to look like
you're having fun. No, I wasn't going to spend a
penny on their pictures.

But with Yvonne spending every waking moment
with Arthur (only her waking moments, mind
you – the one wild week of her life, and she's too
much of a prude to have any fun), I found myself
with some spare time. And so I took a walk down
the hall of farm animals to try to pinpoint the
moment when my sister's betrayal began. Look –
here are Yvonne and Arlette arriving together,
looking as happy as two sisters can be. Here's

Arthur, arriving all by his lonesome. Here are Yvonne and Arlette against a splashy Caribbean backdrop; here they are against a sprinkle of fake stars. And then – here it is, right before your eyes! – Arlette standing by herself on Formal Night, dressed in her prettiest clothes, and there are Yvonne and Arthur posed together like some old married couple at their golden anniversary party. Look at them together. You can see right away they don't match. At least, I thought, with no small amount of glee, at least the picture didn't come out well; Arthur had turned his head at the moment the shutter snapped, so you can hardly even tell it's him. And that's when I noticed something odd. I looked back through all the earlier photos, and I noticed there wasn't a single one of Arthur's face. It would seem that for some reason he didn't want his picture taken. And that's when I thought, This is a man with something to hide.

I was concerned for Yvonne's welfare, of course. You wouldn't know it from the way she dresses or the way she decorates her home, but Yvonne has quite a bit of money. None of us ever expected it, of course – librarians barely make enough to keep themselves in books and donations to public TV stations. But there was a man who used to come into the library where she worked, a little old man who liked to come in each morning to read the paper. And I guess he was sweet on Yvonne. Not that anything ever came of it – story of Yvonne's life, or so everyone thought before

Arthur – but I guess they used to talk to each other, and she'd bend the rules for him and let him drink his coffee while he read, as long as he wasn't too obvious and didn't spill. She used to tell me about this man, about how he'd point out articles she might be interested in, and how after a while he started bringing a cup of coffee for her too, and I'd say, 'You're living a movie-star life, Yvonne. The thrills never stop.' But then one day, the man died in his sleep, and he left Yvonne almost five million dollars. You'd think a man with that much money could've afforded his own newspaper subscription, but anyway. Of course, it was a big surprise to everyone, and there were stories about Yvonne in all the papers. She told the reporters, 'Oh, it won't change my life,' just like those lottery winners who go out and buy helicopters the next day, but for her it was really true. She kept her job at the library, and she still gets her hair cut at the six-dollar place like some no-class nonmillionaire. Pathetic.

So when I saw the way Arthur kept hiding his face in all those pictures, at first I thought he just didn't want to be seen with Yvonne and her six-dollar hair. But when I noticed that he was doing the same thing in all the earlier pictures, the pre-let's-trample-on-Arlette-and-her-big-soft-heart pictures, I realized what was going on. It wasn't that he didn't want to be seen with Yvonne; he just didn't want to be seen, period.

★　★　★

When we got home – never have I been so happy to put my feet on dry land – I decided I was going to find out what Arthur's story was. It was easier than you'd think. I sat down and watched that *America's Most Wanted* show, and I found out they had one of those Web sites. So I turned on the computer Yvonne gave me for my birthday last year, and I had a look around. And wouldn't you know it, I found Arthur in an hour. His real name isn't Arthur, it turns out. It's Martin Edward Jaffe, and he's wanted in connection with the disappearance of a woman he married in Denver. A wealthy woman, a whirlwind courtship. It's such an old story it's almost boring. Honestly, could Yvonne be any more naive? I sent away to Denver for a copy of a newspaper article that had his picture in it, and I waited for the right moment to bring it to Yvonne's attention.

After hanging up the phone with Yvonne, I settle myself against the pillows, and I wait to see whether or not today is going to be the day. It takes her more than an hour to arrive, which is not a point in her favor – honestly, she only lives five minutes away – and at first, I think maybe I won't tell her at all. Serves her right, I think, she's digging her own grave. But when you get right down to it, I'm a big softie, and she is my only sister. Still, it's not an easy thing to bring up; it would kill her to have to cancel the wedding at this late date, poor thing. She's happier than I've seen her in years, and who am I to take that away from her? So while she's downstairs heating up some broth for me, I take the box of Christmas ornaments out of the closet. Inside, wrapped in old newspaper, are all the foolish pieces of glass and glitter she seems to care so much about. God knows why I've held on to them this long. I take one out and unwrap it; it's the little white angel with the chip in its wing. I place the angel on the newspaper clipping from Denver and wrap it up tight, then bury it deep in the box. I hear Yvonne coming up the stairs, and I quickly close the box and get back into bed.

Yvonne comes into the room with a tray of soup and crackers. I can see she's brought saltines instead of Ritz, and I almost decide to call off the whole plan and leave her to find out about Arthur for herself. But I take a deep breath and remind myself that she's my sister. And in any case, she's already seen the box in the middle of the floor.

She sets the tray down on the bed and points at the box. 'What's this?' she asks, even though it's clearly marked and she's seen it a hundred times before. Really, she is the most infuriating creature. Arthur doesn't know what he's gotten himself into.

But I smile and make my voice as sugary as the icing on the tacky wedding cake she's sure to have on Saturday. 'A wedding gift,' I say. 'I know how you've always wanted these.' She gets that look on her face that I've always hated, a sort of tentative, frightened joy, like a dog taking meat from a hand she knows might hit her.

'Arlette, really?' she says. She sounds like she might cry, and I feel like pinching her.

'Well, I expect I'll be coming over to your house for Christmas from now on. It just makes sense.'

'Oh, Arlette!' she cries and throws her arms around me, nearly upsetting my bowl of broth. 'That's why you made me come over here today, isn't it? You're the sweetest sister a person could have!'

'You always could see right through me,' I say and bite into a saltine.

I watch as she picks the box up to carry it down to her car, chattering away about some nonsense or other. I think about the picture of Arthur hidden deep inside, his lying face wrapped around a ruined angel. She'll find it at Christmastime, if her eyes are sharp. And if anything should happen before then, I can hardly be held accountable. I've done everything I can.

And if, God forbid, anything should happen before then, I'm prepared to take the situation into my own hands. I have no doubt that, with a little bit of guidance, Arthur could become the kind of husband I deserve.

A LIFE IN FICTIONS

Kat Howard

He wrote me into a story again.

I told him to stop doing that, after we broke up. In fact, it was one of the reasons that we broke up. I mean, being a muse is all well and good until you actually become one.

The first time it happened, I was flattered. And it wasn't like my normal life was so great that I was going to miss it, you know? So getting pulled into that world – a world he had written just for me, where I was the everything, the unattainable, the ideal – it was pretty powerful.

When he finished the story, and I came back to the real world, the first thing I did was screw him until my thighs ached. It was our first time together. He said it was the best sex of his life.

When I asked him if someone had ever fallen into a story that he had written before, he said not that he knew of. Oh, sure, he had based characters on people he knew, stolen little bits of their lives. A gesture, a phrase, a particular color of eye or way of walking. The petty thievery all writers commit.

I asked what he had done differently this time.

'I was falling in love with you, I guess. You were all I could think of. So when I wrote Marah, there you were in my head. Always.'

I hadn't fallen into the story right away, and I didn't know what happened in the parts where Marah didn't appear. Reading the finished draft was this weird mix of déjà vu and mystery.

Apparently inspired by my real-world sexual abandon, the next thing he wrote me into was an erotic novella. Ali was a great deal more flexible than I was, both physically and in her gender preferences.

I really enjoyed that story, but one night I tried something in bed that Ali thought was fun but that he thought was beyond kinky. After that, the only sex scenes he wrote me into involved oral sex.

Men can be so predictable, even when they are literary geniuses.

Maybe especially then.

The next time he wrote me into something, I lost my job. It was a novel, what he was working on then, and when he was writing Nora, I would just disappear from my life as soon as he picked up his pen. For days, or even weeks at a time, when the writing was going well.

He said he didn't know what happened to me during those times. He would go to my apartment, check on things, water my plants. When he remembered. When he wasn't so deep in the writing that nothing outside registered.

I was always in his head during those times, he said, at the edges of his thoughts. As if that should reassure me.

It happened faster. He would begin to write, and I would be in the story, and I would stay there until he was finished.

The more I lived in his writing, the less I lived in the real world, and the less I remembered what it was like to live in the real world, as a real person, as me.

When the writing was going well, I would be surrounded by the comfortable, warm feeling that someone else knew what was going on, was making all the decisions, was the safety net under the high wire. Everything was gauzy, soft focus, fuzzed at the periphery.

I could have an adventure without worrying about the consequences. After all, I was always at the edges of his thoughts.

Until the day I wasn't. Everything froze, and I was in a cold, white room, full of statues of the people I had been talking to.

I walked from person to person, attempting to start conversations, but nothing happened. Walked around the room again, looking for a way out, but there was nothing. Solid white walls, floor, ceiling. It was a large room, but I could feel the pressure of the walls against my skin.

I walked to the center of the room, and sat, cross-legged, on the floor. Waiting.

Have you ever had your mind go blank? That

space between one thought and the next when your brain is just white noise, when there is not one thought in your head – do you remember that feeling?

Imagine that absence extending forever. There's no way of escaping it, because you don't know – not don't remember, don't know – what you were thinking about before your brain blanked out, and so you don't know what to do to get it started again. There's just nothing. Silence. White.

And there's no time. No way of telling how long you sit in that vast, claustrophobic white room, becoming increasingly less.

I never was able to figure out how long I waited there. But suddenly I was in a room I had never seen before, back in the real world, and he was there.

There were wrinkles at the corners of his eyes, and gray threading through his hair. Writer's block, he explained to me. He had tried to write through it, work on other projects, but nothing helped. Finally, that morning, he had abandoned the novel as unworkable.

I asked if he had tried to bring me back, while he was stuck.

He hadn't really thought of it.

That was when I broke up with him.

He had, I discovered, become quite successful while I was away. A critical darling, praised especially for the complexity, the reality, of his female characters.

Speaking of Marah in an interview, he described her as his one lost love. The interviewer found it romantic.

I found the interviewer tiresome. Being lost was not romantic at all.

Parts of me stayed lost, or got covered over by all those other women I had been for him. Sure, they were me, but they were his view of me, exaggerated, slightly shifted, truth told slanted.

I would turn up a song on the radio, then remember that it was Ali who liked gypsy punk. I abandoned my favorite bakery for two weeks when I convinced myself that I had Fiona's gluten allergy.

For three months, I thought my name was Marah.

During all of this, there were intervals of normalcy. But I still felt the tugs as he borrowed little pieces of me for his fictions. I would lose my favorite perfume, or the memory of the first time I had my heart broken. Tiny bits of myself that would slough away, painlessly. Sometimes they would return when he wrote 'The End.' More often, they did not.

I reminded him that he had promised not to write about me anymore. He assured me he hadn't meant to. It was just bits, here and there. He'd be more careful. And really, I ought to be flattered.

But then a week of my life disappeared. I loved that short story, and Imogen was an amazing character, the kind of woman I wished I was. That wasn't the point.

The point was, he had stolen me from myself again. I was just gone, and I didn't know where I went. And there were more things about myself that I had forgotten. Was green really my favorite color?

I flicked on the computer, started typing madly. Everything I could remember about myself. But when I looked over the file, there were gaps that I knew I had once remembered, and duplications of events.

Panting, I stripped off my clothing and stared at myself, hoping that my body was more real than my mind. But was that scar on my knee from falling off my bike when I was twelve, or from a too-sharp rock at the beach when I was seventeen. Was that really how I waved hello? Would I cry at a time like this?

Anyone would, I supposed.

I tried to rewrite myself. I scoured boxes of faded flower petals, crumpled ticket stubs, paged obsessively through old yearbooks. Called friend after friend to play do you remember.

When I remembered enough to ask. To know who my friends were.

It didn't work. Whatever gift he had or curse that I was under that let him pull me into his stories, it was a magic too arcane for me to duplicate.

And still, the gaps in my life increased. New changes happened. I woke one morning to find my hair was white. Not like an old woman's, but the platinum white of a rock star or some elven queen.

I didn't dye it back.

There was a collection published of his short fiction. He appeared on Best Of lists, and was shortlisted for important literary prizes.

I forgot if I took milk in my coffee.

He called, asked to see me. Told me he still loved me, was haunted by memories of my skin, my voice, my scent. I missed, I thought, those things, too. So I told him yes.

It took him a moment to recognize me, he said, when I walked across the bar to meet him. Something was different. I told him I didn't know what that might be.

He ordered for both of us. I let him. I was sure he knew what I liked.

There was a story, he explained. He thought maybe the best thing he would ever write. He could feel the electricity of it crackle across his skin, feel the words that he would write pound and echo in his brain.

He had an outline that I could look at, see what I thought. He slid a slim folder across the table.

I wondered aloud why, this time, he would ask permission. This one was longer. An epic. He wasn't sure how long it would take him to write it. And after what had happened the last time, when I had . . . Well. He wanted to ask.

I appreciated the gesture.

I drummed my fingers across the top of the folder, but did not open it.

A waiter discreetly set a martini to the right of my plate. Funny. I had thought that it was Madeleine who drank martinis. But I sipped, and closed my eyes in pleasure at the sharpness of the alcohol.

I said yes.

To one more story, this masterpiece that I could see burning in his eyes. But I had a condition.

Anything, he said. Whatever I needed.

I wanted him to leave me in the story when he was finished.

He told me he had wondered if I might ask for that. I was surprised he hadn't known. He nodded agreement, and that was settled.

We talked idly through dinner. Occasionally his eyes would unfocus, and I could see the lines of plot being woven together behind them.

I wondered what he would name me this time, almost asked, then realized it didn't matter. Then realized I wasn't even sure what my own name was anymore. Grace, maybe? I thought that sounded right. Grace.

He started scribbling on the cover of the folder while we were waiting for the check. I watched him write.

'Rafe fell in love with her voice first, tumbled into it when she introduced herself as . . .'

LET THE PAST BEGIN

Jonathan Carroll

Eamon Reilly was handsome and sloppy. He seemed to know everyone, even waitresses in restaurants. When he walked in the door, they beamed and began seriously flirting the minute he sat down at their table. I saw this happen several times at different places, places none of us had ever been to before. I asked if he knew these women but he always said no.

Eamon wore his heart on his sleeve and it worked. People cared about him even when he was being impossible, which was pretty often. He drove an old, badly neglected Mercedes that was filthy inside and out. Whenever you rode in it, he had to move stuff off the passenger's seat and throw it in the back. Sometimes you couldn't believe what was there – a metal dowsing rod; a box of diapers (he was single); a jai alai *xistera*; or once a very intimately autographed, badly wrinkled photo of a famous movie actress. He wrote everything in block letters so precise that you might have guessed it came from a typewriter. He kept a detailed daily diary but no one ever saw what was in it, although he carried the book

97

around with him everywhere. His love life was a constant disaster and we wondered why no woman ever stayed with him for very long.

He had once been together with my girlfriend Ava for a couple of weeks. But she was no help when I finally got up the nerve to ask why she broke up with him. 'We didn't fit.'

'*And?*'

'And nothing. Some people just don't fit together in certain configurations. There are people you can be good friends with, but if you turn it into lovers, the mix is wrong or toxic or . . . something. For me, Eamon is a good guy to hang around with but he wasn't a good boyfriend.'

'Why?'

She narrowed her eyes, which is usually the sign a topic *is* closed and Ava doesn't want to talk about it anymore. But this time was different. 'Sit down.'

'What?'

'Sit down. I'm going to tell you a story. It's kind of long.'

I did as I was told. When Ava tells you to do something, you do it because, well, because she's Ava. The woman likes dessert, foreign politics, the truth, working in perilous situations, and wonder, not necessarily in that order. She's a journalist who goes on assignment to extremely dangerous places around the world like Spinkai Raghzai, Pakistan, or Sierra Leone. You see her on the TV news holding down her hair or helmet as a military helicopter takes off nearby, leaving her and a small camera crew in some forward armed outpost or barren village that was attacked by rebels the night before. She is fearless, self-confident, and impatient. She is also pregnant, which is why she's home these days. We're pretty sure the child is mine but there is a chance that it might be Eamon's.

I've known Ava Malcolm twelve years and loved her for about eleven of them. During those eleven years, she expressed virtually no interest in me save for an occasional late-night telephone call from unimaginable places like Ouagadougou or Aleppo. The reception on these calls was invariably bad and scratchy. More often than not until the birth of satellite telephones, somewhere in the middle of these chats the line would suddenly go dead, as if it had grown tired of our gabbing and wanted to go to sleep.

Later she admitted that for a while she thought I was gay. But when she came back from some assignment at the end of the world and saw I was living with Jan Schick, it put an end to my gay days in Ava Malcolm's mind.

But poor Jan didn't stand a chance. I always assumed I would only get to love Ava from a distance, be grateful for any time she gave me, and go on admiring this brave talented woman as she went about living her larger-than-life life.

Then she got shot. The bitter irony is that it did not happen in some far-flung flyblown,

130-degree-in-the-shade hellhole where the bad guys rode in on animals instead of tanks. It happened at a convenience store four blocks from her New York apartment. A quick trip to the market for a bottle of red wine and a bag of Cheez Doodles coincided with a dunce named Leaky trying to rob his first store with a gun he later said went off accidentally, twice. One of those bullets nicked Ava's shoulder. But since it came from a Glock G36 subcompact pistol, being 'nicked' was an understatement. It probably would not have happened if she'd dropped to the floor like the rest of the people in the store as soon as Leaky started screaming. But Ava being Ava, she wanted to see what was going on, so she just stood there until the gun went off while pointed roughly in her direction.

Ava saw many terrible things in her years as a reporter but had always escaped being hurt. However, as is often the case with people who have been seriously injured, it traumatized her. When she got out of the hospital, she 'traveled, screwed men, and hid for a year.' Her words.

'I came out of the hospital with my arm in a sling and my ass on fire. I was about 142 percent crazy, I'll say that. I wanted to live life twice as hard afterward – see twice as many things, and have as many men as I could. I'd come this close to dying and the only sure thing I learned from the experience was I wanted *more*: more life, more sex, more new places . . .

'So I used up all the frequent-flyer miles I'd accrued over the years in my job. When they were gone, I called in every favor I had due from people who could get me where I wanted to go. I spent a lot of time in southwestern Russia because that area was like the new Wild West, what with all the oil money and exploration going on down there.

'It was in Baku that I met the Yit.'

This was typical Ava storytelling. On her TV reports she gave you relevant information in perfect sound bites and was crystal clear about it. Yet in person she often got so carried away telling you a story or personal anecdote that she overlooked the fact you might not know Baku or, like most people on planet earth, what a 'Yit' was.

'Please explain the last two terms.'

'Azerbaijan,' she said impatiently. 'Baku is the capital of Azerbaijan.'

'Okay, that's Baku. What's a Yit?'

'A *djelloum*.'

'What's a jell-loom?'

'A Yit is another word for a *djelloum* – kind of like a fortune-teller but more shamany. It's a sort of combo fortune-teller and sage. But in Azerbaijan, women are *djelloum*, not men. Which is interesting because it's a very macho, male-oriented society otherwise.'

'Okay – Baku, and a Yit.'

She leaned over and kissed me on one side of my mouth. 'I like how you stop me and ask for clarification. Most people just let me rattle on.'

'Proceed.'

'Okay. So at the end of the trip I wanted to spend some time in Baku because one of my favorite novels, *Ali and Nino*, takes place there. The book makes the city sound like one of the most romantic places on earth. It isn't, but that's beside the point.

'I was visiting a section called Sabunçu. My guide was Magsud, an Azeri fluent in English who we'd used before when I was there on assignment for the network. So I knew the guy pretty well. He knew the sort of things I liked and was interested in. This time, because I wasn't working, I hired him just to show me around.

'When we got to Sabunçu, Magsud said one of the most famous *djelloum* in Russia lived in that part of the city. Would I be interested in visiting her? Things like palmists, astrology, and tarot card readings are like crack for chicks. Seers, shamans, psychics – lead us to 'em. So I said sure, I'd love to meet a Yit.

'Her name was Lamiya, which is Azeri for "educated." She lived in a small apartment in one of those soulless 1950s, gray-cement Communist public-housing projects where every building looks exactly the same and you can easily get lost. I think there were two rooms in the place but we only saw the living room, which was dark even in the middle of the day. Lamiya sat on a couch. Next to it was a baby bassinet. The whole time we were there she kept one hand inside the bassinet, as if she were touching the baby to keep it quiet.

'After we sat down, she asked Magsud if I knew about *lal bala*, which means the silent child. He said no. She told him to explain it to me before she went any further. Of course I didn't understand them because they were speaking Azeri. But I did see him grimace when she finished, like it was going to be tough explaining this in a way that I'd comprehend.

'While Magsud explained *lal bala* to me, Lamiya kept her hand constantly inside the bassinet. I didn't know why until later.' Ava stopped speaking and just stared at me for a few moments. I think she was gathering her energy to go on to the difficult part.

'Now I'm going to tell you the story exactly as it happened. You can believe it or not, but just know that I do with all my heart because of what Lamiya told me about myself. Details and facts no one on earth could know but me. *No one*, do you understand? Not my parents, or my sister, no one. But Lamiya knew. She rattled off the most intimate things about me like she was reading them from a list.

'Let me first explain the silent child. According to legend, there are three of them in Russia at all times. When one dies another is immediately born to replace it. It's kind of like the succession of the Dalai Lama in Tibet: a silent child chooses its mother before it's born.'

'What do you mean, before it's born? Before the *child* is born?'

'Yes. Lamiya said she knew she'd have a silent child the moment she first sensed she was pregnant. So when hers was born, she wasn't surprised or upset to see it.'

'Why would you be upset to see your own baby? Was there something wrong with it?'

Ava looked apprehensive, as if hesitant to tell what must be said next. 'The child is not alive. I mean, it's half alive – half alive and half dead; it lives half in this world and half in the other world too.'

'What "other world"?'

'The afterlife. The baby's half alive and half dead, as I said. It never ages. It lives a certain number of years; they never know how many it'll be. That's different for each child. The day it dies, it looks exactly the same as it did on the day it was born, although some of these children live for decades. It never moves, eats, or breathes. It never opens its eyes. But its heart beats, and most important, it's an oracle.

'After she's told you secret things about yourself that absolutely convinces you beyond a doubt that she's genuine, you're allowed to ask the mother two questions. You can ask anything – about the past, about the future, anything you want. As long as she's touching her silent child, she will answer them. But you are only allowed to ask two.'

'What did you ask?'

Ava shook her head. 'I won't tell you. But part of—' She stopped, got up, and walked to the window. I sat still, waiting for some sign about what to do – go to her, sit, talk, keep quiet . . .

Touching the window glass, she slid her fingers in a long arc across the condensation there. I could almost feel the cold wetness under my own fingertips. What she said next took me completely off guard.

'Did Eamon Reilly ever tell you about his past? About his childhood?'

'*Eamon?* What does he have to do with this?'

'A lot.' Ava began rubbing both hands back and forth very fast on the glass, as if trying to erase something. Then she turned to face me. 'Just go along with me on this – it's all of a piece. Did you ever talk to him about his past?'

'No.'

'Eamon's father was a pilot. He terrorized his family for years, beat them all up and did many other terrible things – a genuine sadist. One of his favorite tortures was to fly really low back and forth over their house in a small plane when he knew everyone was home. Eamon said it was so frightening that the kids and their mother used to all hide under the beds or in the cellar because they were sure one day he'd crash the plane into the house and kill them.'

'What happened to him?'

'The guy was also a drunk who luckily drove his car off a bridge one day and died.'

'Jesus! So that's why Eamon has . . . what, *issues?*'

'Yes. Once I got so fed up with the way he was behaving that I slapped him. Only then did he tell me some of the stories and details of his childhood. Finally I began to understand why he is the way he is. It doesn't make him any less exasperating, but boy, with that background . . .'

'Terrible. Poor guy.'

'Yeah. I don't know if that's the whole reason for him being so peculiar, but it's gotta contribute.'

Crossing my arms over my chest, I asked, 'But what does it have to do with the silent child?'

'One of the things Lamiya told me was that I'm part of a curse.'

I slowly uncrossed my arms and then didn't know what to do with them. 'What do you mean, you're *cursed?*' My voice sounded both skeptical and desperate at the same time. How useless your hands and voice are at moments like that. They're all just in the way; none of them knows what to do or how to behave in a crisis that's suddenly dropped on you in the form of one word – like 'cursed,' or 'dead,' or 'cancer.'

She shook her head. 'No, I'm *part* of a curse. But I guess in some ways I am because of the role I play in this.

'Lamiya said that after I returned to America I'd get pregnant, which I *have*. But my child will

106

be cursed to live exactly the same life as its father whether it wants to or not. Only some unimportant details will be different.' She stopped and said nothing else but continued staring straight at me. I think she was letting her words sink in.

'She didn't say who the father would be?'

'No, she wouldn't. She said whoever made me pregnant, they'd be the one carrying the curse.'

'So that could be me too, Ava.'

'Yes it could, you're right. We'll find out with a DNA test, but I wanted to talk to you first before I did it. You're obviously a big part of this.'

'Yeah, I *guess*,' I said cynically and meanly, although I didn't want to. I never wanted to be mean to her, but why was she telling me this now? Why not before?

More silence.

'I love you Ava, but this is nuts, absolutely nuts. It sounds like one of the Arabian Nights – the silent child, a *djelloum*, a curse . . . How can you know it's true?'

'Because of the things that have happened since I saw her. Things Lamiya said *would* happen. Every single one of them has taken place: the pregnancy, my affair with Eamon, and most of all *you*.'

'What do you mean, me?'

At that moment the washing machine that had been chugging along in the background chose to *ping* and stop. Ava went silent and didn't look like she was going to answer my question anytime soon. I made a face and walked across the room to get the laundry. Opening the door to the machine, I bent down to pull the wet wash out.

'Ava?'

'What?'

'Your washing machine is full of letters.' I pulled out a large white wet K and laid it across my palm. After looking at it, I held it up for her to see. About ten inches long, it appeared to be made of wet cloth. I looked in the machine again and saw that instead of clothes, it was full of a droopy pile of wet capital block letters.

Ava did not seem surprised. In fact, she nodded when I held up the K.

'I put them in there.'

'You put them – where's our laundry?'

'In the bathroom.'

'But why? Why did you do that? What are they? What are they for?'

'Take out four more. Don't look at which ones – just reach in and take out four. I'll tell you why when you're done.'

I wanted to say something but didn't. Reaching into the washing machine, I plunged my hand into the large, soft, wet heap of cloth letters like I was choosing numbers for bingo. When I had four, Ava told me to lay them out together on the floor so that they spelled something. The letters were K, V, Q, R, and O.

'They can't spell anything because there's only one vowel.'

She was far enough away so she couldn't see what they were. 'Tell me which ones you chose.'

'K, V, Q, R, and O.'

She slapped both hands down on her lap. 'Those were the same letters Eamon chose.'

'*What?* Eamon did this too? You also had him take wet letters out of the washing machine?' I realized my voice was way up there, close to shouting.

'Yes, it was a test for both of you. I knew what the answer was going to be, but I had to do it anyway.' The tone of her voice said this was no big deal – why was I making such a fuss?

A test using wet letters from the washing machine? Eamon had done it too? The silent child. A Yit. A curse. For the first time in all the years I had known her, I looked at Ava now like she might be the enemy.

'Do you think Ava's crazy?'

'Of course she's crazy. Why do you think I left her?'

'You left her? She said it was just the opposite – she left you.'

Eamon snorted and pulled his earlobe. 'Do you know the saying – never fall in love with a psychiatrist because they're the craziest people of all? Well, let me amend that to war correspondents too. Never fall in love with a war correspondent either. They've seen too many really bad things. All that pain and death gets into their bones and

109

screws up their heads. Ava's gyroscope is bent, man.

'Did she tell you her story about the silent child? Is that why you're here?' He didn't wait for me to answer. He picked up his vodka and took a sip as if he already knew what I'd say. 'That was all right. It was a mad thing, but at least it was entertaining. It was a really good story. But then came those letters in the washing machine, and then the frozen animals—'

'What frozen animals?'

He slapped my shoulder. 'She hasn't done that to you yet? Ah, more surprises in store for you there, pal! The longer you hang out with Ava, the funnier she gets. I left after the frozen animals. That was it for me. Phew.'

'But what if the child really is yours?'

Eamon put his chin in his hand and looked at the floor. 'Then I'll do everything I can to make sure Ava and the baby are comfortable and well cared for. But I won't live with that woman. Nope. She's as crazy as they come.' He spoke calmly and with resolution. He'd obviously thought all this through and was now at peace with his decisions.

'But wait, Eamon. Just for a minute imagine that what she said was true, *is* true. What if you are the father, and the kid is cursed to live your life?'

'Nothing's the matter with my life. I have a good one.'

'What about your father and the things he did to your family?'

'Yes, that stuff was terrible, but I don't plan on doing the same things to my family if I end up having one someday.' He smiled at me. 'I also don't have a pilot's license, so you don't have to worry that I'm going to fly over Ava's house and dive-bomb it.

'And by the way, what about *your* dad? Was he a good man? What if you're the father of her kid? Does she have anything to worry about with you?'

'I never knew my father. He left my mother when I was two.'

'Well, there you go! I'm sorry to hear that, but in a way it means you could be more dangerous than me if there really is a curse. Because you don't know what kind of guy your father was, or is. He could be much worse than my old man.'

We looked at each other and our silence said we agreed on what he had just said.

Eamon chuckled and shook his head. 'Poor Ava – in a worst-case scenario, if that curse *is* true, she may be doomed either way: me with my monster dad, and you with your mystery dad who could be Jack the Ripper.'

I said weakly, 'But maybe my father's a great guy.'

'Great guys don't abandon their families.'

'You abandoned Ava.'

His voice dropped to a low grumble. 'She's not my family. I never said I wanted to be a father.'

Sometimes people say things, often inadvertently, that make up your mind for you. The

111

moment after Eamon said he didn't want to be a father, it clicked in my mind that I *did* want to be the father to Ava's child – more than anything else in the world. It was as simple as that. I loved her and yearned to be her partner for the rest of my life if she'd have me. I didn't care if her child was Eamon's and I didn't care if there was a curse. Most important, I didn't even care if Ava Malcolm was as crazy as a fly in a jar. I wanted to be with her and would do anything to make that happen.

When I told Eamon that, he raised one arm and crossed the air with it, as if he were a priest giving me a blessing. 'I don't know if you're an idiot, a masochist, or the greatest guy on earth. You know people don't get better as we get older – we just get more of who we are. If Ava's crazy now, she's only going to get crazier.'

'I know. But maybe she's not.'

'True, maybe she's not. But the alternative to her being crazy is that there really *is* a curse and you're going to have to face a whole different bunch of crap. Either way, you're in the hot seat.'

'Maybe but maybe not. You know she's going to the hospital today to get the results of the DNA test.'

Eamon, took a deep breath and let it out in one hard *hush*. 'Call me and let me know the results, will you?'

'I will.' I put out my right hand and we shook for a long time.

He smiled. 'You're a good guy, you really are.

Sticking by Ava like that, no matter what? That's stand-up stuff.'

'Eamon, before I go, tell me about these frozen animals you mentioned before.'

'No, you don't need to hear about that now. Maybe it was just a thing she did to me. Forget I even told you.' He patted me on the shoulder again and walked out of the bar.

When I got back to Ava's apartment, she wasn't there, so I let myself in. On a table in the hallway, impossible to miss, was a sheaf of papers with a yellow note on top. In large black letters it said PLEASE READ. I picked up the papers and saw there was more written in smaller letters on the note.

'This is the DNA report. It says that neither you nor Eamon are the father of my child. I'm a coward and don't have the nerve to be here when you learn that. I'm going to spend the afternoon with my sister and will be back later. Please be here then so we can at least talk about it. I'm so sorry that I lied to you about not being with other men. There have been others since you and I got together.

'Whether it makes any difference to you or not now, I wasn't lying about Lamiya and the curse. I don't know who the father is, although until today I was certain it was either you or Eamon. But Lamiya *was* real. The curse is real. My deepest love and affection for you is real. Please be here later. I don't deserve that, but I can ask.'

Stunned, I tried to look at the other papers in

the sheaf but everything was numbers and graphs and at the end a summary I couldn't understand because my brain was flying south fast and had no more room in it.

Still in my coat, I walked into the living room with the papers in hand and sat down on the couch. The couch where we'd had so many good talks and sex and silent, contented times sitting together and reading or just being. I tried to look at the papers again but it was not possible, so I leaned forward to toss them on the coffee table in front of the couch.

A large-format book of photographs I had never seen before was there. The title of the book was *Freeze Frame*, and every picture inside it was a striking rendering of dead animals, fish, and reptiles . . . the whole animal kingdom, frozen. Every single picture was of dead frozen creatures – on their backs, their sides, on ice in markets, on empty snowy roads where they'd obviously been hit and killed by passing cars. The book was gorgeous, poignant, and macabre all at the same time. As I leafed through it, I kept thinking of Eamon's question about whether I had encountered Ava's frozen animals yet. Was this what he was talking about, this book? Or was there more?

I'd looked at perhaps ten of the photos before I came to the marked page. A green Post-it note was at the top, bent over onto the page by constant use. The photograph was unlike any of the others in the book. It was of a woman dressed in black holding an infant in her arms. It is snowing – the world around her is white. She and the child are the only color there. But the child, or what little we can see of it because the woman is holding it so that it looks like she is hiding it from the photographer, looks dead and so white in her arms that it could be frozen too, like all of the other subjects in the book.

But what is most arresting about the photograph is the look on the woman's face. She is totally serene. If she *is* holding a dead child, she has risen beyond her grief into something holy or inhuman. She is at peace, or a kind of transcendent madness that has given her peace. The image was so powerful and beautiful – there is no other word for it – that I stared at it for what must have been a solid minute. Only after that hypnotic first impression had passed did I look at the bottom of the page where the credits for the pictures all were. The photographer's name was not listed, but the location where it had been taken was Sabunçu, Baku, Azerbaijan.

THE THERAPIST

Jeffery Deaver

One

I met her by chance, in a Starbucks near the medical building where I have my office, and I knew at once she was in trouble.

Recognizing people in distress was, after all, my profession.

I was reading over my patient notes, which I transcribe immediately after the fifty-minute sessions (often, as now, fortified by my favorite latte). I have a pretty good memory, but in the field of counseling and therapy you must be 'completely diligent and tireless,' the many-syllabled phrase a favorite of one of my favorite professors.

This particular venue is on the outskirts of Raleigh in a busy strip mall and, the time being ten thirty A.M. on a pleasant day in early May, there were many people inside for their caffeine fixes.

There was one empty table near me but no chair, and the trim brunette, in a conservative dark blue dress, approached and asked if she could take the extra one at my table. I glanced at her round face, *Good Housekeeping* pretty, not *Vogue*, and smiled. 'Please.'

I wasn't surprised when she said nothing, didn't smile back. She just took the chair, spun it around, clattering, and sat. Not that it was a flirtation she was rejecting; my smile obviously hadn't been more than a faint pleasantry. I was twice her age and resembled – surprise, surprise – a balding, desk- and library-bound therapist. Not her type at all.

No, her chill response came from the trouble she was in. Which in turn troubled *me* a great deal.

I am a licensed counselor, a profession in which ethics rules preclude me from drumming up business the way a graphic designer or personal trainer might do. So I said nothing more but returned to my notes, while she pulled a sheaf of papers out of a gym bag and began to review them, urgently sipping her drink but not enjoying the hot liquid. I was not surprised. With aching eyes, head down, I managed to see that it was a school lesson plan she was working on. I believed it was for seventh grade.

A teacher . . . I grew even more concerned. I'm particularly sensitive to emotional and psychological problems within people who have influence over youngsters. I myself don't see children as patients – that's a specialty I've never pursued. But no psychologist can practice without a rudimentary understanding of children's psyches, where are sowed the seeds of later problems my colleagues and I treat in our adult practices. Children, especially around ten or eleven, are in particularly susceptible developmental stages and can be forever damaged by a woman like the teacher sitting next to me.

Of course, despite all my experience in this field, it's not impossible to make bum diagnoses. But my concerns were confirmed a moment later when she took a phone call. She was speaking softly at first, though with an edge in her voice, the tone and language suggesting the caller was a family member, probably a child. My heart fell at the thought that she'd have children of her own. I wasn't surprised when after only a few minutes her voice rose angrily. Sure enough, she was losing control. 'You did what? . . . I told you not to, under any circumstances . . . Were you just not listening to me? Or were you being stupid again? . . . All right, I'll be home after the conference . . . I'll talk to you about it then.'

If she could have slammed the phone down instead of pushing the disconnect button, I'm sure she would have done it.

A sigh. A sip of her coffee drink. Then back to angrily jotting notes in the margins of the lesson plan.

I lowered my head, staring at my own notes. My taste for the latter was gone completely. I tried to consider how to proceed. I'm good at helping people and I enjoy it (there's a reason for that, of course, and one that goes back to my own childhood, no mystery there). I knew I could help her. But it wasn't as easy as that. Often people don't know they need help and even if they do they resist seeking it. Normally I wouldn't worry too much about a passing encounter like this; I'd give a person some time to figure out on their own that they needed to get some counseling.

But this was serious. The more I observed, the more clear the symptoms. The stiffness of posture, the utter lack of humor or enjoyment in what she was doing with her lesson plan, lack of pleasure in the drink, the anger, the twitchy obsessive way she wrote.

And the eyes. That's what speaks the most, to me at least.

The eyes . . .

So I decided to give it a try. I stood to get a refill of latte and, walking back to my table, I dropped a napkin onto hers. I apologized and collected it. Then laughed, looking at her handiwork.

'My girlfriend's a teacher,' I said. 'She absolutely hates lesson plans. She's never quite sure what to do with them.'

She didn't want to be bothered, but even people in her state acknowledge some social conventions. She looked up, the troubled eyes a deep brown. 'They can be a chore. Our school board insists.'

Clumsy, but at least it broke the ice and we had a bit of a conversation.

'I'm Martin Kobel.'

'Annabelle Young.'

'Where do you teach?'

It was in Wetherby, a good-size town in central North Carolina about an hour from Raleigh. She was here for an education conference.

'Pam, my girlfriend, teaches grade school. You?'

'Middle school.'

The most volatile years, I reflected.

'That's the age she's thinking of moving over to. She's tired of six year olds . . . You put a lot into that,' I said, nodding at the plan.

'I try.'

I hesitated a moment. 'Listen, kind of fortuitous I ran into you. If I gave you our phone number and you've got a few minutes – I mean, if it's no imposition – would you think about giving Pam a call? She could really use some advice. Five minutes or so. Give her some thoughts on middle school.'

'Oh, I don't know. I've only been a teacher for three years.'

'Just think about it. You seem like you know what you're doing.' I took out a business card.

Martin J. Kobel, MS, MSW
Behavioral Therapy
Specialties: Anger Management and Addiction

I wrote 'Pam Robbins' on the top along with the home phone number.

120

'I'll see what I can do.' She slipped the card in her pocket and turned back to her coffee and the lesson plan.

I knew I'd gone as far as I could. Anything more would have seemed inappropriate and pushed her away.

After fifteen minutes, she glanced at her watch. Apparently whatever conference she was attending was about to resume. She gave a chill smile my way. 'Nice talking to you.'

'The same,' I said.

Annabelle gathered the lesson plan and notes and stuffed them back into her gym bag. As she rose, a teenage boy eased past and jostled her inadvertently with his bulky backpack. I saw her eyes ripple with that look I know so well. 'Jesus,' she whispered to him. 'Learn some manners.'

'Hey, lady, I'm sorry—'

She waved a dismissing hand at the poor kid. Annabelle walked to the counter to add more milk to her coffee. She wiped her mouth and tossed out the napkin. Without a look back at me or anyone she pointed her cold visage toward the door and pushed outside.

I gave it thirty seconds then also stopped at the milk station. Glancing into the hole for trash, I spotted, as I'd half expected, my card, sitting next to her crumpled napkin. I'd have to take a different approach. I certainly wasn't going to give up on her. The stakes for her own well-being and of those close to her were too high.

121

But it would require some finesse. I've found that you can't just bluntly tell potential patients that their problems are the result not of a troubled childhood or a bad relationship, but simply because an invisible entity had latched onto their psyches like a virus and was exerting its influence.

In a different era, or in a different locale, someone might have said that the teacher was possessed by a demonic spirit or the like. Now we're much more scientific about it, but it's still wise to ease into the subject slowly.

Annabelle Young had come under the influence of a neme.

The term was first coined by a doctor in Washington, D.C. James Pheder was a well-known biologist and researcher. He came up with the word by combining 'negative' and 'meme,' the latter describing a cultural phenomenon that spreads and replicates in societies.

I think a reference to meme – 'm' version – is a bit misleading, since it suggests something rather more abstract than what a *ne*me really is. In my lengthy book on the subject, published a few years ago, I define a neme as 'a discrete body of intangible energy that evokes extreme emotional responses in humans, resulting in behavior that is most often detrimental to the host or to the society in which he or she lives.'

But 'neme' is a convenient shorthand and every

122

therapist or researcher familiar with the concept uses it.

The word is also beneficial in that it neutrally describes a scientific, proven construct and avoids the historical terms that have muddied the truth for thousands of years. Words like ghosts, spirits, Rudolf Otto's numinous presences, revenants, Buddhism's hungry ghosts, rural countrysides' white ladies, Japanese yurei, demons. Dozens of others.

Those fictional legends and superstitions were largely the result of the inability to explain nemes scientifically in the past. As often happens, until a phenomenon is rationally explained and quantified, folklore fills the gaps. The old belief, for instance, in spontaneous generation – that life could arise from inanimate objects – was accepted for thousands of years, supported by apparently scientific observations, for instance, that maggots and other infestations appeared in rotting food or standing water. It was only when Louis Pasteur proved via controlled, repeatable experiments that living material, like eggs or bacteria, *had* to be present for life to generate that the old view fell by the wayside.

Same thing with nemes. Framing the concept in terms of ghosts and possessing spirits was a convenient and simple fiction. Now we know better.

Growing up, I'd never heard of these things that would later be labeled nemes. It was only after a particular incident that I became aware: the deaths of my parents and brother.

You could say that my family was killed by one.

When I was sixteen we went to one of Alex's basketball games at our school. At some point my father and I hit the hot dog stand. The father of a player on the opposing team was standing nearby, sipping a Coke and watching the game. Suddenly – I can still remember it perfectly – the man underwent a transformation, instantly shifting from relaxed and benign to tense, distracted, on guard. And the eyes . . . there was no doubt that they changed. The very color seemed to alter; they grew dark, malevolent. I knew something had happened, something had possessed him, I thought at the time. I felt chilled, and I stepped away from him.

Then the man suddenly grew angry. Furious. Something on the court set him off. A foul maybe, a bad call. He screamed at Alex's team, he screamed at our coach, at the ref. In his rage, he bumped against my father and dropped his soda, spilling it on his shoes. It was his fault but he seemed to blame my father for the mishap. The men got into an argument, though my father soon realized that the man was out of control, consumed by this odd rage, and ushered us back to the bleachers.

After the game I was still troubled but assumed the matter was over. Not so. The man followed us out into the parking lot and, screaming, bizarrely challenged my father to a fight. The man's wife was crying, pulling him back and apologizing. 'He's never behaved like this, really!'

'Shut up, bitch,' he raged and slapped her.

Shaken, we climbed into the car and drove off. Ten minutes later, driving down I–40, we were sitting in troubled silence when a car veered over three lanes. The man from the game swerved right toward us, driving us off the road.

I remember seeing his face, twisted with anger, over the steering wheel.

In court he tearfully explained that he didn't know what happened. It was like he was possessed. That defense didn't get him very far. He was found guilty of three counts of first-degree manslaughter.

After I got out of the hospital following the crash, I couldn't get out of my head the memory of what had happened to the man. How clear it was to me that he'd changed, in a flash. It was like flipping a light switch.

I began reading about sudden changes in personality and rage and impulse. That research led eventually to the writings of Dr Pheder and other researchers and therapists. I grew fascinated with the concept of nemes, considered a theory by some, a reality by others.

As to their origin, there are several theories. I subscribe to one I found the most logical. Nemes are vestiges of human instinct. They were an integral part of the psychological make-up of the creatures in the chain that led to Homo sapiens and were necessary for survival. In the early days of humanoids, it was occasionally necessary to behave in ways we would consider bad or criminal now. To commit acts of violence, to be rageful, impulsive, sadistic, greedy. But as societies formed and developed, the need for those darker impulses faded. The governing bodies, the armies, the law enforcers took over the task of our survival. Violence, rage, and the other darker impulses became not only unnecessary but were counter to society's interests.

Somehow – there are several theories on this – the powerful neuro impulses that motivated those dark behaviors separated from humans and came to exist as separate entities, pockets of energy, you could say. In my research I found a precedent for this migration: the same thing happened with telepathy. Many generations ago, psychic communication was common. The advent of modern communication techniques eliminated the need for what we could call extrasensory perception, though many young children still have documented telepathic skills. (However, it's interesting that with the increased use of cell phones and computers by youngsters, incidents of telepathy among young people are dramatically decreasing.)

But whatever their genealogy, nemes exist and there are millions of them. They float around like flu viruses until they find a vulnerable person and then incorporate themselves into the psyche of their host ('incorporate' is used, rather than a judgmental term like 'infest' or 'infect,' and never the theologically loaded 'possess'). If someone is impulsive, angry, depressed, confused, scared – even physically sick – nemes will sense that and make a beeline for the cerebrum cortex, the portion of the brain where emotion is controlled. They usually avoid people who are emotionally stable, strong willed, and have high degrees of self-control, though not always.

Nemes are invisible, like electromagnetic waves and light at the far end of the spectrum, though it's sometimes possible to tell they're nearby if you hear distortion on a cell phone, TV, or radio. Usually, the host doesn't sense the incorporation itself; they only experience a sudden mood swing. Some people can outright sense them. I'm one of these, though there's nothing 'special' about me. It's simply like having acute hearing or good eyesight.

Do nemes think?

They do, in a way. Though thought is probably the wrong word. More likely they're like insects, with a sense of awareness and instinct. Survival is very strong within them, too. There's nothing immortal about nemes. When their host passes away, they seem to dissipate also. I myself don't believe they communicate with one another, since I've never seen any evidence that they do.

This isn't to minimize the damage they can do, of course. It's significant. The rage, the impulsive behavior that arises from incorporation leads to rape, murder, physical and sexual abuse, and more subtle harm like substance overuse and verbal abuse. They also affect the physiology and morphology of the host's body itself, as a series of autopsies several years ago proved.

After my devastating personal encounter with nemes, I decided I wanted to work in a field that would help minimize the damage they could do. I became a therapist.

The thrust of my approach is behavioral. Once you're under the influence of a neme, you don't 'cast it out,' as a practitioner (now former) unfortunately joked at a psychotherapy conference in Chicago some years ago. You treat the symptoms. I concentrate on working with my patients to achieve self-control, using any number of techniques to avoid or minimize behaviors that are destructive to them or others. In most cases it doesn't even matter that the patient knows he or she is a host for a neme (some patients are comfortable with the reality, and others aren't). In any case, the methods I use are solid and well established, used by all behavioral therapists, and by and large successful.

There've been occasional defeats, of course. It's the nature of the profession. Two of my patients, in which very potent nemes had incorporated, killed themselves when they were simply unable to resolve the conflict between their goals and the neme-influenced behavior.

There's also something that's been in the back of my mind for years: risk to myself. My life has been devoted to minimizing their effectiveness and spread and so I sometimes wonder if a neme senses that I'm a threat. This is probably according them too much credit; you have to guard against personifying them. But I can't help but think back to an incident several years ago. I was attending a psychology conference in New York City and was nearly mugged. It was curious since the young attacker was a model student at a nice high school near my hotel. He'd never been in trouble with the police. And he was armed with a long knife. An off-duty policeman happened to be nearby and managed to arrest him just as he started after me with the weapon.

It was late at night and I couldn't see clearly, but I believed, from the boy's eyes, that he was being influenced by a neme, motivated by its own sense of survival to kill me.

Probably not. But even if there was some truth to it, I wasn't going to be deterred from my mission to save people at risk.

People like Annabelle Young.

The day after running into her in Starbucks, I went to the North Carolina State University library and did some research. The state licensing agencies' databases and ever-helpful Google revealed that the woman was thirty years old and worked at Chantelle West Middle School in Wetherby County. Interestingly, she was a widow – her husband had died three years ago – and, yes, she had a nine-year-old son, probably the target of her anger on the phone. According to information about the school where she taught, Annabelle would generally teach large classes, with an average of thirty-five students per year.

This meant that she could have a dramatic and devastating impact on the lives of many young people.

Then too was the matter of Annabelle's own well-being. I was pretty sure that she'd come under the influence of the neme around the time her husband died; a sudden personal loss like that makes you emotionally vulnerable and more susceptible than otherwise. (I noted too that she'd gone back to work around that time, and I wondered if her neme sensed an opportunity to incorporate within someone who could influence a large number of equally vulnerable individuals, the children in her classes.)

Annabelle was obviously a smart woman and she might very well get into counseling at some time. But there comes a point when the neme is so deeply incorporated that people actually become accustomed or addicted to the inappropriate behaviors nemes cause. They don't *want* to change. My assessment was that she was past this point. And so, since I wasn't going to hear from her, I did the only thing I could. I went to Wetherby.

I got there early on a Wednesday. The drive was pleasant, along one of those combined highways that traverse central North Carolina. It split somewhere outside of Raleigh and I continued on the increasingly rural branch of the two, taking me through old North Carolina. Tobacco warehouses and small industrial-parts plants – most of them closed years ago – but still squatting in weeds. Trailer parks, very unclosed. Bungalows and plenty of evidence of a love of Nascar and Republican party lines.

Wetherby has a redeveloped downtown, but that's just for show. I noted immediately as I cruised along the two-block stretch that nobody was buying anything in the art galleries and antiques stores, and the nearly empty restaurants, I suspected, got new awnings with new names every eight months or so. The real work in places like Wetherby got done in the malls and office parks and housing developments built around new golf courses.

I checked into a motel, showered, and began my reconnaissance, checking out Chantelle Middle School. I parked around the time I'd learned classes were dismissed but didn't catch a glimpse of Annabelle Young.

Later that evening, about seven thirty, I found her house, four miles away, a modest twenty-year-old colonial in need of painting, on a cul-de-sac. There was no car in the drive. I parked under some trees and waited.

Fifteen minutes later a car pulled into the drive. I couldn't tell if her son was inside or not. The

Toyota pulled into the garage and the door closed. A few minutes later I got out, slipped into some woods beside the house, and glanced into the kitchen. I saw her carting dishes inside. Dirty dishes from lunch or last night, I assumed. She set them in the sink and I saw her pause, staring down. Her face was turned away but her body language, even from this distance, told me that she was angry.

Her son appeared, a skinny boy with longish brown hair. *His* body language suggested that he was cautious. He said something to his mother. Her head snapped toward him and he nodded quickly. Then retreated. She stayed where she was, staring at the dishes, for a moment. Without even rinsing them she stepped out of the room and swept her hand firmly along the wall, slapping the switch out. I could almost hear the angry gesture from where I was.

I didn't want to talk to her while her son was present, so I headed back to the motel.

The next day I was up early and cruised back to the school before the teachers arrived. At seven fifteen I caught a glimpse of her Camry arriving and watched her climb out and stride unsmilingly into the school. Too many people around and she was too harried to have a conversation now.

I returned at three in the afternoon and when Annabelle emerged followed her to a nearby strip mall, anchored by a Harris-Teeter grocery store. She went shopping and came out a half hour later.

She dumped the plastic bags in her trunk. I was going to approach her, even though a meeting in the parking lot wasn't the most conducive place to pitch my case, when I saw her lock the car and walk toward a nearby bar and grill.

At three thirty she wouldn't be eating lunch or dinner and I knew what she had in mind. People influenced by nemes often drink more than they should, to dull the anxiety and anger that come from the incorporation.

Though I would eventually work on getting her to cut down on her alcohol consumption, her being slightly intoxicated and relaxed now could be a big help. I waited five minutes and followed. Inside the dark tavern, which smelled of Lysol and onions, I spotted her at the bar. She was having a mixed drink. Vodka or gin, it seemed, and some kind of juice. She was nearly finished with her first and she waved for a second.

I sat down two stools away and ordered a Diet Coke. I felt her head swivel toward me, tilt slightly as she debated whether she'd seen me before, and turn back to her drink. Then the pieces fell together and she faced me again.

Without looking up I said, 'I'm a professional counselor, Ms Young. I'm here only in that capacity. To help. I'd like to talk to you.'

'You . . . you followed me here? From Raleigh?'

I made a show of leaving money for the soda to suggest that I wasn't going to stay longer than necessary, trying to put her at ease.

'I did, yes. But please, you don't need to be afraid.'

Finally I turned to look at her. The eyes were just as I expected, narrow, cold, the eyes of somebody else entirely. The neme was even stronger than I'd thought.

'I'm about five seconds away from calling the police.'

'I understand. But please, listen. I want to say something to you. And if you want me to leave, I'll head back to Raleigh right now. You can choose whatever you want.'

'Say it and get out.' She took another drink.

'I specialize in treating people who aren't happy in life. I'm good at it. When I saw you the other day in Starbucks, I knew you were exactly the sort of patient who could benefit from my expertise. I would like very much to help you.'

No mention of nemes, of course.

'I don't need a shrink.'

'I'm actually not a shrink. I'm a psychologist, not a doctor.'

'I don't care what you are. You can't . . . can't you be reported for this, trying to drum up business?'

'Yes, and you're free to do that. But I thought it was worth the risk to offer you my services. I don't care about the money. You can pay me whatever you can afford. I care about helping you. I can give you references and you can call the state licensing board about me.'

'Do you even have a girlfriend who's a teacher?'

'No. I lied. Which I'll never do again . . . It was that important to try to explain how I can help you.'

And then I saw her face soften. She was nodding.

My heart was pounding hard. It had been a risk, trying this, but she was going to come around. The therapy would be hard work. For both of us. But the stakes were too high to let her continue the way she was. I knew we could make significant progress.

I turned away to pull a card from my wallet. 'Let me tell you a—'

As I looked back, I took the full tide of her second drink in the face. My eyes on fire from the liquor and stinging juice, I gasped in agony and grabbed bar napkins to dry them.

'Annie, what's wrong?' the bartender snapped, and through my blurred vision I could just make out his grabbing her arm as she started to fling the glass at me. I raised my own arm to protect myself.

'What'd he do?'

'Fuck you, let go of me!' she cried to him.

'Hey, hey, take it easy, Annie. What—?'

Then he ducked as she launched the glass at *him*. It struck a row of others; half of them shattered. She was out of control. Typical.

'Fuck you both!' Screaming. She dug a bill out of her purse and flung it onto the bar.

'Please, Ms Young,' I said, 'I can help you.'

'If I see you again, I'm calling the police.' She stormed out.

'Listen, mister, what the hell d'you do?'

I didn't answer him. I grabbed some more napkins and, wiping my face, walked to the window. I saw her stride up to her son, who was standing nearby with a book bag. So this was the rendezvous spot. I wondered how often he'd had to wait outside for mom while she was in here getting drunk. I pictured cold January afternoons, the boy huddled and blowing breath into his hands.

She gestured him after her. Apparently there'd been something else on the agenda for after school, and, disappointed, he lifted his arms and glanced at the nearby sports store. But the shopping was not going to happen today. She stormed up and grabbed him by the arm. He pulled away. She drew back to slap him, but he dutifully walked to the car. I could see him clicking on his seat belt and wiping his tears.

Without a glance back at the bartender, I too left.

I walked to the car to head back to the motel to change. What had happened was discouraging, but I'd dealt with more difficult people than Annabelle Young. There were other approaches to take. Over the years I've learned what works and what doesn't; it's all part of being a therapist.

The next morning at six I parked behind Etta's Diner, in a deserted portion of the lot. The restaurant was directly behind Annabelle's house. I made my way up the hill along a path that led to the sidewalk in her development. I had to take an oblique approach; if she saw me coming she'd never answer the door, and that would be that.

The morning was cool and fragrant with the smells of pine and wet earth. Being spring, the sky was light even at this early hour and it was easy to make my way along the path. I wondered how different Annabelle's life had been before her husband died. How soon the neme had incorporated itself into her afterward. I suspected she'd been a vivacious, caring mother and wife, completely different from the enraged out-of-control woman she now was becoming.

I continued to the edge of the woods and waited behind the house in a stand of camellias with exploding red blossoms. At about six thirty her son pushed out the front door, carting a heavy book bag, and strolled to the end of the cul-de-sac, presumably to catch his bus.

When he was gone, I walked to the porch and climbed the stairs.

Was I ready? I asked myself.

Always those moments of self-doubt, even though I'd been a professional therapist for years.

Always, the doubts.

But then I relaxed. My mission in life was to save people. I was good at that task. I knew what I was doing.

Yes, I was ready.

I rang the doorbell and stepped aside from the peephole. I heard the footsteps approach. She flung the door open and had only a moment to gasp at the sight of the black stocking mask I was wearing and the lengthy knife in my gloved hand.

I grabbed her hair and plunged the blade into her chest three times, then sliced through her neck. Both sides and deep, so the end would be quick.

Lord knew I didn't want her to suffer.

Two

The job of making sure that Martin Kobel was either put to death or sentenced to life in prison for the murder of Annabelle Young fell to Glenn Hollow, the Wetherby County prosecutor.

And it was a job that he had embraced whole-heartedly from the moment he got the call from county-police dispatch. Forty-two years old, Hollow was the most successful prosecutor in the state of North Carolina, judging in terms of convictions won, and judging from the media since he had a preference for going after violent offenders. A mark of his success was that this was to be his last year in Wetherby. He'd be running for state attorney general in November and there wasn't much doubt he'd win.

But his grander plans wouldn't detract from his enthusiastic prosecution of the murderer of Annabelle Young. In big cities the prosecutors get cases tossed onto their desks along with the police reports. With Glenn Hollow it was different. He had an honorary flashing blue light attached to his dash and, ten minutes after getting the call about the homicide, he was at Ms Young's house while the forensic team was still soaking up blood and taking pix.

He was now walking into the Wetherby County Courthouse. Nothing Old South about the place. It was the sort of edifice you'd find in Duluth or Toledo or Schenectady. One story, nondescript white stone, overtaxed air-conditioning, scuffed linoleum floors, and greenish fluorescents that might engender the question, 'Hey, you feeling okay?'

Hollow was a lean man, with drawn cheeks and thick black hair close to a skullish head – defendants said he looked like a ghoul; kinder reports, that he resembled Gregory Peck in *Moby Dick*, minus the beard. He was somber and reserved and kept his personal life far, far away from his professional life.

He now nodded at the secretary in the ante-office of Judge Brigham Rollins's chambers.

'Go on in, Glenn.'

Inside were two big men. Rollins was midfifties and had a pitted face and the spiky gray hair of a crew cut neglected a week too long. He was in shirtsleeves, though noosed with a tie, of course. He wore plucky yellow suspenders that hoisted his significant tan pants like a concrete bucket under a crane. Gray stains radiated from under his arms. As usual the judge had doused himself with Old Spice.

Sitting opposite was Bob Ringling – the circus jokes all but dead after these many years of being a defense lawyer in a medium-size town, and, no, there was no relation. Stocky, with blondish brown hair carefully trimmed, he resembled a forty-five-year-old retired army major – not a bad deduction, since Fayetteville wasn't terribly far away, but, like the circus brothers, not true.

Hollow didn't like or dislike Ringling. He was fair, though abrasive, and he made Hollow work for every victory. Which was as it should be, the prosecutor believed. God created defense lawyers, he'd said, to make sure the system was fair and the prosecution didn't cheat or get lazy. After all, there *was* that one-in-a-hundred chance that the five-foot-eight black gangbanger from Central High presently in custody wasn't the same five-foot-eight black gangbanger from Central High who actually pulled the trigger.

Judge Rollins closed a folder that he'd been perusing. He grunted. 'Tell me where we are with this one, gentlemen.'

'Yessir,' Hollow began. 'The state is seeking special-circumstances murder.'

'This's about that teacher got her throat slit, right?'

'Yessir. In her house. Broad daylight.'

A distasteful grimace. Not shock. Rollins'd been a judge for years.

The courthouse was on the crook of Route 85 and Henderson Road. Through one window you could see Galloway-belted cows grazing. They were black and white, vertically striped, precise, as if God had used a ruler. Hollow could look right over the judge's shoulder and see eight of them, chewing. Out the other window was a T.K. Maxx, a Barnes & Noble, and a multiplex under construction. These two views pretty much defined Wetherby.

'What's the story behind it?'

'This Kobel, a therapist. He was stalking her. They met at a Starbucks when she was in Raleigh at an educational conference. Got witnesses say he gave her his card but she threw it out. Next thing he tracked her down and shows up in Wetherby. Got into a fight at Red Robin, near Harris-Teeter. She threw a drink in his face. One witness saw him park at Etta's, the diner, the morning she was killed—'

'Tonight's corned beef,' the judge said.

'They do a good job of that,' Ringling added.

True, they did. Hollow continued, '—and he hiked up into those woods behind her place. When she opened the door, he killed her. He waited till her boy left.'

'There's that, at least,' Rollins grumbled. 'How'd the boys in blue get him?'

'Unlucky for him. Busboy on a smoke break at

Etta's saw him coming out of the forest, carrying some things. The kid found some blood near where he'd parked. Called the police with the make and model. Kobel'd tossed away the knife and mask and gloves, but they found 'em. Fibers, DNA, fingerprints on the *inside* of the gloves. People always forget that. They watch *CSI* too much . . . Oh, and then he confessed.'

'*What?*' the judge barked.

'Yep. Advised of rights, twice. Sang like a bird.'

'Then what the hell're you doing here? Take a plea and let's get some real work done.'

The judge glanced at Ringling, but the defense lawyer in turn cast his eyes to Hollow.

Rollins gripped his ceramic coffee mug and sipped the hot contents. 'What isn't who telling who? Don't play games. There's no jury to impress with your clevers.'

Ringling said, 'He's completely insane. Nuts.'

A skeptical wrinkle on the judge's brow. 'But you're saying he wore a mask and gloves?'

Most insane perps didn't care if they were identified and didn't care if they got away afterward. They didn't wear ninja or hit-man outfits. They were the sort who hung around afterward and fingerpainted with the blood of their victims.

Ringling shrugged.

The judge asked, 'Competent to stand trial?'

'Yessir. We're saying he was insane at the time of commission. No sense of right or wrong. No sense of reality.'

The judge grunted.

The insanity defense is based on one overriding concept in jurisprudence: responsibility. At what point are we responsible for acts we commit? If we cause an accident and we're sued in civil court for damages, the law asks, would a reasonably prudent person have, say, driven his car on a slippery road at thirty-five miles per hour? If the jury says yes, then we're not responsible for the crash.

If we're arrested for a crime, the law asks, did we act knowingly and intentionally to break a law? If we didn't, then we're not guilty.

There are, in fact, two ways in which sanity arises in a criminal court. One is when the defendant is so out of it that he can't participate in his own trial. That US Constitution thing: the right to confront your accusers.

But this isn't what most people familiar with *Boston Legal* or *Perry Mason* think of as the insanity defense and, as Bob Ringling had confirmed, it wasn't an issue in *State v. Kobel*.

More common is when defense lawyers invoke various offshoots of McNaghten rule, which holds that if the defendant lacked the capacity to know he was doing something wrong when he committed the crime, he can't be found guilty. This isn't to say he's going scot-free; he'll get locked up in a mental ward until it's determined that he's no longer dangerous.

This was Bob Ringling's claim regarding Martin Kobel.

But Glenn Hollow exhaled a perplexed laugh. 'He wasn't insane. He was a practicing therapist with an obsession over a pretty woman who was ignoring him. Special circumstances. I want guilty, I want the needle. That's it.'

Ringling said to Rollins, 'Insanity. You sentence him to indefinite incarceration in Butler, Judge. We won't contest it. No trial. Everybody wins.'

Hollow said, 'Except the other people he kills when they let him out in five years.'

'Ah, you just want a feather in your cap for when you run for AG. He's a media bad boy.'

'I want justice,' Hollow said, supposing he was sounding pretentious. And not caring one whit. Nor admitting that, yeah, he did want the feather, too.

'What's the evidence for the looney tunes?' the judge asked. He had a very different persona when he was in chambers compared with when he was in the courtroom, and presumably different yet at Etta's Diner, eating corned beef.

'He absolutely believes he didn't do anything wrong. He was saving the children in Annabelle's class. I've been over this with him a dozen times. He *believes* it.'

'Believes what exactly?' the judge asked.

'That she was possessed. By something like a ghost. I've looked it up. Some cult thing on the Internet. Some spirit or something makes you lose control, lose your temper and beat the crap out of your wife or kids. Even makes you kill people. It's called a neme.' He spelled it.

'Neme.'

Hollow said, 'I've looked it up too, Judge. You can look it up. We all can look it up. Which is just what Kobel did. To lay the groundwork for claiming insanity. He killed a hot young woman who rejected him. And now he's pretending he believes in 'em to look like he's nuts.'

'If that's the case,' Ringling said gravely, 'then he's been planning ever since he was a teenager to kill a woman he met two weeks ago.'

'What's that?'

'His parents died in a car crash when he was in high school. He had a break with reality, the doctors called it. Diagnosed as a borderline personality.'

'Like my cousin,' the judge said. 'She's awkward. The wife and I never invite her over, if we can avoid it.'

'Kobel got involuntary commitment for eight months back then, talking about these creatures that possessed the driver who killed his family. Same thing as now.'

'But he had to go to shrink school,' the judge pointed out. 'He graduated. That's not crazy in my book.'

Hollow leaped in with, 'Exactly. He has a master's in psychology. One in social work. Good grades. Sees patients. And he's written books. For God's sake.'

'One of which I happen to have with me and which I will be introducing into evidence. Thank

145

you, Glenn, for bringing it up.' The defense lawyer opened his briefcase and dropped a 10-pound stack of 8?-by-11 sheets on the judge's desk. '*Self*-published, by the way. And written by hand.'

Hollow looked it over. He had good eyes but it was impossible to read any of the text except the title because it was in such tiny hand-writing. There had to be a thousand words per page, in elegant, obsessive script.

Biblical Evidence of Malevolent
Emotional ENERGY Incorporated into Psyches
By Martin Kobel
© All rights reserved

'All rights reserved?' Hollow snorted. 'Who's going to plagiarize this crap? And what's with the capitalization?'

'Glenn, this is one of about thirty volumes. He's been writing these things for twenty years. And it's the smallest one.'

The prosecutor repeated, 'He's faking.'

But the judge was skeptical. 'Going back all those years?'

'Okay, he's quirky. But this man is dangerous. Two of his patients killed themselves under circumstances that make it seem like he suggested they do it. Another one's serving five years because he attacked Kobel in his office. He claimed the doctor provoked him. And Kobel broke into a

146

funeral home six years ago and was caught fucking around with the corpses.'

'*What?*'

'Not that way. He was dissecting them. Looking for evidence of these things, these nemes.'

Ringling said happily, 'There's another book he wrote on the autopsy. Eighteen hundred pages. Illustrated.'

'It wasn't an autopsy, Bob. It was breaking into a funeral home and fucking around with corpses.' Hollow was getting angry. But maybe it's just a neme, he thought cynically. 'He goes to conferences.'

'Paranormal conferences. Wacko conferences. Full of wackos just like him.'

'Jesus Christ, Bob. The people who cop insanity pleas're paranoid schizos. They don't bathe, they take Haldol and lithium, they're delusional. They don't go to fucking Starbucks and ask for an extra shot of syrup.'

Hollow had used the *f* word more times today than in the past year.

Ringling said, 'They kill people because they're possessed by ghosts. That's not sane. End of story.'

The judge lifted his hand. 'You gentlemen know that when the earth was young, Africa and South America were right next to each other. I mean, fifty feet away. Think about that. And here you are, same thing. You're real close, I can tell. You can work it out. Come together. There's a song about that. It's in your interest. If we go to trial,

147

you two're doing all the work. All I'm gonna be doing is saying "sustained" and "overruled."'

'Bob, he killed that girl, a schoolteacher. In cold blood. I want him away forever. He's a danger and he's sick . . . What I can do, but only this, I'll go with life. Drop special circumstances. But no parole.'

The judge looked expectantly toward Bob Ringling. 'That's something.'

'I knew it'd come up,' Ringling said. 'I asked my client about it. He says he didn't do anything wrong and he has faith in the system. He's convinced there're these things floating around and they glom onto you and make you do bad stuff. No, we're going for insanity.'

Hollow grimaced. 'You want to play it that way, you get your expert and I'll get mine.'

The judge grumbled. 'Pick a date, gentlemen. We're going to trial. And, for Christ sake, somebody tell me, what the hell is a neme?'

The *people of the State of North Carolina v. Kobel* began on a Wednesday in July.

Glenn Hollow kicked it off with a string off witnesses and police reports regarding the forensic evidence, which was irrefutable. Bob Ringling let most of it go and just got a few errant bits of trace evidence removed, which Hollow didn't care about anyway.

Another of Hollow's witnesses was a clerk from Starbucks in Raleigh, who testified about the business card exchange. (Hollow noted the troubled looks on the faces of several jurors and people in the gallery, leaving them wondering, he supposed, about the wisdom of affairs and other indiscreet behavior in places with observant baristas.)

Other witnesses testified about behavior consistent with stalking, including several who'd seen Kobel in Wetherby on the days before the murder. Several had seen his car parked outside the school where Annabelle Young taught. If there's any way to put your location on record, it's to be a middle-aged man parked outside a middle school. Eight concerned citizens gave the police his tag number.

The busboy at Etta's Diner gave some very helpful testimony with the help of a Spanish translator.

As for Kobel himself, sitting at the defense table, his hair was askew and his suit didn't fit right. He frantically filled notebook after notebook with writing like ant tracks.

Son of a bitch, thought Hollow. It was pure performance, orchestrated by Bob Ringling, Esq., of course, with Martin Kobel in the role of schizophrenic. Hollow had seen the police interview video. On screen the defendant had been well scrubbed, well spoken, and no twitchier than Hollow's ten-year-old Lab, known to take naps in the middle of tornados.

Any other case, the trial would've been over with on the second day – with a verdict for the People, followed by a lengthy appeal and an uncomfortable few minutes while the executioner figured out which was the better vein, right arm or left.

But there was more, of course. Where the real battle would be fought.

Ringling's expert psychiatrist testified that the defendant was, in his opinion, legally insane and unable to tell the difference between right and wrong. Kobel honestly believed that Annabelle Young was a threat to students and her son because she was infested by a neme, some spirit or force that he truly believed existed.

'He's paranoid, delusional. His reality is very, very different from ours,' was the expert's conclusion.

The shrink's credentials were good, and since that was about the only way to attack him, Hollow let him go.

'Your Honor,' Ringling next said. 'I move to introduce defense exhibits numbers one through twenty-eight.'

And wheeled up to the bench – literally, in carts – Kobel's notebooks and self-published treatises on nemes, more than anybody could possibly be interested in.

A second expert for the defense testified about these writings. 'These are typical of a delusional mind.' Everything Kobel had written was typical of a paranoid and delusional individual who had lost touch with reality. He stated that there was no scientific basis for the concept of neme. 'It's like voodoo, it's like vampires, werewolves.'

Ringling tried to seal the deal by having the doctor read a portion from one of these 'scientific treatises,' a page of utterly incomprehensible nonsense. Judge Rollins, on the edge of sleep, cut him off. 'We get the idea, Counselor. Enough.'

On cross-examination, Hollow couldn't do much to deflate this testimony. The best he could do was: 'Doctor, do you read the Harry Potter books?'

'Well, as a matter of fact, yes, I have.'

'The fourth was my favorite. What was yours?'

'Umm, I don't know really.'

'Is it possible,' the prosecutor asked the witness, 'that those writings of Mr Kobel are merely attempts at writing a novel? Some big fantasy book.'

'I . . . I can't imagine it.'

'But it's possible, isn't it?'

'I suppose. But I'll tell you, he'll never sell the movie rights.'

Amid the laughter, the judge dismissed the witness.

There was testimony about the bizarre autopsy, which Hollow didn't bother to refute.

Bob Ringling also introduced two of Kobel's patients, who testified that they had been so troubled by his obsessive talk about these ghosts or spirits inhabiting their bodies that they quit seeing him.

And then Ringling had Kobel himself take the stand, dressed in the part of a madman in his premeditatedly wrinkled and dirty clothes, chewing his lip, looking twitchy and weird.

This idea – insane in its own right – was a huge risk, because on cross-examination Hollow would ask the man point-blank if he'd killed Annabelle Young. Since he'd confessed once, he would have to confess again – or Hollow would read the sentence from his statement. Either way the jury would actually hear the man admit to the crime.

But Ringling met the problem head-on. His first question: 'Mr Kobel, did you kill Annabelle Young?'

'Oh, yes, of course I did.' He sounded surprised.

A gasp filled the courtroom.

'And why did you do that, Mr Kobel?'

'For the sake of the children.'

'How do you mean that?'

'She was a teacher, you know. Oh, God! Every year, thirty or forty students, impressionable young people, would come under her influence. She was going to poison their minds. She might even hurt them, abuse them, spread hatred.' He closed his eyes and shivered.

And the Academy Award for best performance on the part of a crazed murder suspect goes to . . .

'Now, tell me, Mr Kobel, why did you think she would hurt the children?'

'Oh, she'd come under the influence of a neme.'

'That's what we heard a little about earlier, right? In your writings?'

'Yes, in my writings.'

'Could you tell us, briefly, what a neme is?'

'You could call it an energy force. Malevolent energy. It attaches to your mind and it won't let go. It's terrible. It causes you to commit crimes, abuse people, fall into rages. A lot of temper tantrums and road rage are caused by nemes. They're all over the place. Millions of them.'

'And you were convinced she was possessed?'

'It's not possession,' Kobel said adamantly. 'That's a theological concept. Nemes are purely scientific. Like viruses.'

'You think they're as real as viruses?'

'They are! You have to believe me! They are!'

'And Ms Young was being influenced by nemes.'

'One, just one.'

'And was going to hurt her students.'

'And her son. Oh, yes, I could see it. I have this ability to see nemes. I had to save the children.'

'You weren't stalking her because you were attracted to her?'

Kobel's voice cracked. 'No, no. Nothing like that. I wanted to get her into counseling. I could have saved her. But she was too far gone. The last thing I wanted to do was kill her. But it was a blessing. It really was. I had to.' Tears glistened.

Oh, brother . . .

'Prosecution's witness.'

Hollow did the best he could. He decided not to ask about Annabelle Young. Kobel's murdering her was no longer the issue in this case. The whole question was Kobel's state of mind. Hollow got the defendant to admit that he'd been in a mental hospital only once, as a teenager, and hadn't seen a mental health professional since then. He'd taken no antipsychotic drugs. 'They take my edge off. You have to be sharp when you're fighting nemes.'

'Just answer the question, please.'

Hollow then produced Kobel's tax returns for the past three years.

When Ringling objected, Hollow said to Judge Rollins, 'Your Honor, a man who files a tax return is of sound mind.'

'That's debatable,' said the ultraconservative judge, drawing laughter from the courtroom.

Oh, to be on the bench, thought Glenn Hollow. And maybe after a few years' stint as the attorney general I will be.

Rollins said, 'I'll let 'em in.'

'These are your returns, aren't they, sir?'

'I guess. Yes.'

'They indicate you made a fair amount of money at your practice. About forty thousand dollars a year.'

'Maybe. I suppose so.'

'So despite those other two patients who testified earlier, you must have a much larger number of patients you treat regularly and who are satisfied with your services.'

Kobel looked him in the eyes. 'There're a lot of nemes out there. Somebody's gotta fight 'em.'

Hollow sighed. 'No further questions, Your Honor.'

The prosecutor then called his own expert, a psychiatrist who'd examined Kobel. The testimony was that, though quirky, he was not legally insane. He was well aware of what he was doing, that he was committing a crime when he killed the victim.

Ringling asked a few questions, but didn't belabor the cross-examination.

Toward the end of the day, during a short break, Glenn Hollow sneaked a look at the jury box; he'd been a prosecutor and a trial lawyer for a long time and was an expert not only at the law but at reading juries.

And, goddamn it, they were reacting just the way Bob Ringling wanted them to. Hollow could tell they hated and feared Martin Kobel, but because he was such a monster and the things he was saying were so bizarre, he couldn't be held to the jury's standards of ethics and behavior. Oh, Ringling had been smart. He wasn't playing his client as a victim, he wasn't playing him as somebody who'd been abused or suffered a traumatic childhood (he barely referred to the deaths of Kobel's parents and brother).

No, he was showing that this *thing* at the defense table was not even human.

Like his expert said, 'Mr Kobel's reality is not *our* reality.'

Hollow stretched his skinny legs out in front of him and watched the tassels on his loafers lean to the side. I'm going to lose this case, he reflected. I'm going to lose it. And that son of a bitch'll be out in five or six years, looking for other women to stalk.

He was in despair.

Nemes . . . shit.

Then the judge turned away from his clerk and said, 'Mr Hollow? Shall we continue with your rebuttal of Mr Ringling's affirmative defense?'

It was then that a thought occurred to the prosecutor. He considered it for a moment and gasped at where the idea led.

'Mr Hollow?'

'Your Honor, if possible, could we recess until tomorrow? The prosecution would appreciate the time.'

Judge Rollins debated. He looked at his watch. 'All right. We'll recess until nine A.M. tomorrow.'

Glenn Hollow thanked the judge and told his young associates to gather up the papers and take them back to the office. The prosecutor rose and headed out the door. But he didn't start sprinting until he was well out of the courthouse; he believed that you never let jurors see anything but your dignified self.

At a little after nine the next morning, Glenn Hollow rose to his feet. 'I'd like to call to the stand Dr James Pheder.'

'Objection, Your Honor.' Bob Ringling was on his feet.

'Reasons?'

'We received notice of this witness last night at

156

eight P.M. We haven't had adequate time to prepare.'

'Where were you at eight?'

Ringling blinked. 'Well, Your Honor, I . . . the wife and I were out to dinner.'

'At eight *I* was reading documents in this case, Mr Ringling. And Mr Hollow was – obviously – sending you notices about impending witnesses. Neither of us were enjoying the buffet line at House O'Ribs.'

'But—'

'Think on your feet, Counselor. That's what you get paid those big bucks for. Objection overruled. Proceed, Mr Hollow.'

Pheder, a dark-complexioned man with a curly mop of black hair and a lean face, took the oath and sat.

'Now, Mr Pheder, could you tell us about your credentials?'

'Yessir. I have degrees in psychology and biology from the University of Eastern Virginia, the University of Albany, and Northern Arizona University.'

'All of which are accredited four-year colleges, correct?'

'Yes.'

'And what do you do for a living?'

'I'm an author and lecturer.'

'Are you published?'

'Yessir. I've published dozens of books.'

'Are those self-published?'

157

'Nosir. I'm with established publishing companies.'

'And where do you lecture?'

'All over the country. At schools, libraries, bookstores, private venues.'

'How many people attend these lectures?' Hollow asked.

'Each one is probably attended by four to six hundred people.'

'And how many lectures a year do you give?'

'About one hundred.'

Hollow paused and then asked, 'Are you familiar with the concept of neme?'

'Yessir.'

'Is it true that you coined that term?'

'Yessir.'

'What does it refer to?'

'I combined the words "negative" and "meme." "Negative" is just what it sounds like. "Meme" is a common phenomenon in society, like a song or catchphrase, that captures the popular imagination. It spreads.'

'Give us the gist of the concept of neme, that's *n-e-m-e*, if you would.'

'In a nutshell?'

'Oh, yessir. I got Cs in science. Make it nice and simple.'

Nice touch, Hollow thought of his improvisation. Science.

Pheder continued. 'It's like a cloud of energy that affects people's emotions in destructive ways.

158

You know how you're walking down the street and you suddenly feel different? For no reason at all. Your mood swings. It could be caused by any number of things. But it might be a neme incorporating itself into your cerebrum.'

'And you say, "negative." So nemes are bad?'

'Well, bad is a human judgment. They're neutral, but they tend to make us behave in ways society characterizes as bad. Take a case of swimming in the ocean. Sharks and jellyfish aren't bad; they're simply doing what nature intended, existing. But when they take a bite out of us or sting us, we call that bad. Nemes are the same. They make us do things that to them are natural but that we call evil.'

'And you're convinced these nemes are real?'

'Oh, yessir. Absolutely.'

'Are other people?'

'Yes, many, many are.'

'Are these people scientists?'

'Some, yes. Therapists, chemists, biologists, psychologists.'

'No further questions, Your Honor.'

'Your witness, Mr Ringling.'

The defense lawyer couldn't, as it turned out, think on his feet, not very well. He was prepared for Hollow to introduce testimony by experts attacking his client's claim of insanity.

He wasn't prepared for Hollow to try to prove nemes were real. Ringling asked a few meaningless questions and let it go at that.

Hollow was relieved that he hadn't explored Pheder's history and credentials in other fields, including parapsychology and pseudoscience. Nor did he find the blog postings where Pheder claimed the lunar landings were staged in a film studio in Houston, or the ones supporting the theory that the Israelis and President George Bush were behind the 9/11 attacks. Hollow had particularly worried that Pheder's essay about the 2012 apocalypse might surface.

Dodged the bullet there, he thought.

Ringling dismissed the man, seemingly convinced that the testimony had somehow worked to the defense's advantage.

This concluded the formal presentations in the case and it was now time for closing statements.

Hollow had been writing his mentally even as he'd fled the courthouse yesterday, in search of Pheder's phone number.

The slim, austere man walked to the front of the jury box and, a concession to camaraderie with the panel, undid his suit jacket's middle button, which he usually kept snugly hooked.

'Ladies and gentlemen of the jury. I'm going to make my comments brief, out of respect to you and respect to the poor victim and her family. They – and Annabelle Young's spirit – want and deserve justice, and the sooner you provide that justice, the better for everyone.

'The diligent law officers involved in this case have established beyond a reasonable doubt that

Martin Kobel was, in fact, the individual who viciously and without remorse stabbed to death a young, vibrant schoolteacher; window; and single mother, after stalking her for a week, following her all the way from Raleigh, spying on her, and causing her to flee from a restaurant while she waited to meet her son after school. Those facts are not in dispute. Nor is there any doubt about the validity of Mr Kobel's confession, which he gave freely and after being informed of his rights. And which he repeated here in front of you.

'The only issue in this case is whether or not the defendant was insane at the time he committed this heinous crime. Now, in order for the defendant to be found not guilty by reason of insanity, it must – I repeat, *must* – be proven that he did not appreciate the difference between right and wrong at the time he killed Annabelle. It must be proven that he did not understand reality as you and I know it.

'You have heard the defendant claim he killed Annabelle Young because she was infected by forces called nemes. Let's think on that for a moment. Had Mr Kobel been convinced that she was possessed by aliens from outer space or zombies or vampires, maybe that argument would have some validity. But that's not what he's claiming. He's basically saying that she was infected by what he himself described as a virus . . . not one that gives you a fever and chills but one that makes you do something bad.'

A smile. 'I have to tell you, when I first heard this theory, I thought to myself, brother, that's pretty crazy. But the more I thought about it, the more I wondered if there wasn't something to it. And in the course of this trial, listening to Mr Kobel and Dr Pheder and spending all last night reading through Mr Kobel's lengthy writing, I've changed my mind . . . I too now believe in nemes.'

The gasp throughout the courtroom was loud.

'I'm convinced that Martin Kobel is right. Nemes exist. Think about it, ladies and gentlemen: what else can explain the random acts of violence and abuse and rage we find in people who were previously incapable of them.'

Yes . . . some of the jurors were actually nodding. They were with him!

Hollow's voice rose. 'Think about it! Disembodied forces of energy that affect us. *We* can't see them but doesn't the moon's gravitation affect us? Doesn't radiation affect us? We can't see them either. These nemes are the perfect explanation for behaviors we otherwise would find impossible to understand.

'There was a time when the concept of flight by airplane would have been considered sorcery. The same with GPS. The same with modern medical treatments. The same with lightbulbs, computers, thousands of products that we now know are rooted in scientific fact but when first conceived would seem like black magic.'

Hollow walked close to the rapt members of the jury. 'But . . . but . . . if that's the case, if nemes exist, as Mr Kobel and I believe, then that means they're part of the *real* world. They are part of *our* society, our connection with one another, for good or for bad. Then to say that Annabelle Young was infected with one is exactly the same as saying that she had a case of the flu and might infect other people. Some of those infected people, the elderly or young, could die. Which would be a shame, tragic . . . But does that mean it would be all right to preemptively murder her to save those people? Emphatically no! That's not the way the world works, ladies and gentlemen. If, as I now believe, Annabelle Young was affected by these nemes, then as a trained professional, Martin Kobel's responsibility was to get her into treatment and help her. Help her, ladies and gentlemen. Not murder her.

'Please, honor the memory of Annabelle Young. Honor the institution of law. Honor personal responsibility. Find the defendant in this case sane. And find him guilty of murder in the first degree for taking the life of a young woman whose only flaw was to be sick, and whose only chance to get well and live a content and happy and productive life was snatched from her grasp by a vicious killer. Thank you.'

His heart pounding, Glenn Hollow strode to the prosecution table through an utterly quiet courtroom, aware that everyone was staring at him.

He sat. Still, no voices, no rustling. Nothing. Pin-drop time.

After what seemed like an hour, though it was probably only thirty seconds, Bob Ringling rose, cleared his throat, and delivered his closing statement. Hollow didn't pay much attention. And it seemed no one else did either. Every soul in the courtroom was staring at Glenn Hollow, and, the prosecutor believed, replaying in their minds what was the most articulate and dramatic closing argument he'd ever made. Turning the whole case on its ear at the last minute.

If, as I now believe, Annabelle Young was affected by these nemes, then as a trained professional, Martin Kobel's responsibility was to get her into treatment and help her. Help her, ladies and gentlemen. Not murder her.

Glenn Hollow was inherently a modest man but he couldn't help but believe he'd pulled off the coup of his career.

And so it was a surprise, to say the least, when the good men and woman on the jury panel rejected Hollow's argument completely and came back with a verdict finding Martin Kobel not guilty by reason of insanity after one of the shortest deliberations in Wetherby County history.

Three

I avoided the sunroom as much as I could.

Mostly because it was full of crazy people. Lip-chewing, Haldolpopping, delusional crazies. They

164

smelled bad, they ate like pigs at a trough, they screamed, they wore football helmets so they didn't do any more damage to their heads. As if that were possible. At my trial I was worried that I was overacting the schizo part. I shouldn't have worried. My performance in the courtroom didn't come close to being over the top.

The Butler State Hospital doesn't include the words 'for the criminally insane' in the name because it doesn't need to. Anybody who sees the place will get the idea pretty fast.

The sunroom was a place to avoid. But I'd come to enjoy the small library and this was where I'd spent most of my time in the past two months since I was committed here.

Today I was sitting in the library's one armchair, near the one window. I usually vie for the chair with a skinny patient, Jack. The man was committed because he suspected his wife of selling his secrets to the Union army – which would've been funny except that as punishment for her crime he tortured her for six hours before killing and dismembering her.

Jack was a curious man. Smart in some ways and a true expert on Civil War history. But he'd never quite figured out the rules of the game: that whoever got into the library first got the armchair.

I'd been looking forward to sitting here today and catching up on my reading.

But then something happened to disrupt those plans. I opened this morning's paper and noticed a reference to the prosecutor in the case against me, Glenn Hollow, whose name, I joked with my attorney Bob Ringling, sounded like a real estate development. Alarming Ringling somewhat since I wasn't sounding as crazy as he would have liked – because, of course, I'm not.

The article was about party officials pulling all support for Hollow's bid for attorney general. He'd dropped out of the race. I continued to read, learning that his life had fallen apart completely after failing to get me convicted on murder one. He'd had to step down as county prosecutor and no law firm in the state would hire him. In fact, he couldn't find work anywhere.

The problem wasn't that he'd lost the case, but that he'd introduced evidence about the existence of spirits that possessed people and made them commit crimes. It hadn't helped that he was on record as stating that nemes were real. And his expert was a bit of a crackpot. Though I still hold that Pheder's a genius. After all, for every successful invention, da Vinci came up with a hundred duds.

In fact, Hollow's strategy *was* brilliant and had given me some very uncomfortable moments in court. Bob Ringling, too. Part of me was surprised that the jury hadn't bought his argument and sent me to death row.

These revelations were troubling and I felt sorry for the man – I never had anything personal against him – but it was when I read the last paragraph that the whole shocking implication of what had happened struck home.

> *Before the Kobel trial, Hollow had been a shoo-in to become the attorney general of the state. He had the best conviction record of any prosecutor in North Carolina, particularly in violent crimes such as rape and domestic abuse. He actually won a premeditated murder case some years ago for a road rage incident, the first time any prosecutor had convinced a jury to do so.*

Reading this, I felt like I'd been slugged. My God . . . My God . . . I literally gasped. I'd been set up.

It was suddenly clear. From the moment Annabelle Young had sat next to me in Starbucks, I was being suckered into their plan. The nemes . . . they knew I'd take on the mission of trying to become her therapist. And they knew that I'd see that the neme within her was so powerful and represented such a danger to those around her that I'd have to kill her. (I'd done this before, of course; Annabelle was hardly the first. Part of being a professional therapist is matching the right technique to each patient.)

And where did the nemes pick their host? In the very county with the prosecutor who represented perhaps the greatest threat to them. A man who was winning conviction after conviction in cases of impulsive violence – locking away some of their most successful incarnations in the country: abusers, rapists, murderers . . .

Well, that answered the question that nobody had been able to answer yet: yes, nemes communicate.

Yes, they plot and strategize. Obviously they'd debated the matter. The price to eliminate Glenn Hollow was to get me off on an insanity plea, which meant that I would be out in a few years, and back on the attack, writing about them, counseling people to guard against them.

Even killing them if I needed to.

So, they'd decided that Glenn Hollow was a threat to be eliminated.

But not me. I'd escaped. I sighed, closing my eyes, and whispered, 'But not me. Thank God, not me.'

I saw a shadow fall on the newspaper on my lap. I glanced up to see my fellow patient Jack staring down at me.

'Sorry, got the chair first today,' I told him, still distracted by the stunning understanding. 'Tomorrow . . .'

But my voice faded as I looked into his face.

The eyes . . . the eyes.

No!

I gasped and started to rise, shouting for a guard, but before I could get to my feet, Jack was on me, 'My chair, you took my chair, you took it, you took it! . . .'

But then, as the razor-sharp end of the spoon he clutched slammed into my chest again and again, it seemed that the madman began to whisper something different. My vision going, my hearing fading, I thought perhaps the words slipping from these dry lips were, 'Yes you, yes you, yes you . . .'

PARALLEL LINES

Tim Powers

It should have been their birthday today. Well, it was still hers, Caroleen supposed, but with BeeVee gone the whole idea of 'birthday' seemed to have gone, too. Could she be seventy-three on her own?

Caroleen's right hand had been twitching intermittently since she'd sat up in the living room daybed five minutes ago, and she lifted the coffee cup with her left hand. The coffee was hot enough but had no taste, and the living room furniture – the coffee table, the now-useless analog TV set with its forlorn rabbit-ears antenna, the rocking chair beside the white-brick fireplace, all bright in the sunlight glaring through the east window at her back – looked like arranged items in some kind of museum diorama; no further motion possible.

But there was still the gravestone to be dealt with, these disorganized nine weeks later. Four hundred and fifty dollars for two square feet of etched granite, and the company in Nevada could not get it straight that Beverly Veronica Erlich and Caroleen Ann Erlich both had the same birth date, though the second date under Caroleen's name was to be left blank for some indeterminate period.

BeeVee's second date had not been left to chance. BeeVee had swallowed all the Darvocets and Vicodins in the house when the pain of her cancer, if it had been cancer, had become more than she could bear. For a year or so she had always been in some degree of pain – Caroleen remembered how BeeVee had exhaled a fast *whew*! from time to time, and the way her forehead seemed always to be misted with sweat, and her late-acquired habit of repeatedly licking the inner edge of her upper lip. And she had always been shifting her position when she drove, and bracing herself against the floor or the steering wheel. More and more she had come to rely – both of them had come to rely – on poor dumpy Amber, the teenager who lived next door. The girl came over to clean the house and fetch groceries, and seemed grateful for the five dollars an hour, even with BeeVee's generous criticisms of every job Amber did.

But Amber would not be able to deal with the headstone company. Caroleen shifted forward on the daybed, rocked her head back and forth to make sure she was wearing her reading glasses rather than her bifocals, and flipped open the brown plastic phone book. A short silver pencil was secured by a plastic loop in the book's gutter, and she fumbled it free –

– And her right hand twitched forward, knocking

the coffee cup right off the table, and the pencil shook in her spotty old fingers as its point jiggled across the page.

She threw a fearful, guilty glance toward the kitchen in the moment before she remembered that BeeVee was dead; then she allowed herself to relax and looked at the squiggle she had drawn across the old addresses and phone numbers.

It was jagged, but recognizably cursive letters:

Ineedyourhelpplease

It was, in fact, recognizably BeeVee's handwriting.

Caroleen's hand twitched again, and scrawled the same cramped sequence of letters across the page. She lifted the pencil, postponing all thought in this frozen moment, and after several seconds her hand spasmed once more, no doubt writing the same letters in the air. Her whole body shivered with a feverish chill and she thought she was going to vomit; she leaned out over the rug, but the queasiness passed.

She was sure that her hand had been writing this message in the air ever since she had awakened.

Caroleen didn't think BeeVee had ever before, except with ironic emphasis, said *please* when asking her for something.

She was remotely glad that she was sitting, for her heart thudded alarmingly in her chest and she was dizzy with the enormous thought that BeeVee was not gone, not entirely gone. She gripped the edge of the bed, suddenly afraid of falling and knocking the table over, rolling into the rocking chair. The reek of spilled coffee was strong in her nostrils.

'Okay,' she whispered. 'Okay!' she said again, louder. The shaking in her hand had subsided, so she flipped to a blank calendar page at the back of the book and scrawled *OKAY* at the top of the page.

Her fingers had begun wiggling again, but she raised her hand as if to wave away a question, hesitant to let the jiggling pencil at the waiting page just yet.

Do I want her back, she thought, *in any sense?* No, not *want*, not *her*, but – in these past nine weeks I haven't seemed to exist anymore, without her paying attention, any sort of attention, to me. These days I'm hardly more than an imaginary friend of Amber's next door, a frail conceit soon to be outgrown, even by her.

She sighed and lowered her hand to the book. Over her *OKAY* the pencil scribbled,

Iambeevee

'My God,' Caroleen whispered, closing her eyes. 'You think I need to be told?'

Her hand was involuntarily spelling it out again, breaking the pencil lead halfway through but

173

continuing rapidly to the end, and then it went through the motions three more times, just scratching the paper with splintered wood. Finally her hand uncramped.

She threw the pencil on the floor and scrabbled among the orange plastic prescription bottles on the table for a pen. Finding one, she wrote, *What can I do? To help*

She wasn't able to add the final question mark because her hand convulsed away from her again, and wrote,

touseyourbodyinvitemeintoyourbody

and then a moment later,

imsorryforeverythingplease

Caroleen watched as the pen in her hand wrote out the same two lines twice more, then she leaned back and let the pen jiggle in the air until this bout, too, gradually wore off and her hand went limp.

Caroleen blinked tears out of her eyes, trying to believe that they were caused entirely by her already-sore wrist muscles. But – for BeeVee to apologize, to her . . . ! The only apologies BeeVee had ever made while alive were qualified and impatient: *Well, I'm sorry if . . .*

Do the dead lose their egotism? wondered Caroleen, their onetime need to limit and dominate earthly

174

households? BeeVee had maintained Caroleen as a sort of extended self, and it had resulted in isolation for the two of them; if, in fact, they had added up to quite as many as two during the last years. The twins had a couple of brothers out there somewhere, and at least a couple of nieces, and their mother might even still be alive at ninety-one, but Caroleen knew nothing of any of them. BeeVee had handled all the mail.

Quickly she wrote on the calendar page, *I need to know – do you love me?*

For nearly a full minute she waited, her shoulder muscles stiffening as she held the pen over the page; then her hand flexed and wrote,

yes

Caroleen was gasping and she couldn't see the page through her tears, but she could feel her hand scribbling the word over and over again until this spasm, too, eventually relaxed.

Why did you have to wait, she thought, *until after you had died to tell me?*

But *use your body, invite me into your body.* What would that mean? Would BeeVee take control of it, ever relinquish control?

Do I, thought Caroleen, *care, really?*

Whatever it might consist of, it would be at least a step closer to the wholeness Caroleen had lost nine weeks ago.

Her hand was twitching again. She waited until

the first couple of scribbles had expended themselves in the air before touching the pen to the
page. The pen wrote,

yesforever

She moved her hand aside, not wanting to spoil
that statement with echoes.

When the pen had stilled, Caroleen leaned
forward and began writing, *Yes, I'll invite you*, but
her hand took over and finished the line with

exhaustedmorelater

Exhausted? Was it strenuous for ghosts to lean
out or in or down this far? Did BeeVee have to
brace herself against something to drive the pencil?

But, in fact, Caroleen was exhausted, too – her
hand was aching. She blew her nose into an old
Kleenex, her eyes watering afresh in the menthol-
and-eucalyptus smell of Ben Gay, and lay back
across the daybed and closed her eyes.

A sharp knock at the front door jolted her awake,
and though her glasses had fallen off and she
didn't immediately know whether it was morning
or evening, she realized that her fingers were
wiggling, and had been for some time.

She lunged forward and with her left hand
wedged the pen between her twitching right
thumb and forefinger. The pen began to travel

lightly over the calendar page. The scribble was longer than the others – with a pause in the middle – and she had to rotate the book to keep the point on the page until it stopped.

The knock sounded again, but Caroleen called, 'Just a minute!' and remained hunched over the little book, waiting for the message to repeat.

It didn't. Apparently she had just barely caught the last echo – perhaps only the end of the last echo.

She couldn't make out what she had written. Even if she'd had her glasses on, she'd have needed the lamplight, too.

'Caroleen?' came a call from out front. It was Amber's voice.

'Coming.' Caroleen stood up stiffly and hobbled to the door. When she pulled it open, she found herself squinting in the noon sunlight that filtered through the avocado tree branches.

The girl on the doorstep was wearing sweatpants and a huge T-shirt and blinking behind her gleaming round spectacles. Her brown hair was tied up in a knot on top of her head. 'Did I wake you up? I'm sorry.' She was panting, as if she had run over here from next door.

Caroleen felt the fresh air – smelling of sun-heated stone and car exhaust – cooling her sweaty scalp. 'I'm fine,' she said hoarsely. 'What is it?' Had she asked the girl to come over today? She couldn't recall doing it, and she was tense with impatience to get back to her pen and book.

'I just –' said Amber rapidly – 'I liked your sister, well, you know I did really, even though – and I – could I have something of hers, not like valuable, to remember her by? How about her hairbrush?'

'You want her hairbrush?'

'If you don't mind. I just want something—'

'I'll get it. Wait here.' It would be quicker to give it to her than to propose some other keepsake, and Caroleen had no special attachment to the hairbrush – her own was a duplicate anyway. She and BeeVee had, of course, matching everything – toothbrushes, coffee cups, shoes, wristwatches.

When Caroleen had fetched the brush and returned to the front door, Amber took it and went pounding down the walkway, calling 'Thanks!' over her shoulder.

Still disoriented from her nap, Caroleen closed the door and made her way back to the daybed, where she patted the scattered blankets until she found her glasses and fitted them on.

She sat down, switched on the lamp, and leaned over the phone book page. Turning the book around to follow the newest scrawl, she read,

bancaccounts
getmyhairbrushfromhernow

'Sorry, sorry!' exclaimed Caroleen; then in her own handwriting, she wrote, *I'll get it back.*

She waited, wondering why she must get the hairbrush back from Amber. Was it somehow necessary that all of BeeVee's possessions be kept together? Probably, at least the ones with voodoo-type identity signatures on them – DNA samples, like hair caught in a brush, dried saliva traces on dentures, Kleenex in a forgotten wastebasket. But—

Abruptly her chest felt cold and hollow.

But this message had been written down *before* she had given Amber the hairbrush. And Caroleen had been awake only for the last few seconds of the message transmission, which, if it had been like the others, had been repeating for at least a full minute before she woke up.

The message had been addressed to Amber next door, not to her. Amber had read it somehow and had obediently fetched the hairbrush.

Could all of these messages have been addressed to the girl?

Caroleen remembered wondering whether BeeVee might have needed to brace herself against something in order to communicate from the far side of the grave. Had BeeVee been bracing herself against Caroleen, her still-living twin, in order to talk to Amber? Insignificant *Amber*?

Caroleen was dizzy, but she got to her feet and padded into the bedroom for a pair of outdoor shoes. She had to carry them back to the living room – the bed in the bedroom had been BeeVee's, too, and she didn't want to sit on it in order to pull the shoes on – and on the way she leaned into the bathroom and grabbed her own hairbrush.

★　★　★

179

Dressed in one of her old church-attendance skrits, with fresh lipstick, and carrying a big embroidered purse, Caroleen pulled the door closed behind her and began shuffling down the walk. The sky was a very deep blue above the tree branches and the few clouds were extraordinarily far away overhead, and it occurred to her that she couldn't recall stepping out of the house since BeeVee's funeral. She never drove anymore – Amber was the only one who drove the old Pontiac these days – and it was Amber who went for groceries, reimbursed with checks from Caroleen . . . and the box of checks came in the mail, which Amber brought in from the mailbox by the sidewalk. If Caroleen alienated the girl, could she do these things herself? She would probably starve.

Caroleen's hand had begun wriggling as she reached the sidewalk and turned right, toward Amber's parents' house, but she resisted the impulse to pull a pen out of her purse. *She's not talking to* me, she thought, blinking back tears in the sunlight that glittered on the windshields and bumpers of passing cars; she's talking to stupid *Amber*. I won't *eavesdrop*.

Amber's parents had a Spanish-style house at the top of a neatly mowed sloping lawn, and a green canvas awning overhung the big arched window out front. Even shading her eyes with her manageable left hand Caroleen couldn't see anyone in the dimness inside, so she huffed up the widely spaced steps, and while she was catching her breath on the cement apron at the top, the front door swung inward, releasing a puff of cool floor-polish scent.

Amber's young, dark-haired mother – Crystal? Christine? – was staring at her curiously. 'It's . . . Caroleen,' she said, 'right?'

'Yes.' Caroleen smiled, feeling old and foolish. 'I need to talk to Amber.' The mother was looking dubious. 'I want to pay her more, and see if she'd be interested in balancing our, my, checkbook.'

The woman nodded, as if conceding a point. 'Well, I think that might be good for her.' She hesitated, then stepped aside. 'Come in and ask her. She's in her room.'

Caroleen got a quick impression of a dim living room with clear plastic covers over the furniture, and a bright kitchen with copper pans hanging everywhere. Amber's mother then knocked on a bedroom door and said, 'Amber honey? You've got a visitor,' then pushed the door open.

'I'll let you two talk,' the woman said, and stepped away toward the living room.

Caroleen stepped into the room. Amber was sitting cross-legged on a pink bedspread, looking up from a cardboard sheet with a rock, a pencil, and BeeVee's hairbrush on it. Lacy curtains glowed in the streetside window, and a stack of what appeared to be textbooks stood on an otherwise bare white desk in the opposite corner. The couple of pictures on the walls looked like pastel blobs. The room smelled like cake.

Caroleen considered what to say. 'Can I help?' she asked finally.

Amber, who had been looking wary, brightened and sat up straight. 'Shut the door.'

After Caroleen had shut the door, Amber went on, 'You know she's coming back?' She waved at the cardboard in front of her. 'She's been talking to me all day.'

'I know, child.'

Caroleen stepped forward and leaned down to peer at the cardboard, and saw that the girl had written the letters of the alphabet in an arc across it.

'It's one of those things people use to talk to ghosts,' Amber explained with evident pride. 'I'm using the rock crystal to point to the letters. Some people are scared of these things, but it's one of the good kinds of crystals.'

'A Ouija board.'

'That's it! She made me dream of one over and over again just before the sun came up, because this is her birthday. Well, yours, too, I guess. At first I thought it was a hopscotch pattern, but she made me look closer till I got it.' She pursed her lips. 'I wrote it by reciting the rhyme, and I accidentally did *H* and *I* twice, and left out *J* and *K*.' She pulled a sheet of lined paper out from under the board. 'But it was only a problem once, I think.'

'Can I see? I, uh, want this to work out.'

'Yeah. She won't be gone. She'll be in me, did she tell you?' She held out the paper. 'I drew in lines to break the words up.'

'Yes. She told me.' Caroleen slowly reached out to take the paper from Amber, and then held it up close enough to read the pencilled lines:

I/NEED/YOUR/HELP/PLEASE
Who R U?
I/AM/BEEVEE
How can I help U?
I/NEED/TO/USE/YOUR/BODY/INVITE/
ME/IN/TO/ YOUR/BODY
IM/SORRY/FOR/
EVERY/THING/PLEASE
R U an angel now? Can U grant wishes?
YES
Can U make me beautiful?
YES/FOR/EVER
OK. What do I do?
EXHAUSTED/MORE/LATER
BV? It's after lunch. Are U rested up yet?
YES
Make me beautiful.
GET/MY/HAIRBRUSH/FROM/MY/SIST
ER
Is that word 'hairbrush'?
YES/THEN/YOU/CAN/INVITE/ME/IN/T
O/YOU
How will that do it?
WE/WILL/BE/YOU/TOGETHER

183

+ What will we do?
GET/SLIM/TRAVEL/THE/WORLD
Will we be rich?
YES/I/HAVE/BANC/ACCOUNTS
GET/MY/HAIRBRUSH/ FROM/HER/
NOW
I got it.
NIGHT/TIME/STAND/OVER/GRAVE/B
RUSH/YR/HAIR/INVITE/ME/IN
ME/IN

'That should be B-A-N-K, in that one line,' explained Amber helpfully. 'And I'll want to borrow your car tonight.'

Not trusting herself to speak, Caroleen nodded and handed the paper back to her, wondering if her own face was red or pale. She felt invisible and repudiated. BeeVee could have approached her own twin for this, but her twin was too old; and if she did manage to occupy the body of this girl – a more intimate sort of twinhood! – she would certainly not go on living with Caroleen. And she had eaten all the Vicodins and Darvocets.

Caroleen picked up the rock. It was some sort of quartz crystal.

'When . . .' she began in a croak. She cleared her throat and went on more steadily, 'When did you get that second-to-last message? About the bank accounts and the hairbrush?'

'That one? Uh, just a minute before I knocked on your door.'

184

Caroleen nodded, wondering bleakly if BeeVee had even known that she was leaving *her* with carbon copies – multiple, echoing carbon copies – of the messages.

She put the crystal back down on the cardboard and picked up the hairbrush. Amber opened her mouth as if to object, then subsided.

There were indeed a number of white hairs tangled in the bristles.

Caroleen tucked the brush into her purse.

'I need that,' said Amber quickly, leaning forward across the board. 'She says I need it.'

'Oh, of course, I'm sorry.' Caroleen forced what must have been a ghastly smile, and then pulled her own hairbrush instead out of the purse and handed it to the girl. It was identical to BeeVee's, right down to the white hairs.

Amber took it and glanced at it, then laid it on the pillow, out of Caroleen's reach.

'I don't want,' said Caroleen, 'to interrupt . . . you two.' She sighed, emptying her lungs, and dug the car keys out of her purse. 'Here,' she said, tossing them onto the bed. 'I'll be next door if you . . . need any help.'

'Fine, okay.' Amber seemed relieved at the prospect of her leaving.

Caroleen was awakened the next morning by the pain of her sore right hand flexing, but she rolled over and slept for ten more minutes before the telephone by her head conclusively jarred her out

185

of the monotonous dream that had occupied her mind for the last hour or so.

She sat up, wrinkling her nose at the scorched smell from the fireplace and wishing she had a cup of coffee, and still half-saw the Ouija board she'd been dreaming about.

She picked up the phone, wincing. 'Hello?'

'Caroleen,' said Amber's voice, 'nothing happened at the cemetery last night, and BeeVee isn't answering my questions. She spelled stuff out, but it's not for what I'm writing to her. All she's written so far this morning is – just a sec – she wrote, uh, *"You win – you'll do – we've always been a team, right—"* Is she talking to you?'

Caroleen glanced toward the fireplace, where last night she had burned – or charred, at least – BeeVee's toothbrush, razor, dentures, curlers, and several other things, including the hairbrush. And today she would call the headstone company and cancel the order. BeeVee ought not to have an easily locatable grave.

'Me?' Caroleen made a painful fist of her right hand. 'Why would she talk to me?'

'You're her twin sister, she might be—'

'BeeVee is dead, Amber, she died nine weeks ago.'

'But she's coming back. She's going to make me beautiful! She said—'

'She can't do anything, child. We're better off without her.'

186

Amber was talking then, protesting, but Caroleen's thoughts were of the brothers she couldn't even picture anymore, the nieces she'd never met and who probably had children of their own somewhere, and her mother who was almost certainly dead by now. And there was everybody else, too, and not a lot of time.

Caroleen was resolved to learn to write with her left hand, and, even though it would hurt, she hoped her right hand would go on and on writing uselessly in the air.

At last she stood up, still holding the phone, and she interrupted Amber: 'Could you bring back my car keys? I have some errands to do.'

THE CULT OF THE NOSE

Al Sarrantonio

First mention of the cult in the literature is found in a tract of the Germanic heretic Jacobus Mesmus, which I have dated to somewhere near 1349 A.D.; it mentions, amidst an account of an outbreak of plague in the town of Breece, that 'a band of townsfolk had spied this day two figures, a man and a woman, prancing gaily on the outskirts of the village, wearing the feared Nose. They were driven out with fire clubs and a hail of stones.' Mesmus goes on to say that the appearance of figures wearing the Nose continues – sometimes there are two figures mentioned, sometimes three: a man, woman and small child; the text is partly destroyed and confusing – throughout the reign of the plague, abruptly terminating with the last case of the disease, although there is one cloudy passage toward the end of the treatise (which, as a sidelight, deals mainly with weather) mentioning that a 'nosed person' was spotted in the church bell tower intermittently for some time afterward.

There is, actually, a case for the Cult's being traced to well before this time; scant evidence and

188

brief mentions exist that might date it to the Egyptian dynastic era. There is a legend that one of the noses itself was found in the burial chamber of Ramses II, though there is no surviving physical evidence or corroborating testimony to support this.

After Jacobus Mesmus, accounts of the Cult become more frequent. A figure wearing the Nose appears in one of Brueghel's triptychs; there are several appearances of Cult members in the work of Bosch, as might be expected. There is also, curiously, an appearance of a figure bearing the Nose in a little-known (and by reason of the appearance of the adornment, thought to be spurious) painting by Pierre-Auguste Renoir: a tiny grinning figure, peeking out from behind a child holding a red parasol, is seen wearing a Nose utilizing a strap to keep it upon its face. The story is that the young girl in the painting was the daughter of M. Ebrezy, a prominent minister, and that the girl died mysteriously soon after posing for the artist.

There are mentions of the Nose in the works of Maupassant; Emily *and* Charlotte Brontë; and, in the Americas, Hawthorne and, quite often, in the later works of Twain.

There is a false, and dangerously misleading, conception that the Nose is a modern concoction, that it was not only invented for the foolish pleasure of children and childlike adults, but that it was promoted for this use alone, and for the further and more arcane uses to which it is currently being put by the modern Cult. It must be understood that the Nose is not only an ancient instrument, but that its use can be traced back nearly to the dawn of recorded history (see my opening remarks). The Nose has doubtless gone through periods – it might be hypothesized that these periods were ones of relative calm and social and religious stability – where it has been relegated to the position of toy. It has been determined, though, that these times of tranquility have always been rather brief, and, further, that the Nose has always regained its position of mysterious authority – and of feared nebulosity.

Such a period is, of course, where we find ourselves at the moment.

I might add at this point that my interest in the Cult is not a recently flowering one; I have been gathering references to it and carefully formulating my theories for many years.

For the record, my interest was sparked during the waning months of the free world's involvement in the Vietnam War. At that time I was a special attaché aligned with a covert arm of American intelligence, checking black-and-white photographs taken by spies and insurgents behind Communist lines – these were photos smuggled out of prisoner-of-war camps and such. I might also add that this was a period in which I was seeking to forget an unfortunate incident in my personal life: my young spouse, understandably lonely due to my lengthy absence, took up with another man and had a child by him. I sought solace by immersing myself in my work.

I began to notice in some of the photos I handled a recurring and curious phenomenon. Here and there, tucked in a corner or peering out from behind a barracks, was a peculiar figure wearing what seemed to be a false nose upon its face. Often the figure was identifiably male; at other times it appeared to be a female, or even a child. Many prisoners of war at that time, due to malnutrition and concurrent emaciation, were barely identifiable by their gender – or their age – so it must be remembered that any sort of positive identification was difficult. Many of the nose-wearing figures appeared beside, or within (though they were apparently not dead) mass graves.

I put these photographs aside, thinking that, though there was little here to interest my superiors, there might yet be something to investigate further.

I began to dream of figures, birdlike, resembling Bosch's horrid hell beasts, wearing false, beaklike noses.

My collection of photographs grew. I realized that as the scenes of horror increased – by this time we were receiving covert daily pictures from death camps holding Americans and Vietnamese Buddhists – the number of nose-bearing figures increased. In one photograph – one I keep to this day folded in my wallet – a man, woman and child, in a long line of tired and bleakly hopeless prisoners, most of them in tatters of clothes hanging on barely enough bones to stand, being led meekly to an open pit by machine gun-bearing guards, have turned their faces toward the camera, three in a row, and are smiling a death's-head smile. There seems to be a bit more meat on their bones than on those in front and in back of them.

They each wear the Nose.

Other activities soon saved me from complete absorption in the manner of these curious photographs, and it was not until well after the war's resolution, after I had settled in Montreal, far away from my ex-wife, her son and husband (who traveled extensively) that I came across a small bundle of the grainy pictures in a box (the above-mentioned photo was among them) and all of my former interest was rekindled. I began to search other sources – having a bit of influence, due to my war service, in being able to access materials not easily available by the public – and began to come across other photos taken in other sectors of the war in which figures bearing the Nose appeared.

I then broadened my research, and found similar artifacts among World War II memorabilia. I came across one precious bit of evidence (alas, recently lost to fire) that depicted a Third Reich rally in which two separate nosed figures could plainly be discerned. I remember this photo clearly, because one of the figures stood a few scant feet from Hitler himself, and grinned maliciously at the camera.

Eventually, my interest once again waned, until I picked up one morning in 1979 a London newspaper that contained a news-service photo on the front page presenting the dead body of the assassinated president of South Korea, Park Chung Hee. To the right of the body, barely visible in the deep background, was a figure with the Nose on its face.

I immediately researched other photos that were taken at the time but came up with nothing useful.

However, another reference turned up in a photograph of a train derailment that killed forty-five passengers in Ohio the same week: among the twisted metal a head could be seen poking through with the false appendage attached to it by a thin silver strap. The figure it belonged to, which was surrounded by dead commuters, was clearly alive.

I began to comb picture morgues and newspaper files, turning up hundreds of photos with similar figures in them. Most depicted disasters or near disasters; I began to notice that the number – and demeanor – of the figures often depended on the amount of destruction that surrounded them. Their faces glowed with pleasure in ratio to the amount of mayhem and carnage. This was by no means a strictly quantifiable thing, but the correlation, in general, seemed to exist.

Most of these photos, unfortunately, have also been destroyed by fire.

I began to notice small, easily missed references to the Nose, or the Cult of those wearing the Nose, in literature, and naturally broadened my research to include that area also, as I have already mentioned.

I had apparently stumbled onto something that had gone nearly undetected by the general populace, something that had stayed just outside the general consciousness since the beginning of recorded history. Here was a sect so arcane, nefarious and secret (a kind of truly devilish Freemasonry?) that no more than widely scattered references to it remained, or had ever existed. There were no prime source materials; the only evidence to point to its existence were the photos few and far between and a symbol – the Nose – so thoroughly steeped in the general notion of tomfoolery as to virtually ensure safety from detection.

The next step, of course, was to search for the modern remnants of the Cult.

My task of discovery proved to be a long and difficult one. It would take me days to recount the numerous blind alleys and dead ends I encountered; the false leads, misinformation (deliberate, some of it), the intrigue, deception, the attempts (yes) on my life. For years, I meticulously pored over each scrap of evidence that might at last lead me to the discovery of the true aspect of the Cult.

Eventually, despite all attempts to stop me, I succeeded.

In the spring of this year my obsession led me to Paris, where I hoped to meet with a man under the pyramidic shadow of the Eiffel Tower. I was to wait at a certain café until three o'clock in the afternoon, and then I was to ask the waiter to change my table to the one next to mine. It was a half-gray, half-sunny day in early April; there were breezes in the air that gave hope of a coming warmth mixed with the threat of a quick return to a latent wet winter. I had a coat and muffler on, and a black bowler hat. I carried a folded umbrella. In these things, too, I had followed instructions. I felt like a figure model in a painting by Magritte, felt I should somehow be floating in midair above the redbrick shop across the street, stiff and sharp as a cardboard cutout. Three o'clock came. I changed my table, tipped my waiter for his trouble and waited. Nothing happened. I bought a paper from a passing vendor, unfolded it before me and began to read. This kind of thing had happened too many times before; I would wait another ten minutes and then make my way, undaunted, back to my hotel. On the front page of the paper was a picture of a man with a black bowler hat on and a false nose. I heard the sound of the metal chair at the table I had just vacated scrape across the patio floor and the man in the photo, in the flesh, sat down across

195

from me. He wore the Nose. The photo in the paper, I now saw, had been pasted on.

'You follow instructions, I see,' he said in clipped, neutral English, the schoolroom English taught all over the world. He did not wait for me to answer, but held out an envelope.

'Take this and continue to follow instructions.'

In the envelope was a ticket to a baseball game in New York City.

Two days hence found me in crowded Yankee Stadium. The seat beside me remained empty for eight full innings; by this time the home team had a commanding lead and many of the spectators had left. I took little notice when the seat was finally occupied by a young boy who had, I surmised, come down from higher, cheaper seats; it was happening all around me.

It was only when he turned toward me that I saw that, under his ball cap, the boy wore the Nose. He smiled crookedly, handed me another envelope and slipped away.

The next weeks found me at a succession of similar rendezvous in public locations – theaters, restaurants, the London Zoo and Piccadilly Circus, a San Francisco streetcar. Always the pattern was the same. A messenger, identified by the Nose, approached and handed me an envelope with a ticket, or a short, untraceable note in it.

I always did as I was told. My obsession had become a compulsion: I was determined to find the source of the mystery.

I began to see false noses everywhere – in lines, in food markets, rising suddenly out of a mass of people on a street as if the wearer had put a box down and stepped up on it to elevate himself above those around him. My dreams were haunted. I would wake in the middle of the night calling for the Nose to confront me and be done with it. I had visions of my father and mother bathing me as a young boy, bending down over my shallow tub and splashing water on me, laughing. They wore the Nose – golden versions of it, tied with bright red ribbons behind their heads. One morning in Seattle, Washington, sick from lack of sleep, I hallucinated a man into my hotel bedroom doorway who bore a silver Nose in a tin box. The man himself had no face, only a blank oval of flesh.

And then, abruptly, on the same day as this hallucination, the Cult finally made its secrets known to me.

After the vision dissipated I spent the entire morning in the bath. My eyes were tightly closed; I sought a wakeful kind of sleep.

There came a knock at my hotel room door. I ignored it. The knock was repeated.

I called out tentatively, fearfully.

I was answered by a trill of tinkling, insubstantial laughter from behind the door, which I had left unlocked. I stepped dripping from the bath into the living area in time to see the doorknob turning. I waited for the man with no face to reveal himself again.

The door opened to reveal an empty hallway.

I dressed quickly, in my Magritte outfit – black bowler, umbrella, black laced shoes – and put my research material hurriedly into my briefcase, snapping it closed with a jerk. As I did so a picture, the one depicting the führer and his nosed shadow, dropped out, to the floor. I retrieved it, and now saw that there were more cultish figures in the frame than I had at first noticed.

The platform on which Hitler stood was filled by figures with noses on.

I shoved the picture back into my case and closed it. I took the morning paper from the table by the door. The front-page photograph was of a gangster who had been drowned in his own bathtub – what looked like a false nose floated on the water near the submerged face.

On a hunch, I moved to the window, and just caught sight of a man, woman and child disappearing into the entrance to the hotel, eight floors below. I was plainly visible, but they did not peer back up at me.

I straightened my tie. On a hunch, I turned back to the window and there, sure enough, were the man, woman and child. They had retreated from the front entrance to the curb and stood staring up at me expectantly. The child waved.

He was the boy I had seen at the baseball park, with the crooked smile.

The man was the same one I had seen under the shadow of the Eiffel Tower.

The woman looked familiar also.

The three of them wore the Nose.

They reentered the hotel and I turned quickly from the window and set my briefcase by the doorway.

On the table where the newspaper had been was a can of fluid. I unscrewed its top carefully, avoiding the sharp industrial smell, and began to splash its contents around the room. When the can was empty I placed it by the briefcase. I removed a cigarette lighter from my coat pocket and casually flipped it open.

Flame burst up unexpectedly, burning my finger, and I was forced to drop the lighter. It did not go out, but instead fell into the liquid.

The fire before me burst to hot life. I was blinded momentarily. When I regained my sight the room was filling rapidly with smoke. I could hear voices beginning to build outside the window on the street, a few cries of alarm.

The man, woman and child, wearing their Noses, had somehow made their way into the room, and stood smiling at me as they quickly bound one another with ropes.

Gasping, I groped for the door, yanked it open and lurched out into the hallway and down the fire stairs. I stopped before the door to the street to brush and straighten my clothes.

I heard screams behind me. Like the tinderbox

it was, the cheap hotel was exploding into roaring flames.

I eased open the door to the street. Television crews had already arrived with cameras; one of those pictures would undoubtedly grace tomorrow's front page. I reached inside my coat to make sure that my ticket home to Montreal was in place. It was. Many of the reporters and spectators on the street wore Noses. A woman, wearing the Nose, fell, screaming, on fire, to the pavement in front of me. She was the one I had seen in my hotel room. Her hands were still bound behind her.

It was at that point that I realized with shock that I had left my briefcase behind.

I turned and, though a wall of flames met me, I went back.

As you can imagine, it is very painful for me in this condition. I cannot see through these bandages; I have not been told if I will have my sight back when they are removed.

And now, to my horror, I find my testimony on the Cult of the Nose disputed.

The literary references to the Cult are real, though they are scattered with the loss of my notes and would have to be researched once more. Other documentation exists; since the destruction of my valuable material it would have to be reassembled. I am told that my one remaining photograph, which was in my wallet, and which the unesteemed prosecutor contends I snapped myself, that of the man, woman and child in line, has been tampered with, and so cannot be used as evidence in my defense: the death camp has somehow been doctored into an amusement park, and now only the child wears the true Nose. The others bear noses that, oddly, have been drawn on with a felt-tip pen, and it appears that whoever did take the photograph was hiding in a hedge, since there are branches and small leaves visible in the forefront.

Obviously, I have been the victim of fraud and chicanery.

But this does not discourage me.

Nothing does.

Why?

Because I possess the most revealing bit of evidence proving the existence of the Cult of the Nose.

I know, without a shred of doubt, that it exists.

How?

It is obvious.

Because:

Despite all of the testimony that has been given against me here today; despite all of the lies and accusations; despite the spurious contention by the unesteemed prosecutor that I set the blaze in that ramshackle hotel deliberately, in order to murder my ex-wife, her son and husband, merely because she left me to have another man's child while I was overseas, which, the unesteemed prosecutor contends, caused me to become obsessed, to track them for months, even years and, eventually, to murder them; despite all of this, I know that if my bandages were removed; if my ruined and melted face were restored and my eyes made whole; if I could look through the inches of useless salve and acres of white gauze that enfold my head – I know with certainty that if I could do these things I would see, upon the face of each of the twelve of you who have given me this sentence of death, the Adornment of which I have so eloquently spoken.

HUMAN INTELLIGENCE

Kurt Andersen

He found it almost physically painful to lie, which was unfortunate for someone who had spent most of his life as a spy.

Back when everything was proceeding according to plan, year after year after year, he had gotten a little sloppy, allowing bystanders to see the aircraft in flight, sometimes even announcing to children and their childlike parents who he was and where he lived. What did it matter, back then? Besides, he told himself, his openness created a rapport with the natives. But mainly it relieved his loneliness.

When people asked his occupation, his standard answer for a long time had been 'a writer' or 'an anthropologist.' But lately, once again, he was responding to such questions with a more dangerous version of the truth. These gestures toward self-revelation felt exciting, like precursors to intimacy. But he never put himself in real jeopardy. In America in the twenty-first century, who was going to be anything but charmed and amused by a well-dressed, well-groomed, intelligent, alert, friendly old Anglo-Saxon-looking gentleman who made a fantastic remark or two? 'I'm a spy,' he'd started telling the curious with a smile and a wink, 'here on a long-term intelligence-gathering operation. But it's super-top-secret, so if you don't mind, that's really all I can say about it.'

He had looked like an old man even when he was younger because, early on, before he took up the posting, he'd grown a full beard to conceal the purple cross-hatching of surgical scars on his chin and upper neck. Now that he was genuinely elderly, it pleased him that appearance and reality had come into sync. He looked old and, by any standard, he was old. One less lie to live.

Of course, if he told the whole truth, anyone but a lunatic would consider him a lunatic. Then the authorities would be notified, and even in this comparatively enlightened era he would lose his freedom for the rest of his life. The project to which he'd devoted such vast time and effort – dutifully, yes, but with enthusiasm as well – would be for naught.

On the other hand, with the passing years that downside calculus had changed. Incarceration and 24/7 gawking would be unpleasant, no doubt, but the rest of his life was looking like a manageably brief time.

As for aborting the operation, he doubted that anyone at headquarters was any longer aware of him or his mission – if headquarters still existed. Doing his job had become easier and easier over the years, especially with television and the

Internet – although, of course, the promiscuous availability of information also tended to make his job moot. Maybe the project was already for naught.

Yet he had continued to adhere to the four main directives of the contingency plan, almost as articles of faith: remain at the last position reported to headquarters, maintain all necessary discretion and secrecy, continue to chronicle the people and their society to whatever extent possible, and await retrieval. 'Retrieval' is the closest English translation of the word in the orders, not 'rescue,' a bit of stoic bureaucratese he had come to resent ever since the crash. (Had he gone native? Probably.)

So here he was, living in a city now a thousand times larger than when he arrived, chronicling and waiting, chronicling and waiting, chronicling and still waiting.

After he read *End Game* and *Waiting for Godot* at the Chicago Public Library one pleasantly frigid afternoon near the end of December 1959, he wrote a long, effusive fan letter to Samuel Beckett in Paris, describing the two plays as 'perhaps the most profound works of literature since Shakespeare.' Discovering them, he gushed, had 'made this Christmas one of my merriest ever.' In response he received a curt, generic form letter, mimeographed, which struck him as almost funny. Since the stranding, he has not been an outwardly jovial man, but he's never lost his sense of humor. By nature and by training, he takes the long view.

And so he was more intrigued than anxious when

the little light on the remote beacon had, for the first time ever, started flashing. He wasn't sure exactly when the flashing began, because he kept the device hidden at the back of a high shelf in his bedroom closet. He'd been checking it only once every month or so, grudgingly, feeling like a chump each time he lifted it down, pushed the test button, for the ten thousandth time heard the beep confirming that it worked and the connection was secure – *Takes a Licking and Keeps on Ticking! Nothing Outlasts the Energizer Bunny!* – and then, after waiting ten seconds for the flashing signal that never came, put the thing back up on the shelf.

Until the remarkable evening of September 16, 2007, when he first saw the throb of purple light and shouted so loudly that his young downstairs neighbor called up to see if he was all right. According to the contingency-plan instructions, the light on his box could flash in one or more of nine different colors, each color corresponding to a particular alert condition. Purple means that sensors on the exterior of the station, 2,400 miles away, are now exposed to sunlight.

When the station was set up all those years ago, covered by dozens of feet of ice even at the height of summer, its secrecy seemed guaranteed. Nobody else, not Peary or Amundsen or Byrd or free-ranging Inuits, had traveled so far north. But for the last several decades, more of the Arctic ice had been melting each summer – and in 2007 the summer melt radically spiked, turning a third of the polar ice cap into open sea. The top of the station, a 150-foot oval of tubing and tanks suspended just beneath the water's surface, must be visible. And now there are permanent research stations scattered all over the high Arctic, and surveillance satellites shooting high-resolution pictures of every rod and furlong of the no-longer-trackless wastes.

What was taking them so long to find it? Seasonal ice may still grow back to hide the base in winter, but for each of the last three summers he has waited for the news bulletins (HIGH-TECH 'ATLANTIS' FOUND NEAR NORTH POLE) and the resulting global hysteria. He does worry that the discovery will discombobulate people en masse – the 'unforeseeable cultural and ontological impacts,' as headquarters' boilerplate put it. But he also has a hopeful hunch that a critical, controlling fraction of humanity had matured, and would, after some initial breathlessness, learn to accommodate the new facts.

Selfishly, he's also eager to see pictures of the station again after all this time, to compare his hazy memories with fresh digital images. And although it felt vaguely insubordinate (to whom?), or even traitorous (to what?), he was excited by the prospect of everyone on earth learning all at once the truth that he alone had known for so long.

As her flight from Oslo approaches O'Hare, Nancy Zuckerman thinks once again of the cliché uttered sooner or later by everyone who spends time in Svalbard, including herself: *This is what it must be like to live on another planet.* NASA actually runs a research station on the other side of the North Pole, in the Canadian Arctic, where they simulate the conditions of a Martian space colony.

She had always liked spending time outdoors, and when she was seven could stick a live worm on a fishing hook and set up a tent herself. But it was the second *Indiana Jones* sequel, which came out the summer she turned eight, that decided her on becoming an explorer when she grew up. In earlier generations, adults would have smiled at a little *girl* who said she wanted to be an explorer. But at the turn of the twenty-first century in Boulder, Colorado, adults smiled and patronized little Nancy Zuckerman not because of her gender but because her cute dream job no longer existed.

Fortunately, she was both collegial and self-reliant, a cheerful team player as well as a cheerfully independent loner. 'If I could be a superhero,' she used to say, 'I'd be totally willing to be like a second-string member of X-Men or the Justice League.' And so science in general and her chosen field in particular – exploration geophysics, specializing in the Arctic – suited her. She hadn't minded spending the last year and a half on a postdoc in Longyearbyen, a town in the Svalbard islands, northernmost Norway, 1,200 miles up from Oslo and 600 miles below the North Pole. It was and it wasn't a fortress of solitude. Her fellow researchers and faculty were a cosmopolitian, caffeinated assortment of English speakers from all over the world, chatty good company for the six months of perpetual sunlight. And Einar, a single young coal miner who'd grown up in Svalbard and had no idea how handsome he was, made the six months of subzero darkness tolerable, even though (or maybe because) he spoke very little English. She played squash, she swam in the indoor pool, she took pictures.

She was attached to one team drilling experimental wells to store captured CO_2 in a sandstone aquifer, and part of another project testing the feasibility of thickening the polar cap by pumping seawater onto the ice and letting it freeze. Good data had been collected. Techniques had been refined. Reasonable progress had been made. It wasn't heroic exploration of the kind she'd imagined as a kid, but as she approached thirty she had made her peace with the exigencies of incremental science and the real world.

Or so she had thought until a few weeks ago. She was five days into an excursion aboard the university's sixty-eight-foot research vessel, the *Dauntless*, taking a group of new undergraduates on a tour of the southern edge of the ice cap. Around two A.M. on the morning of July 11, unable to sleep, she'd gotten up and taken one of the motorboats out alone to cruise close to the ice, looking for polar bears to photograph. It was warm, 46°F, the sky almost cloudless, and, of course, the sun high in the sky. The sea was calm. Thirty yards from the ice, at the mouth of a recently formed inlet, she cut the motor and let herself drift along, sitting cross-legged on the deck at midships, watching, camera and long lens at the ready. She was exploring. A half hour passed. Some terns flew over, but she saw no seals and no bears.

When she heard and felt the thud, she figured she'd struck a chunk of submerged ice. As she stood to investigate, the boat rocked freely in the water even though it was stuck more or less in place, knocking against some underwater structure to its left and its right. It was as if the boat had slid into a marina slip.

What the fuck?

She started probing underwater with the tip of an oar blade, and a foot and a half beneath the surface found not ice, but what felt like pipe, a big pipe, a pipe with a diameter – she scraped and stroked the hard surface – of several feet. She climbed over to the starboard side to probe some more, and found an apparently identical pipe, running parallel to the other. The distance between them was ten, maybe twelve feet.

Completely bizarre.

A sunken ship? Even the fleeting thought made her feel childish and silly. The water was a mile deep. No way a wreck could float to the surface, and ditto for stray lengths of oil or gas pipeline. Unless, *shit*, she'd discovered some hitherto unknown shoal or reef in the Arctic Ocean! She had discovered *something*. More to the point, *she* had *discovered* something.

Kneeling on the deck, she started to use the oar as a push pole, levering it against the underwater pipe on the port side to propel the boat back – shove, coast a couple of yards, shove, coast – toward the opening through which she must have drifted.

But then, abruptly, the dinghy stopped moving, caught between the mysterious pipes. The pipes didn't run parallel, it turned out, but came together at an angle, and she was now wedged near their apex. She stood. The boat barely budged. She tried and failed to pole herself forward. She was stuck fast. Crouching and leaning out next to the raised motor, she stuck the oar into the water directly behind the boat – and found another smooth, hard underwater surface. But this was different, not a pipe but some kind of funnel. She used both hands to plunge the oar straight down into the funnel's neck.

She gasped as she felt the blade end of the oar being smartly, mechanically grabbed, then slowly pulled into the water another foot. She let go. The oar's hand grip protruded straight up between waves. She stared down, bewildered.

Then she was shocked beyond belief, and terrified. The ocean beneath the boat and in a long, narrow strip beyond began to churn, forming into a 100-foot-long tubular wave – but the very opposite of a breaking surf, for this wave had depth

211

instead of height, its crest not a peak but a trough ten feet below the water's surface. She thought of her mother and brothers, of her late father, and of the fact that she wouldn't get any credit at all for discovering this freakish inverted tsunami before it killed her.

But the boat wasn't swamped or sucked under, and the upside-down wave, instead of crashing, just kept rolling and rolling. In other words, a ten-foot-wide ditch had formed in the sea, with ten-foot sides of smooth water and a sloshing, foamy bottom. Nancy Zuckerman was sitting in a boat suspended by metal pincers – the two big pipes, now fully exposed – at the top of this perfect, impossible ditch.

As in Exodus 14, the waters of the sea had been divided, the waters being a wall on her right hand and on her left. But even at that supremely dream-like moment, Nancy Zuckerman's faith in reason and science was unshaken. Miracles are a function of ignorance, inexplicability a temporary condition. By some mechanical means, a hundred thousand gallons of seawater were being sucked away to form a semicylindrical void. It was amazing, but it was also like one of the rides at Water World, off I-25 in Denver.

She had the presence of mind to push the button on her GPS, and press again to record the reading: longitude 14° 48' 3" east, latitude 86° 19' 27" north.

And then she was vindicated – although also freshly terrified – when a rubbery blue sleeve rose from the pit beneath the boat and wrapped itself tightly around the hull with a vaccum-packing *thrrrooooop*. Definitely a machine at work, not God or Satan. As the dinghy started moving smoothly and slowly into the slot in the sea, she considered escape – she might be able to dive out past the edge of the slot and swim away, might make it to the ice and pull herself out of the water before hypothermia set in, might be rescued by searchers from the *Dauntless* after they discovered her and the dinghy missing. But curiosity kept her in the boat. As the machine moved her down into the mists and darkness, Nancy was careful to notice everything she heard and saw and smelled. She was an explorer.

Twelve days ago, his beacon – now out of the closet and sitting on the coffee table in the living room – had started alternating a chartreuse throb with each purple one. Chartreuse meant that someone had entered the station. And the station's mapping console, assuming it still worked, would give the intruders the precise location of the remote beacon. He thought of getting rid of the device, leaving it on the El or heaving it into the Chicago River, to put the hounds off his scent. But then he admitted, once and for all, that he wants to be tracked down. He craves being found.

And so he has gotten all his documents and images in order, the entire chronicle. He has packed a suitcase, and straightened up the apartment. He has been watching cable news and surfing the Web constantly. Surely it is only a matter of time.

But he's surprised when the front-door buzzer buzzes. He had expected helicopters and flood-lights and grappling hooks and special-ops troopers in black visors and haz-mat suits bursting through the doors and windows with automatic weapons and gas canisters, and had even prac-ticed dropping to the floor and putting his hands over his head. The Obamas' Hyde Park house is ten minutes from his apartment, which he'd figured would make the brouhaha all the more spectacular. As he stands at the intercom speaker, he looks out the window down at Kimbark Avenue: cars driving past, people strolling by and hanging out as on any summer afternoon, no evac-uation of the block, no emergency vehicles, no perimeter secured.

The doorbell buzzes again. He wonders if it's the UPS guy.

'Yes?'

'Hello?' A woman, sounding tentative.

'Yes?'

'I'm looking for someone who, um, also lives at 86 degrees, 19 minutes, 27 seconds north?'

He grins, and buzzes her in.

Opening the apartment door, he's surprised all over again: she's alone, apparently unarmed, and very young. She extends her right hand.

'I'm Nancy Zuckerman.'

'Hello. I'm Nicholas Walker.'

'I'm a scientific researcher,' she says. 'From the Arctic.'

'Really?' He smiles, and motions her inside. 'So am I! How very fortunate. For the both of us.'

They sit. She sets aside the cardigan he'd handed her, and explains herself in a nervous rush. Why she had been in the Arctic, how she happened to drift over the station and accidentally jimmy the entry system with her oar. How she'd figured, at first, that it must be some military facility, American or Russian or Chinese, but then, as she spent hours exploring the interior – the peculiar materials and shapes and technology interfaces, the very peculiar quality of artificial light, the unrecognizable written language, the images displayed – how she had developed a new hypo-thesis. How she had photographed everything, including the mapping console with its one, tiny blinking light in the middle of North America, and then, on her computer back in Longyearbyen, had transposed a longitude and latitude grid over her image to find the precise location of the blinking light – 41 degrees, 47 minutes, 54.1475 seconds north and 87 degrees, 35 minutes, 41.7095 seconds west, South Kimbark Avenue between 53rd and 54th Streets, Chicago. How she had taken a few things from the station – including a small plastic picture of him, which she had just shown to a lady downstairs in order to find his apartment. She hands him the picture.

'My goodness,' he says, 'I was young. So young!'
He puts the picture down and turns to look at
her. They've talked for ten minutes, yet she hasn't
asked where he's from or what he's doing here.
Which is fine by him. He's in no particular hurry.

She's a little flummoxed. 'I have to tell you I am
incredibly excited. This is beyond surreal. It's like
I'm having a stroke, or been drugged, or gone to
heaven. It's – it's a new category of excitement.'
She takes a deep breath. 'I'm also scared.'

'Scared? Of me? Oh, don't be. No, no, no.'

'No, scared that I haven't *told* anyone about any
of this – not my colleagues, not my bosses, not
any government people, not my mom, no one. I
don't know what the rules are, but I sure as shit
haven't followed them.'

How interesting. 'Why have you kept it secret?'
He knows about keeping secrets.

'Well, I guess possibly I worried that . . . no, I'll
tell you why. Because I want to be the one who
gets to *reveal* it, to tell the whole story. To be, you
know, "the discoverer." Like Columbus or
Magellan or Galileo or Einstein. I'm sorry – do
you know who they are?'

He smiles. 'Yes.'

'Before the rest of the world finds out and rushes
in and pushes me out of the way, I want to learn
as much as I can. I want to be *the expert.*'

He likes this girl. He will give her the gift she
wants.

'Oh, *Jesus.*' She reaches into a bag, searching for

her two tape recorders. 'May I record our conversation?'

'Of course.' He spots something in the bag. 'You found the gold? At the station?'

She blushes, and pulls out a half-pound golden cylinder the size of a lipstick. 'You can have it back. I took one, as a research sample.'

He strokes the ingot with one finger. 'And you said you saw images at the station?'

'Projected on those big spherical monitors in the, like, office.'

'To the left and straight back as you entered?'

'Hundreds of pictures on those monitors, 3-D photographs, in color, of huts and houses and towns and farm animals and pots and carts and soldiers and children and temples, it looked like from all over the world, Europe, Asia, Africa—'

He hates to seem smug, which he's afraid is about to become his default affect, but he can't suppress a knowing smile, and interrupts her. 'I know. I took them.'

'Shot from overhead, mostly, I guess with a very long lens?'

'Intelligence gathering is supposed to be clandestine. And I tried to minimize the Hawthorne effect – people behaving differently when they know they're being watched.'

'A lot of the images look extremely old. Unbelievably old. Not the *pictures*, I mean, but the people and buildings and so on.'

'They are.'

She hesitates before asking the next question. 'So, you were takeing photographs all over the world before . . . before photography was invented?' This is precisely what she'd hypothesized, that he must be at least two hundred years old. *Incredible*.

'And moving pictures as well – videos, more or less. From when I arrived until the day the camera was destroyed. By the time the technology existed . . . indigenously, it seemed pointless for me to start up again.'

'May I ask your age?'

This time it's he who pauses, anticipating her reaction. 'The station was established in 429, CE.'

She stares, saying nothing. Her skepticism races to catch up with her astonishment.

He restates his answer, trying to help her register the fact. 'I arrived fifteen hundred and eighty-one years ago.'

'You're *sixteen hundred* years old?'

'Eighteen hundred and seven. Which is fairly ancient even on my planet.'

Finally, she thinks, *yes: 'on my planet.'* It had seemed impossible, but it also seemed like the only plausible explanation. She tries not to hyperventilate. 'Where – what planet are you from?'

'We call it –' for an instant his voice slips into an inhuman half hiss, half buzz – 'Vrizhongil' – and then back to English with no trace of an accent: 'It's a moon, really, which orbits a large planet.

218

Which orbits our sun, of course. About sixty-two light-years away. Very close by, in the scheme of things. But far enough, if turns out, that it made me expendable.'

Nancy says nothing, and continues to stare. Can this be happening? Can all of this possibly be real?

He had imagined this encounter hundreds of times, thousands, even rehearsed it. 'You're wondering if I'm insane, I expect. Well, there have been moments over the years when I've begun wondering that very thing: Am I mad? Is this story – spy from another planet stationed on Earth and abandoned by his superiors, almost two thousand years old, undersea polar base – is this all delusion, some sorry old man's schizophrenic gibberish? And when I've reached those moments of existential crisis, this is one of the things I do, to prove to myself that I'm sane, that I am who I believe I am.'

He picks up a pair of nail scissors from the coffee table and jabs hard into the palm of his right hand. His blood is a kind of Day-Glo orange, and as it drips from his hand onto the table it sizzles and burns the wood like acid.

'Of course,' he says, grabbing a tissue to wipe his hand and the wood, 'a skeptic would think this is a trick, some theatrical special effect. But you, Ms Zuckerman, you have seen the Arctic station. And you found my picture there.'

'Yes.'

'So given the evidence, perhaps I don't need to

perform any further mortifications to establish my bona fides.' He's smiling. He really does not want to remove his eyes from their sockets, or show her that he has a bifurcated phosphorescent penis and no anus at all.

'I believe you,' she tells him.

He explains that his government established a system to monitor civilizations on planets feasible for Vrizhongilians to reach, and that Earth was one of those 116 designated planets when he embarked on his 83-year-long flight here. The big ship carried four other intelligence agents headed for four other planets in the vicinity, along with their terrestrial stations in prefabricated pieces and individual expeditionary aircraft. A reconnaissance probe was sent to the surface to photograph humans, so that the necessary reconstructive surgery – remodeling ears, removing external neck cartilage, giving his skin a convincingly soft texture and pinkish tint, and so on – could be performed by doctors aboard the mother ship. His station was installed beneath the polar ice. And, voilà, he was on his own.

Sending a message between Earth and Vrizhongil took sixty-two years, so communication was impractical. He spent six weeks each year doing the field work – flying around the world, observing human settlements, taking pictures, making videos, scribbling notes – and the rest of his time organizing and distilling his material.

'Huh,' she says.

'What?'

'That's so much time for assembling and editing.'

'Well, yes. Our productivity problem. You see, we sleep twenty or twenty-one hours a day. It's the single thing I envy most about you. About people here, I mean.' Eating and digestion, he did not add, were what he found monstrous about humans. No doubt all intelligent species have their horrific and pathetic outliers, the psychopaths and murderers, the self-mutilators and televangelists. But on Earth, *every single person* chews food and swallows and shits, and it still disgusts him.

Once each century, he says, a mother ship would visit to resupply him and take back home a copy of his meticulous multimedia chronicle of another Earth century. And by the way – every one of his first six chronicles received the highest possible rating from headquarters.

'So your people, back on your planet, were only seeing your reports of life on Earth a hundred years after the fact.'

'Or longer.'

'And you wouldn't hear back from them for another hundred years after that.'

He shrugs. 'The speed of light is the speed of light.'

At the end of his standard eight hundredth tour of duty, which fell in the thirteenth century, he was to have been replaced by a young agent, and return to Vrizhongil for a headquarters job for

221

another five hundred years before retiring. But no mother ship arrived in 1229. No mother ship ever showed up again. He's been waiting ever since. And he never retired. The chronicle, he tells her, 'is rather absurdly up to date.'

He explains that his people possess, by human standards, an uncanny ability to learn languages, so that during his biannual field expeditions, the northern hemisphere in December and the southern in June, he could move among people incognito. When he was threatened with harm or capture, he protected himself with a weapon, a long wand, which temporarily paralyzed every creature ('except, oddly, marsupials') within 200 feet. He used the weapon, according to his records, 373 times in 1,442 years.

Quite often, however, when his aircraft hovered for long periods at very low altitudes, people saw it and became alarmed. To demonstrate his peaceful intentions, he would give away tokens, beads and bits of gold.

'The way that poll takers,' he says, a little defensively, 'offer small cash payments in exchange for participating in a survey. It was one of our standard protocols.'

'And the station was established in the Arctic,' she asks, 'for secrecy's sake?'

He nods. 'Yes, and for my personal comfort as well. Vrizhongil is a cold planet. During these hellish months,' he says, nodding toward the windows, 'I give thanks every day for the invention of air-conditioning.' Outside it was almost ninety degrees, but Nancy had put on his sweater. 'The region of my birth is considered warm, and temperatures there are the equivalent of Fairbanks. Or were, anyway.'

'But so – why are you here now, in Chicago? Why aren't you in the Arctic?'

'Because it's my kind of town?'

She doesn't get the joke.

'An accident,' he says. He was wrapping up one of his annual northern field surveys, having just revisited and filmed the large Indian city of Cahokia, at the confluence of the Mississippi and Illinois rivers. Flying north, back toward the station, he suddenly lost power, and crash-landed in Lake Michigan. He managed to get gold, as well as the paralyzer, video equipment, and portable beacon – he touched the blinking device on the table – into the emergency raft. His aircraft sank.

'Our orders were unequivocal – remain as close as possible to one's last position and wait for . . . rescue. Besides, back then I had no means of returning to the Arctic. So I built a home in the woods and coexisted with the natives. Every so often I brandished the paralyzer to reestablish my bona fides.' He smiles. 'And I'm afraid I never disabused them of their "White God from the Heavens" idea.'

'But what about, you know, the Europeans, the settlers?'

'They came later. Much later.' He pauses,

possibly for dramatic effect. 'Three hundred and fifty-six years later. I crashed in February 1317. When the French arrived, fortunately, they ignored the stories the Indians told about me. I was just another supernatural character in one of the savages' supernatural myths. Fiction.'

'So for food, you hunted and gathered?'

'I don't eat. As such. My body absorbs nutrients from the air.' This tangent makes him dread that she will ask to use his bathroom. He has no toilet paper.

He tells her about moving into Chicago not long after it was founded, about buying what he needed with pieces of his gold, about working at odd jobs in order to conserve the gold, about losing his video camera and paralyzer in the great fire of 1871, about the difficulty of employment in this era of income taxes and Social Security and government IDs. He has, of course, never sought medical care from a physician, and has kept changing residences so that neighbors don't get too curious about why he doesn't seem to age, or die. This is his fourteenth apartment. But except for the years he spent up in Winnetka, from the 1940s through the 1960s, in order to experience suburban life firsthand – 'Once an anthropologist, always an anthropologist' – he has lived in Chicago since 1837.

They had talked for more than three hours, and Nicholas had awoken three hours before she arrived. He's getting drowsy.

'You've told me almost nothing about your planet,' she says. 'Your people, your history. We have so much to talk about. So much.'

'We do indeed. But if you don't mind, perhaps we can finish for the day and continue our conversation tomorrow?'

'Oh, yes, of course, yes, absolutely.' But what if he runs away? What if he dies overnight? Then she reassures herself. She had today's recordings. She'd taken pictures of him. She'd photographed the station, and knows its location exactly. Everything would be okay. She reaches over and touches his shoulder.

'Thank you. This is so extraordinary, I can't . . . words really don't . . . *thank* you.'

'I'm pleased, too. Extraordinarily pleased that it was *you* who made the discovery. I'm very, very lucky.'

'*You're* lucky? Well, this is – I mean, I've won the lottery to end all lotteries, right? It's Christmas in July!'

He chuckles, and the chuckle becomes, as he sits back, a full-throttle guffaw.

She's horrified. Is he about to tell her that this has all been a practical joke, a hoax? That he's an actor in some incredibly elaborate reality show?

'I'm sorry,' he says finally, still chuckling. 'My fatigue has ruined my manners. I'm so sorry.'

'What?'

'There's another part of the story you need to

225

know. I was going to save it for tomorrow. But now that I've upset you, that won't do.'

He begins by describing his aircraft in more detail than he had before: small, just twenty-six feet long, a large transparent canopy, landing rails instead of wheels, and a thicket of navigational probes extending from the front of the fuselage.

'When the people of the north, the Nordics and the Lapps and the rest, saw me flying, cruising at low altitudes through their midwinter skies nine hundred years ago, eleven hundred years ago, what do you suppose they thought they were seeing?'

Nancy shakes her head. She has no idea what he's getting at.

'A *flying sleigh*, driven by a large bearded man who had given them gifts.'

'Oh my God.'

'And a flying sleigh pulled by what? By nothing? Literally unimaginable, so the array of antennae on the nose of the aircraft appeared to them as – what?'

'Oh my God.'

'Antlers, on a team of flying reindeer.'

'Oh my *God*.' She's had three weeks to get used to the idea that she'd discovered an extraterrestrial base, and that she might actually find a creature from another planet. But this – *meeting Santa Claus* – is almost too shocking to process.

'When people would ask my name, I gave the one I'd always used, adapted to the local language – Nikolaos, Nikola, Nicholas. And when they asked where I lived, I saw no reason to conceal the truth –

"beyond the mountains of Korvatunturi," I told them, "near the top of the world." Although I don't believe I ever said, "At the North Pole.'"

When she arrives the next afternoon, he doesn't answer the buzzer. Oh, *Christ*, no. She presses again. As she's about to press a third time she hears his voice over the speaker.

'Nancy? Very sorry! Come right up.'

Has she ever been so thrilled? He's still here, still friendly, his windows still improbably frosty. And she sees he has been scanning through downs still improbably frosty. And she sees he has been scanning through his documentary videos. He invites her to sit next to him on the sofa and watch on a small, black spherical device that reminds her of Magic 8-Ball.

'I'm afraid I've never figured out a way to hook it up to the television,' he tells her as he touches the Play button.

'Holy Christ, they've got *sound*!' Nancy says, embarrassing herself. 'Excuse me. I'm an idiot. Of course they have sound.'

She sees aerial panoramas of Lakota Indians chasing a bison over a cliff in the Sand Hills, junks and gondolas on the Tigris in Baghdad, China's Great Wall half built. She watches and listens to slightly furtive-looking shots inside a bustling Viking tavern in northern England, men packing a piece of bronze statuary into a crate in eleventh-century Benin, a mock sea battle at the Colosseum in Rome, a smiling toddler in Edo speaking Japanese directly to the camera, a tall beardless man delivering a speech in Chicago in the summer of 1858. 'Yes,' he tells her, 'Abraham Lincoln.'

She is wonderstruck. She could keep watching forever. But after yesterday she's more conscious of the time. Before long, he would get sleepy again.

'I want to discuss with you, Nicholas, exactly how you'd like us to proceed.'

'We can watch some more of this footage. We can talk. As you wish.'

'I mean longer term. I'll do whatever you say. If you want, I could take you back up to the station, and you could see if the people on Vreezhonk, Vreez . . . I'm sorry. You could see if your headquarters has sent any messages to you, there, during the last seven hundred years. And couldn't you send them a message?'

'And then wait 124 years for a reply? If there's anyone there to reply.' He shakes his head. If he could cry, he might cry.

She says nothing for a few seconds. 'Well, if I have your permission to tell your story to the world – I mean, if you prefer that I wait until after you, after you're *gone* to reveal everything, posthumously, I would completely understand. If you want to maintain your privacy, I mean.'

'Thank you. *Thank* you. But while I am very old, it's true, I might have another thirty or forty or fifty years left. Vrizhongilians have lived to be two thousand.'

'Good!'

'But I think you would find it a great burden and disappointment to be obliged to wait that long, would you not? And when someone else stumbles across the station in the meantime?' He leans forward. 'I'm tired of keeping my secret. All right, Nancy? I'm ready.' He'd thought about saying, 'All right, Ms Zuckerman, I'm ready for my close-up,' but figured she probably wouldn't get it.

She wipes away tears. 'I thought I was going to have to convince you.'

'You know, my dear, I've had more than enough time to consider this.'

He lays out his thinking, his concerns, his plan. The biggest problem, he believes, will be persuading the world that the Arctic station is not some kind of military base, that no invasion of Earth is imminent. Before anything becomes public, he thinks it might make sense to get Rupert Murdoch on board, possibly even offer him some kind of media exclusive, in order to keep Fox News from terrifying Americans unnecessarily. Nancy thinks he's joking. He assures her he is not.

'Now I know this will sound corny in the extreme. Especially given the "Santa" business. But I believe the best way for us to create good-will from the outset is to describe what I have in mind as, quote, "Gifts to the People of Earth."'

He will hand over his chronicle – all 2.4 million words he has written and, 'far more interesting, I should think,' all 73,496 of hours of video that he shot on every continent but Antarctica in every year from the early fifth century to the late nineteenth century.

He will tell everything he knows about life in our part of the Milky Way, corroborated by the library of text and images stored at the station. 'It's all badly out of date, of course,' he says, 'but it's better than nothing.'

And he will give to the people of Earth his surviving pieces of technology – in particular the batteries that power the video player and portable beacon and Arctic station, all still operating 1,581 years after installation. 'I should think,' he says, 'that some bright scientists somewhere will be able to reverse-engineer them.'

As she wonders how many billions of dollars his Vrizhongilian batteries might be worth, she feels a jolt of self-loathing. 'This is going to be unbelievable, Nicholas.'

He smiles. 'Let's hope not.'

'I mean, this will be the biggest thing . . . *ever*.'

'I suppose. I do hope that people, anyway most people, will be glad to learn, finally, definitively, that they're not alone in the universe.' *Because*, he thinks to himself, *I know I am inexpressibly happy that my loneliness is finally about to end.*

'Nicholas?'

'Yes?'

'May I hug you?'

STORIES

Michael Moorcock

This is the story of my friend Rex Fisch who blew out his complicated brains in his Lake District library all over his damned books one Sunday afternoon last September. Naturally the place was a horror to clean, but Rex never really cared much about the mess he left in his wake. What pissed me off was the waste: each blasted cell was a story he'd never tell; a story no one else would ever tell. Rex knew how to hurt himself and the old friends who loved him. Only a few of us are now left. Cancer took Hawthorn, Hayley, Slade and Allard that same year. The first three had shared digs with Rex when he first lived in London. It didn't seem fair of the bastard to deliberately deplete what remained of our joint memory.

As I said at his funeral Rex had more fiction in him than could ever come out, no matter how long he'd lived. A superb raconteur, he produced stories in every form, from dry, funny narrative verse to self-dramatising social lies. Novels, plays, short stories, comic strips, operas, movies, RPGs: throughout his career he was never stuck for a narrative. In that respect we were pretty much alike and shared a kind of discomfort at our own facility. We both identified with Balzac, sharing a fascination for Jacques Collin, his sinister and ubiquitous many-named master villain who set out to ruin La Torpille in *Splendeurs et misères des courtisanes*. Rex discovered that most people prefer a good story and a bit of conventional prejudice to honest ambiguity; they made their most profound life decisions based on tales they saw in the tabloids or on reality TV. That didn't stop Rex telling the truth when it frequently occurred to him. Truth was always in there somewhere, even when he thought he was lying. For all his later right-wing posturing, he had, like Balzac, a way of tapping into poor people's dreams and understanding what they wanted most in the world. I envied him his empathy, if not his ambition. There was one story he couldn't write. I think it was what we were all waiting for and which might have brought him the literary recognition he longed for. But he believed *Paris Review* editors could 'smell the pulp writer on you,' while as an editor I rejected stories because I could smell *Paris Review* on them. I believed we were too good for the reviews even when we appeared in them. The conventions of genre were staler in literary writing than Harlequin romances: exactly why Rex turned out to be the writer we most needed on *Mysterious*.

We were both six-two and shared the same colouring and humour, though Rex was already balding. I guess our differences came from our backgrounds. I was a Londoner. Rex had been born and raised in Wrigley, Texas, pop. 1,204, about forty miles from Waco. He'd believed everything they told him until he went to Austin where he found out how to doubt his small-town certainties, trading them for the snobberies of the UT literary enclave. Dumping his provincialism a little late, he never lost his reverence for academia. Furiously cynical, he was determined to tell readers what fools they were to believe his stories. Despite this, he seemed oddly innocent when he turned up in London fresh from the UT campus via Spain, with the remnants of his jaundice, an uncompleted creative-writing degree and a few sales to the American crime and sci-fi digests, to be disgusted by our rates, even lower than the US, but delighted when we bought whatever he wrote, at whatever length he did it. When we met we were both twenty-five. Literary powers like Julie Mistral had already called him the James M. Cain of his generation. Angus Wilson had compared me to Gerald Kersh and Arnold Bennett.

The 'digests' were the pulps' attempts to look more sophisticated, with abstract expressionist covers and cooler titles, but I had grown up reading the real pulps with their powerful pictures and raving shout lines (*Donna was a dame who dared to be different – Kelly was a cop who craved to kill!*). The quality of the fiction didn't alter, just the presentation.

I found it hard to come in at the end of that era, working on the Falcon and Sexton Blake Library, but it had proved one thing to me. There were no such things as pulp writers. Bad writers like Carroll John Daly and brilliant ones like Dashiell Hammett just happened to write for the pulps. Mostly their reputation had to do with context. Jack Trevor Story would write a novel for Sexton Blake then, with minor modifications, turn it into a novel for Secker and Warburg.

By the time I took it over, Hank Janson's *Mystery Magazine* was about the last of the UK thriller digests and I had some crackbrained notion to lift it away from genre altogether and make it into something addressing the widest possible readership. By 1964 there were few short story mags left and most of those were generic. They ran romances, military adventures, mysteries and sci-fi. To get published and paid you had to adapt your work, usually by inserting a clunky rationalised plot. That way you earned a bit as you learned a bit. We didn't want to write what we called Englit-fic: the styles and themes of which came out of universities in sad imitation of the great modernists. We wanted to write something that had the vitality of good commercial fiction and the subtle ambition of good literary fiction, reflecting the sensibilities and events of our times: stuff that would get us high with the sense of enthusiasm and engagement of Proust or Faulkner but with the disciplined vitality of genre fiction pulsing from every page.

A few of us talked about a 'two-way street' to reunite junk, middle-brow and highbrow fiction. Some people out there had to be as frustrated as us, dissatisfied by pretty much everything on offer, literary or commercial. For ages people had discussed the 'two cultures.' We might just be the guys to unite them: writing for a reader who knew a bit about poetry, painting and physics, enjoyed Gerald Kersh, Elizabeth Bowen and Mervyn Peake, merging realism with grotesquerie and doing it elegantly, eloquently. By 1963 we were publishing a few examples in the digests and with Billy Allard and Harry Hayley, my two closest writer friends; we made plans for a 'slick' quarto magazine bringing together designers, artists, scientists, poets, but of course the cost of the art paper alone made publishers shake their heads.

Then Len Haynes, the decent old drunk who ran it forever, proposed that I take over *Janson's* when he retired to live with his daughter in Majorca.

Married less than a year, Helena Denham and I lived in Colville Terrace, still Rachman's Notting Hill fiefdom. We'd had our first daughter, Sara, and Helena, beautiful as ever with her pageboy chestnut hair framing a heart-shaped face, was furiously pregnant with Cass, our second. I'd been fired from *Liberal Topics*, the party magazine whose wages I'd taken in spite of promising Winston Churchill, when I was eleven, never to become a Liberal. So I needed Janson's money. More important, it would be a chance to do what we'd been saying we should do for so long. I talked it over with Helena and the others.

When I went back to Dave and Howard Vasserman, the publishers, I made only three conditions: that I decide policy, that they let me change the title gradually and if our circulation went up they give me the paper and size I wanted. I would help them get mainstream distribution with their more upmarket titles. I convinced them I could make their imprint respectable enough to be taken on by the high-street retailers. Then I got my friends busy. We lacked a decent designer but I did my best. Our first issue would not merely offer a manifesto, we would attempt to demonstrate policy – and we'd have a lot of illustrations, one of the secrets, in my experience, of a successful periodical. They were Jack Hawthorn's job.

Hayley started finishing a novella he'd been talking about, a weird thing in which the detective's dreams informed his case. Allard began writing us a new serial, full of brooding metaphysical imagery borrowed from Dali and Ernst. Helena finished her alternate-world Nazi creeper. I drafted my editorial about pulp influences on William Burroughs, and Burroughs gave us a chapter from his new book. American beats and British pop artists had something in common with noir movies, our other great enthusiasm. Allard produced a guest editorial arguing that 'the space age' needed a new lexicon, new literary ideas. I did a short under a regular pseudonym and the rest came from Janson's stable of favourites.

All three of us were English but had known little conventional upbringing. Hayley had been orphaned by a buzz bomb, taken a job on a local paper before being conscripted into the RAF, studied metaphysics at Oxford where he'd met Allard who'd been raised in occupied France with an Anglo-Jewish mother who'd been on one of the last transports to Auschwitz, worked for the Resistance as a kid then come home not to prewar Mayfair fantasy but despairing suburban austerity, the world Orwell captured. After his conscription served in the RAF, he did physics at Oxford, where he met Harry. They both dropped out after a few terms, writing features and noirish sci-fi stories for mags like *Authentic* or *Vargo Statten's*. Allard was qualified to fly obsolete prop planes, Hayley was a qualified radio operator and I'd done a couple of miserable ATC years before they abolished conscription about a nanosecond before I was due to be drafted, edited juvenile story papers, trade mags and Sexton Blake, so I had loads of editorial experience but little formal education.

We'd spent half our lives in the pub discussing why modern fiction was crap and why it needed an infusion of the methods and concerns of popular fiction, all of us having sold a bit to the surviving thriller and science fantasy pulps. I think we felt we knew what we were talking about, having been raised in the social margins, thanks to one trick of fate or another, and loved surrealism, absurdism, French new wave movies as well as Pound, Eliot, Proust and the rest. In common with a few other restless autodidacts of our day we loved anything containing Gabin's smoking .38, Mitchum's barking .45 or Widmark's glittering knives, all mixed up with Brecht and Weill, Camus' Fascist *Caligula* screaming 'I'm still alive' and the black bars crossing the faces of Sartre's *Huis Clos*, emphasizing the prisons in which we place ourselves. Into that mix we threw James Mason in *Odd Man Out*, Harry Lime, Gerald Kersh's *Night and the City*, Bester's *Demolished Man*, Bradbury's *Fahrenheit 451*, Household's *Rogue Male*, Lodwick's *Brother Death*. We'd met the likes of Francis Bacon, Somerset Maugham and Maurice Richardson at the Colony, read Beckett, Miller and Durrell in Olympia Press and generally got our education from the best novelists, journalists and artists of our day. Allard liked Melville more than I did, Hayley preferred Kafka and I loved Meredith. We were agreed that their lessons needed to be brought back into contemporary culture via the popular arts. Borges, too, though his stuff was only just being done into English via Ferlinghetti's City Lights press. We also thought that fiction should be able to carry as many narratives per paragraph as possible, using techniques borrowed from absurdism, futurism and combined with new ideas of our own. We'd thought there were hundreds of writers dying for the chance to do the same as us, but though a lot more readers welcomed what we made of *Mysterious*, contributors were slow in coming.

By 1965 we'd at least laid the foundations of the two-way street. Pop art came one way, pulp the other. The Beatles and Dylan were doing the sound track. They broke new ground and got paid for it, but most people had no real idea what we meant when we talked about combining 'high' and 'low' arts, in spite of the two cultures being as popular a subject in features pages as the big bang and planet-size computers. We wanted to rid pop fiction of its literalism, taking exaggeration for granted in ambitious work, but were only slowly developing a critical vocabulary, trying to bring a deeper seriousness to the novel, but were still frustrated, reckoning we were still missing a piece in the equation. Whittling the title slowly down to one word hadn't been enough. We needed writers desiring to emulate modern classicism to help build a genuine bridge able to take the weight of our two-way traffic.

It took Rex turning up in 1965 to show us what we needed to convince readers and writers of our authority. Like Allard or Hayley, he wrote better than any other contemporary I knew. His sardonic style was deceptively simple. He, too, was a Balzac fan with a special love of Jacques Collin/Vautrin. We were almost exactly the same age. Like me, he'd supported himself since the age of sixteen.

He'd climbed out of a family of father-dominated German Catholic drunks, dropping out of the University of Texas after selling a few stories to the digests which got him a couple of book contracts to fund the trip to Europe he felt was the next rung on his career ladder, which he planned with his friend Jake Slade, a fellow Texan Catholic and a master ironist.

I was only familiar with Rex's world through what little fiction I'd read of Jim Thompson or what he'd described himself in *Paine in Congress* or *The Clinic*. I'd certainly never been to Texas and only knew Manhattan. Jake's stories had never seen print; they were dry, sly and ticking with the energy of unexploded bombs. Rex's were like Henry James on speed. Quick-mouthed contemporary clarity; good fast fiction fresh off the calendar and with plenty of class. Rooted in our familiar world.

Jake and Rex had planned to write a mystery together in Spain, travel around Europe for a while, then return either to Austin or to New York. But they hadn't anticipated catching jaundice from bad acid in Spain and having to stay with friends in London until they could finish the book. Rex, having read about us in Juliette Masters's *NYT* column, came to see me in the hope of raising some living money. He also brought some of Jake's manuscripts and I immediately knew we were in luck. Neither had come from populist traditions but they thirsted for pulp. They brought the best academic ambitions to the subject matter we featured. They were exactly what I'd been looking for, roaring down from the other end of the two-way street and bringing a bunch of new writers and readers after them. Two for the price of one. Murder and the human soul. The face of society and the fabric of the future. Their intensity and intelligence lacked the hesitancy or vulgarity I'd rejected when posh literary agents thought they'd found somewhere to dump their clients' awful bits of generic slumming, neither did they stink of the creative-writing class.

Sociable, a little formal, a knowing catalyst, Rex introduced me to friends he had known at UT, including the talented fine artists Peggy Zorin, Jilly Cornish and her husband, Jimmy, as well as others who were yet to leave Texas en route for *Mysterious* and London. At last we had a full set of talented contributors who could give us a substantial inventory, interacting with increased gravity, attracting other writers who added superb stories to our contents list, the best anyone had read in ages, combining a sophistication and vitality taken for granted today but representing a quantum jump at the time and making us the most celebrated fiction magazine of our day. The debate was suddenly over. We could demonstrate everything we'd discussed. That was what Rex Fisch did for *Mysterious* and the rough-and-ready movement we'd always denied was a movement. We entered a golden age.

Almost every story we published was anthologized. A good many won prizes.

I knew of course that our little revolution would collapse rapidly once we achieved what we hoped for and our individual careers were made. Real life grew darker after those good years. The first tragedy was Jane Allard's death on a trip back to the family home near Nantes. Billy moved to Streatham to bring up his kids. We drove over with our own to visit from time to time. Next, Rex took part in a poetry tour with several well-known poets, including the notoriously omnisexual Spike Allison. He came back gay (no surprise to his friends) and monstrously troubled about it after Spike dumped him on their return to London. Our relationships were only just surviving the divorces, rearrangements and general infighting. People join revolutions until they get what they want as individuals, then start quarrelling over the spoils, however imaginary. I was surprised by how many of our friendships remained intact. Writing mostly nonfiction, Jake settled down with a local girl, Daisy Angelino, in Portobello Road, near our offices. Rex met Chick Archer, who was from Maine, at an S & M bar in Paris. They fell in love, travelled for a few years, then bought their lovely freezing old house in the English Lakes. The place couldn't be more Wordsworthy with its hard, driving cloud banks bringing relentless rain, rewarding you with bursts of sunshine, the whole fell moving like a living body in its contours and shadows, over which Rex presided with a rather proprietorial air at his huge sitting-room windows. Sometimes the wind bawled against the long scar of Wattendale Edge, creating waves across the black tarn. You can see those landscapes, beautifully drawn by Chick in their *Mary Stone* comic. They're still syndicated. Almost nobody knew Rex wrote that great, gritty newspaper strip which made them more money than anything else and which explained why their home smelled so strongly of well-loved wealth.

Rex and I still made each other laugh uncontrollably, much to Chick's silent disgust. This of course drove the sadistic Rex to increase Chick's discomfort. I suspect that's why we didn't get invited up so often. Harry went to live in Ireland with his Dublin-born wife, to look after her mother who lived on a miserable council estate just outside Cork. Stuck there, Harry grew increasingly depressed and began a long book on Nietschze. I saw him occasionally when he came to do research at the British Library. Jimmy and Jill Cornish settled near the old mill in Tufnell Hill. He wrote reviews, criticism for the *LRB* and nonfiction guides. She produced commercial posters to supplement her gallery shows. Others continued to get novels published and exhibitions arranged with increased success. Pete Bates disappeared on a cycling holiday in France. His bike was found at the bottom of a sea cliff in Brittany. Other good writers and artists came and went.

Charlie Ratz joined us as our designer. I performed and made records with the Deep Fix.

I thought we were extending the '60s golden age but really it was the end. I continued to publish *Mysterious* but now it was edited by others as affairs and relationships collapsed dramatically across four continents. Gender roles rolled in every possible direction. Stable quartets became full orchestras; ramshackle duets became rock-solid trios. If you visited friends in San Francisco, you needed a complicated chart to know who was with whom, why, when and where. As he and Rex settled in to do the old Alan Bennetts, Chick now wore the slightly self-conscious air of a resting chorus boy down from London for the weekend. Rex had exchanged his Texan brogue for a rather attractive Cowardian drawl which disappeared on the few occasions he phoned home. Chick's tones grew increasingly clipped. They were models of moral righteousness, so thoroughly faithful that when AIDS came it gave them no hint of anxiety. They adopted a very superior attitude to everyone else, of course. And particularly, it turned out, to me. With three much-loved offspring to care for, I weakly divorced Helena, married again and moved across the street with my child bride, Jenny.

Though I had suffered with Rex through his sexual transition and every minor treachery practiced on and by him, he chose to see my breakup with Helena as perhaps the most infamous deed since Eddie's in *Death of the Heart*. My separation from Helena was reasonably amicable, I thought. I was still supporting everyone. I'd done it pretty straightforwardly. But the first time I took Jenny up to Wattendale to see them and a group of friends they'd invited, I thought the murmured commentary from Rex would never end. If Kim and Di Stanley hadn't as usual conned me into giving them a lift up from Bury I would have gone back on the Saturday morning. I was furious and very close to ending our friendship on the spot.

Jenny talked me out of it. 'I love hearing you and Rex tell your stories.' She grinned. 'You're such great liars.'

I hardly saw Rex or Chick for the next three years. Chick sent a card at Christmas with just his signature on it. Jenny sent one from us. But I'd had enough. Rex wasn't the only moody bastard writing for *Mysterious* and I just didn't have the energy to work at anything more. At least he was still sending his stuff in, via Charlie Ratz, the new editor. Charlie still saw him regularly. His parents had retired to a massive house outside Keswick, only a couple of miles from Rex and Chick. Whenever Charlie returned to London, he had a new story or two with him. Or Jake Slade would go up and bring something back.

Rex knew the prestige of publishing in the mag. The public saw no ruptures. We were getting more praise than was probably healthy. In fact, a critic brought about our reconciliation. Julie Mistral, the *NYT* reviewer who had been our early champion, now lived about half the year in England. She threw one of her so-called A-list parties and we were all invited. The party was held in the huge rundown hotel restaurant she rented.

Jenny and I were amongst the first to arrive. Rex and Chick were already there, sipping Jacquesson from dusty flutes. Rex spotted me, came over and greeted us with all his old, amused affection. The Great Big Hi as Jake called it. We were embraced. We were kissed. We were mystified.

I was wise enough not to ask how or why this had happened but Jenny found out later from Chick. Rex had come across a review written by Helena for *Tribune*, which had a circulation of about twenty. She had failed to praise *Lost Time Serenade*, Rex's Proustian parody, as much as Rex felt it should be praised. It wasn't a bad review, given I knew she'd found the whole thing pretentious and unworthy of such a good writer, but with Rex you were expected as a friend either to praise him to the skies or not review him at all. Now I knew why Helena hadn't been invited and since I'd never made that particular error of diplomacy I was back in favour again. Then Chick came up and gave me that look of wordless disgust, which was his way of maintaining friendships when Rex blew hot and cold. I was still unsure of him. I was a bit unsure of everything, in fact, because Jenny was just getting into what she'd call her experimental phase, which would enliven our sex life and destroy our marriage. Fourteen years younger than me, she felt she hadn't experienced enough of the world.

I have to admit our sexual experiments were funny to me at first. There's not a lot of sexual pleasure to be got from hopping shouting around your bedroom having failed to wallop your wife's bottom and whacked your own leg instead. I had no instinct for it. Eventually though I was able to play the cruel Sir Charles with reasonable skill. A bit like faking an orgasm.

Ever since we'd been together Jenny had a fantasy about me watching one of my friends fuck her. There were a thousand scenarios in her little head and scarcely one in mine. I think I used up all my stories while I was working. I didn't dream either. I needed a rest from tale spinning at the end of the day. But I did my best. I hated to disappoint her.

I had an idea of the scenario she planned one evening when Rex turned up holding a bottle of Algerian red in one hand and his dripping cap and overcoat in the other, beaming. 'Hi!' A wild giggle at his own physical discomfort. Charming. On his best and happiest behaviour. He embraced us in his soft gigantic arms. He had some meetings with Universal Features and wanted to stay for a bit. I thought the evening was to be a celebration of our reborn friendship. Jenny was all over him, flirting like a fag hag, bringing Rex out all atwitter. So we dined. While I washed up, she whispered in his ear.

It turned out Jenny loved threesomes but mostly with her looking on frigging herself blind while waiting to get fucked by the least exhausted bloke. Mostly that was me, as Rex jerked off. That image is no more appealing to me than to you. After three or four nights and days of this, I realised that Rex was getting most of his buzz from knowing Chick had no suspicion of what he was up to.

Of course, to add to his own wicked relish Rex told Chick what he'd done with us. He had to. He never could resist a good story, particularly if he was telling it. Our few nights of passionless sex had become a means of manipulating Chick. This time Chick cut us.

Inevitably Jenny and I grew further apart as our games got more fantastic. Rex had already been through all that with Chick in Paris. Real-life fantasies are distractions for a working writer. Years before Rex told me that himself. 'It's as bad as going to law. The story starts to take over. Like falling in love. All sentimentality and melodrama. The scenarios are repetitive, conventional. All they offer arc the comforts of genre.' He was right. Sex games are more boring than an Agatha Christie novel.

Anyway Jenny, despite our investment in special clothing and sex aids, wasn't getting a big enough buzz out of my efforts. It's like horror movies or superhero comics, you either stop and give them a rest or you have to keep heightening the action.

Even if the games didn't bore me, our widening circle of acquaintances did. I wasn't finding enough time alone. Individuals, couples, whole fucking communes got involved. If they gave me a good paragraph or two, I wouldn't have minded so much, but there was an infantile sameness about their scenarios. Jenny and I were driven further apart by what the courts call intimacy. I tried to get to see Rex and Chick on their own, desperately needing to find out how they had rescued themselves from the crack of the crop, the smell of damp leather, the spell of repetition. Did you just grow out of it? Sometimes Jenny seemed to be flagging until some fresh variation on a familiar theme perked her up again. She was a natural addict. I've never been seriously addicted to anything. So I started trying to get her off the habit. It didn't work. She made excuses, started doing stuff in secret. I hate ambiguity in my day-to-day life. There's enough in my work. A writer needs routines and certainties. What can I say? As well as losing real intimacy with old friends, I lost it with Jenny. In a halfarsed attempt to restore our earlier closeness, she told me some of her new adventures. Then I got hooked for a while. I started pumping her for more revelations. She owed me that, I decided. They added nothing but did become pretty chilling. The seduction of underage girls. Things my friends liked to do. It amazed me how so many women took the odd rape for granted. Too many secrets revealed. Friendships frayed. Rex came back in the picture. I moved out.

I took my kids, whom I'd been missing anyway, on a long trip round the USA. It made us feel better. To my relief we grew back together. Feeling my old self I got home, bought a short lease on a little flat in Fulham, just when Notting Hill turned into a gentrified suburb. I saw enough of Jenny to know it was thoroughly over. I didn't like what she'd done to herself. She'd dyed her hair bright blond and her brown eyes had a vaguely dazed, mirror-like quality, as if they only reflected and no longer saw anything. She'd lost her sense of humour, too, and was into various odd relationships, still searching for the good life. When I shifted the last of my stuff she made a halfhearted attempt to patch things up. She wanted to have a baby, she said, and get back into our old domestic routine. Even while she proposed this deal, a bloke I vaguely knew was sleeping upstairs in what had been our bed, where once, like Proust, I'd done most of my writing. From being a place of concentration in which I conceived stories it had become a place of distraction, where real stories died. I said she could keep the place. All she had to do was pay the mortgage.

'But I love you.' She wept. She made an awkward attempt to remind me of the old days. 'I love just lying in your arms at night while you tell me a story.'

I was sad. 'It's too late, Jenny.' Those stories were over.

I went up to Windermere, phoned Rex and Chick, but Chick was frosty. Did I know I had almost broken them up? I apologized. I said how much I regretted what had happened. Rex, just as distant and haughty, put the phone down on me. I saw them in Kendal once or twice and in Grasmere. They wouldn't speak to me. Once, over his shoulder, Rex gave me the most peculiar leer. Did he wish we were still deceiving Chick? It made me shudder. Was something wrong with him?

Of course I longed to be back with Helena but she'd settled down with a jolly Scottish chef and was doing her best work. Why would she want to change that?

Even though our pillow talk inspired a couple of shorts, I really hated having been part of Jenny's daisy chain. Some of those people I never wanted to see again, others I needed distance from; I wasn't ready to see Charlie Ratz or Jonny Fowler yet. Pete was still missing in France, presumed dead. I gave up any interest in *Mysterious*, which was now doing fine without me, bought a house near Ingleton, West Yorks, and settled in first with Emma MacEwan, who couldn't stand the rain and cold, and then started seeing a local woman who disapproved of central heating. I desperately hoped to restore my friendship with Rex, even after I met Lucinda, to this day the love of my life. Lu found my obsession weird, I know, until she eventually met Rex in Leeds, at a Ted Hughes literary weekend we'd all been invited to. Lu's teenage daughter loved Rex's work and wanted him to autograph her books. She was too shy to ask him, so Lucy, her fair hair flying and blue eyes blazing, marched up to the table where he was sitting and said: 'I gather you're Mike's old friend. Well, I'm his new wife and this is my daughter, who's read most of your work and loves it. I think it's pretty good, too. So what about some autographs and while you're at it why don't you two shake hands?' And, that being just one of her powers, we did.

Later at the bar Rex told me Chick blamed me for the infamous 'seduction.' At that idea we continued to laugh for the rest of the day, until the next, when Chick turned up, glaring when he saw us, and Lucinda, nearly six feet herself, took him in hand as well. 'It's all over,' she said. 'If you're going to blame anyone, blame that poor, barmy bitch Jenny. She got you all involved in her folly and now look at you.' And when Chick grumbled that Rex was still seeing Jenny, which surprised me, Lu said: 'Well, she's poison as far as I can tell, and he doesn't need her now he has Mike back.' Chick teared up then. He told her I was the best friend Rex had ever had but I had betrayed them both. Which again I admitted. And the following weekend Lu and I went up and stayed with them. On our way home she said: 'You two could make Jeremiah roll about on the floor laughing himself sick.'

I didn't know why Rex went on seeing Jenny,

unless he simply enjoyed wounding Chick. He still had that cruel streak in him. Chick and I talked about it. Chick thought it had to be directed at him, too. He guessed Jenny was a substitute for me, especially when Rex dropped Jenny so soon after we were reconciled. She still phoned him.

I saw Jenny myself a few times after that. She seemed more her old self in some ways. She'd had twins and was living with her mother in Worthing, on the Sussex coast. She had the washed-out look of so many single mothers, said she was happy, if poor, and even suggested my 'sexual conservatism' had dulled me down. Next time I bumped into her in Kensington High Street she was again pale, overpainted, dyed up. She looked as if all the vitality had been sucked from her. I thought she was doing junk. Her eyes were back to blank. Was she living in London? Did she have someone? She laughed and looked even more devitalized. 'None of your business,' she said. I couldn't argue with that.

Of course, I was curious to know what she and Rex had been up to. I guessed she hadn't accepted that he'd dropped her. At a party in Brighton a year or two later she looked worse than ever, clinging to Rupert Herbert, one of those new Low Tories on the *Spectator*. More make-up, too blond and getting through a packet of Gauloises a minute. I did really feel sorry for her. Then Rex turned up and snubbed her so royally he pissed me off, so I made a point of going over to talk to her but she snubbed me in turn. Lucinda came over and murmured 'poor bitch' and meant it. Between us the *Mysterious* crew had ruined a nice, unimaginative girl, she thought. Not entirely fair. You could hear Jenny over the general buzz talking about some famous film producer she'd lived with. He'd been the one who bought *The Vices of Tom* from Rex and then turned it into that pot of toss. 'The bastard . . . ,' she was saying. You could guess the rest. Maybe Lu was right.

For the next ten years or so life settled into routines nobody felt like messing with though Rex grew increasingly unreasoning in his arguments with editors, then publishers, then agents until almost nobody would work with him. His books didn't sell enough for any editor to bother keeping him sweet. He took offence easily and frequently and, through his vengeful verse, publicly. Chick said he could no longer manage him. I would have thought this a good thing. I believed Chick's natural leanings towards convention and literary respectability pushed Rex away from his saving self-mocking vulgarity. Balzac and Vautrin were less his models than Proust or Albertine. His work seemed to apologise for itself. He lost his popular touch without gaining critical prestige. Only *Mary Stone* went on making money for them. His short stories came out less frequently, but he kept his habit of phoning and often reading the whole thing to you. And he still enjoyed inventing a story when he got your answering machine. 'Oh, I know what you're doing. You've met that good-looking farmer again and gone badger watching with him.' Usually the time would be up before he could complete his fantasy. His new novels tended to peter out after a few chapters. I'd get frustrated and consider continuing them for him. They were wonderful ideas. Occasionally they would re-emerge when a way of telling them occurred to him. His aptitude for ironic narrative verse never left him. I'd labour for hours to get anything close to what usually took him minutes. Chick helped him develop his taste for classical music, which is how he came to write his three operas, one of which he based on Kersh's *The Brazen Bull* and another on Balzac's *Illusions Perdues* but he became snobbish about popular music or he'd have written some great lyrics. I used a few of his verses in my own music stuff. I inserted another into one of my hack thrillers, its redeeming feature. His only opera to reach the stage was a version of Firbank's *Cardinal Pirelli*. Rex delighted in upsetting Catholics, although his attacks meant little to most of us.

Then, as we limped into our sixties, we began to suffer from real illnesses, as opposed to passing scares. Rex was diabetic, arthritic. Chick was the first of us to be diagnosed with cancer. I think it was colon, he wouldn't say. Even Rex refused to betray him on that occasion. His surgery seemed to cure him. We heard Jenny survived a stroke. By that time she hardly saw any old friends. When she had an operation, I'm not sure what for. Rex didn't speak of the years when he'd seen her regularly, even as we grew closer than ever, all living up in those northern hills, from Todmorden to Kendal. Harry, of course, was still in Ireland. Billy Allard went to Corfu after his children grew up. Pete continued to be presumed dead. Peggy Zoran returned to New York and was very successful. The Cornishes moved to Kirkby Lonsdale. I had a hernia operation which went wrong. Bad stitching cut off an artery and caused problems in my leg. I couldn't walk or climb anymore. Rex's diabetes was complicated by drinking. Chick successfully got him on the wagon. In 2005, while we were at our place in Paris, I got an e-mail from Rex referring casually to Chick's return to Airedale General, so I phoned the hospital at once. 'It's spread a bit,' Chick said. 'I'll be out in a few days.' So we flew home and drove over. Chick had lost a lot of weight. He was ghastly white but Rex pretended nothing was wrong. A lot of surgery was involved. Chick started a short story called 'Over the Knife.' He showed it to us. Very mystical and sardonic. He got me to ask Jack Hawthorn if he'd take over *Mary Stone*, but Jack wasn't up to it. The next thing we knew he was admitted again and we made the first of several trips to Skipton. Chick was bitter about friends who couldn't find time to visit or phone. 'Or send a bloody Hallmark card and a bunch of fucking flowers.' Rex, sometimes there when I was, echoed all this. I did what

I could to make friends visit. Very few did. People were fighting to keep some sort of income, I suppose. At the hospital we made the usual jokes, complimented Chick on his courage. He found this amusing. 'You're just thanking me for not making you feel bad. It's easy to be brave when everyone's attention's focused on you.' He could do the best wan smile, remembered Rex, giggling later. Chick asked us to stop sending flowers. The smell reminded him too much of funerals. I remembered my mother making the same complaint.

Rex was still pretty much in denial. Who could blame him? His responses became more and more monosyllabic, either because he didn't want to cry or because he didn't want to be reminded of what was happening. His partner of nearly forty years, however, spoke more freely. He had so little time. Subsequent operations were done to 'repair' his intestines. When he went home he was only there for a matter of weeks, even days, before they sent him back again. Another series of surgeries was proposed but Chick refused any more. He wanted to die with a semblance of dignity. A quietly practicing Anglican for some years, he was ready to go. I asked if he was scared. 'In a way,' he said, 'as if I were going for a job interview.' He chiefly needed promises that we'd keep an eye on Rex, make sure he paid bills, had repairs done, all the jobs Chick had taken on so Rex could write without worry. 'I know it's hard, but you're the best friends he has.' A kind of blackmail. I didn't resent it. He probably said the same to others. 'He mustn't start drinking. He won't look after the place unless you pester him. There's still a bit on the mortgage. He'll let the pool go. Make sure he gives you a key. Oh, and he has a gun. Get the bullets if you can. You know what a drama queen he can be.' Next time we saw him he had written out a list in his educated American hand. Where the stopcocks were, what needed watering when, the names and numbers of the oil-delivery people, the gas and electricity people, the best plumber, the most reliable electrician. Their handyman, the local rates office: all the details of their domestic lives. We promised to do all we could.

His thin, grey face with its grey toothbrush moustache became earnest. 'In spite of anything Rex says?'

We promised.

'Or anything he tells you? Or I tell you?' This was puzzling, but we agreed. Once he had our promises, he drew a long breath. Then: 'You know, don't you, what he was doing with Jenny?'

'We don't want to.' Lucinda spoke before I could answer. Of course I wanted him to tell me.

'Okay.' Chick turned on his pillows. 'Probably just as well.'

Lu and I drove home in unspeaking silence.

Chick died a few days later. In late August many friends were on holiday and couldn't make it to the funeral. Rex blamed them, of course. If Chick's

frail old dad could make the trip, then surely . . . ?
I went to stay with him. He was dazed. He'd found
Chick's diaries before we could. 'I never realised
what he gave up. Why he was so unhappy.' I
pointed out that journals are almost always
misleading. We use them to record miseries, frustrations of the moment, anger we don't want to
put into the air. We didn't need them when we
were content. But he refused to be comforted. He
had failed Chick. That's all he had to say. He was
drinking again.

Rex was very particular about the funeral,
insisting we wear what he called 'full mourning,'
which meant black hats and veils for women, suits
and ties for men. There were only seven of us in
the Grasmere cemetery where Chick wanted to
be buried. Rex bore his grief through his familiar
haughty disguise. Lucinda had organized the
funeral meats, such as they were. Rex had insisted
on everything being simple. Chick had wanted the
same. After we had all gone to bed or home, Rex
sat down in his study and phoned everyone who
hadn't been able to make it. If they didn't pick
up, he left messages on their machines. Not the
usual whimsical tales. He told them what he and
Chick had always said behind their backs about
their lack of talent, their ugly child, their gigantic
ego, their terrible cooking, their bad taste. When
Rex hurt, everyone got hurt. Next day, high on
his own vengeance, he told me in a series of
vignettes what he'd done. Some of the people

phoned me next. Many were in tears. Almost all tried to forgive him. Several wanted to know if he was right. My daughter Cass had given him Helena's regards and been snubbed so badly by Rex she was still crying when she got through to me. She was readier to forgive him than I was.

About a week later, while Lu visited her hypochondriacal mother, I went over to see how Rex was doing. He'd been drinking heavily. 'I'm glad you came,' he said. 'I wanted you to know about a favour I did you a few years back.' I cooked us dinner, after which he told me what he'd done for me. He was sure I'd be pleased, he said. I didn't know who he was mocking. Gasping and yelping with pain from the arthritis brought on by the booze, he poked up the fire and poured us cognacs. Then he started with the slow, dramatic relish he reserved for his readings. I suppose you could call it a revenge tale, with all the elements he enjoyed in Balzac and the Jacobeans. Soon after Jenny and I split up, and blaming her for 'luring' him into the threesome with which he had taunted Chick, Rex became, in his words, her confessor, suggesting ideas to her for sexual adventures, often helping her make specific contacts and introducing her to what he called his list of 'forty famous perverts.' He had sometimes accompanied her to dinners and parties, encouraging her to risks she'd never have dared take on her own. 'I drove her farther and farther down that road, Mike. You'd have loved it! Whenever she faltered

I was there encouraging her to stay the course. I told her heroin wasn't addictive!' (Luckily he'd only been able to persuade her to snort it.) 'I convinced her she was a natural whore. I became her best friend, just as Vautrin took Emma under his wing!' That terrible, self-approving chuckle followed as he sat there in his big leather chair overlooking the darkening fell, staring in sardonic satisfaction at the sky, speaking in the tones of measured mockery usually reserved for his satirical verse. '*I* knew you wanted to do it but couldn't. So I took your revenge *for* you, Mike!'

'Jesus, Rex. She didn't deserve . . . I would never . . .'

'Oh, Mike, you *know* what she deserved. *You'd* never do it, but Vautrin could, eh? I learned the lessons of Balzac better than you ever did!' At that point, as the world grew darker and the fire reflected on his face, he was every inch Balzac's monster, apparently completely mad. I felt physically sick, concerned for his sanity, deeply sorry for Jenny. I wondered if Lucinda had guessed what had gone on. Was that why she had refused to let Chick tell us anything? Rex relished every revelation. Giggling, he explained how he persuaded her to do something particularly demeaning. I was no sadist but of couse he was. He could hate women. He went on for ages, offering chapter and verse, names, places, bringing all the horror and misery back. He explained little mysteries, offered anecdotes, consequences, a whole catalogue of betrayal.

Chick could not have known the half of it. I wanted to walk out on him there and then but I was too fascinated. Besides, I had promised Chick I would stand by Rex. I couldn't abandon him. This was Rex's way of being my friend. I knew how much he relished revenge. He sincerely believed others merely pretended not to take the same pleasure in it.

I had promised to stay the night. By the time I went to bed, I had nothing to say to him. I knew how kind he could often be, how kind he had been to Jenny. I could hardly imagine such complicated, elaborate cruelty. Around three A.M. I took a couple of sleeping pills and woke up at eight on a wonderful sunny morning. Under a clear grey-blue sky the granite glittered and the grass glowed. Rex was down in the big, stone-flagged kitchen making breakfast. I ate it as if it might be poisoned. Standing in his drive beside my car, I hugged him. 'I love you, Rex,' I said. And I did, even at that moment, when I could barely look at him. He paused, appearing to consider this. Then he teared up, making that muted humming sound I became used to hearing when he searched for an appropriate word, the little smack of his lips and intake of breath when he'd found it.

'I love you, too,' he said at last.

I got home that afternoon. I'd had to pull over twice to collect myself. Lucinda was still out. I'd hoped so much she would be home before me. The message light was flickering on the phone. I had a sickening premonition something had happened to her. But it was Rex sounding dramatically cheerful, a sure sign he'd been drinking. 'Hi, Mike! I know you're off ratting with your friend the vicar and your Jack Russells. Clearly you've no time to spend for poor old Rex . . .'And so on until the machine cut him off. I was relieved I'd taken longer getting home. When Lu finally arrived with fish and chips from the local, she was too full of her own frustrations with her mother to notice my mood so I explained how I was tired from staying up all night with Rex.

We saw a bit more of Rex after that. Because I would never know anything different, I decided to treat most of what he'd told me that night as an elaborate fiction. I was probably right. A couple of months later, as if he had been practising on me with the Jenny story, he began writing again. At first I was relieved, but we eventually realised he was unable to finish anything. He had lost his gift for narrative, his sense of the future. We did all we could to encourage him, to keep him engaged. The ideas themselves were as brilliant as ever. He phoned to read me a couple of opening paragraphs over the answer machine and they were so good, so typical of Rex at his best, Lucinda wouldn't let me erase them. When I was home he might read several pages, even a chapter. But two chapters were the most he could manage of anything. Chick had always been the one to help with construction. After I stopped editing he wouldn't let me do it any more. He claimed Chick's diary had left him unable to complete a story. 'Maybe because I know how it finishes. How they all finish.'

Rex had spent his whole life telling stories. There wasn't much I could say. He was still writing narrative verse and every fortnight or so he would phone again with the start of a new story, still leaving it on the machine if we weren't in.

Then his troubles began to increase. Phoning him I learned how he was threatened by the VAT authorities because of his failure to send in his forms or how a builder had gone off on a second job in the middle of fixing the library roof, how rain was drenching his books. I'd go over and do what I could but eventually I'd have to return home. I felt horribly guilty, recalling my promise to Chick. Not that I failed to remind Rex of what Chick had mentioned, but I couldn't be there the whole time. Often he seemed to resent our help. I suppose the boxed wine he bought by mail order didn't help. He ate a lot, but badly for a diabetic, and for all the various domestic disasters, which his friends coped with pretty well among us, things appeared to improve with time. If anything his grasp on reality seemed to strengthen. He broke down less and began going to a few parties and conferences. He made his peace with the friends he'd insulted and was mostly forgiven. Optimistically, we spoke of him as becoming his old self again. He was introspective in a positive way.

When another August came round he seemed pretty positive. He might start off feeling miserable but conversation soon cheered him up. We'd share a piece of gossip or make fun of a good friend. That was how we were. He joked about Chick, too. I saw that as another sign of healing. Lucinda could always tell who was on the phone because of the laughter. I spoke to him on the first Monday in September. He was drunk, but no more than usual. He'd sent me an e-mail, he said. This was unusual. He hated e-mail as a rule. So I went to my PC and there it was. Rex rarely offered that amount of self-revelation and this had the feel of a continuing conversation, maybe with himself. It knocked me back a bit. So much that I made plans to see him the following weekend. It was as short as it was shocking:

'The story I never wrote was the story of my life, my unhappiness at failing to convince my father of my worth. I tried so hard, but I never had the courage or the method to tell that story. I wrote to impress. The verses always had to be witty, the prose clever. You remember me telling you, when we were young, how scared I was about dropping my guard. Truth wasn't as important as success to me. I needed to impress the people my dad approved of. Nobody else's opinion meant much. Either he saw me in the *Saturday Evening Post* or I simply didn't exist as a writer.' I think he'd planned to say more, but that's all there was.

On the Thursday, Jimmy Cornish called and told

me Rex was dead. The rest was in the obits. Gone but not forgiven.

I had failed to keep my word to Chick. I hadn't found the bullets. I should have spoken to his accountant. I should have helped him back to AA. I've never understood booze. People have to be rolling in the gutter singing 'Nellie Dean' before I get the picture. I missed all the signs and fell down on a solemn promise. Not for the first time. I never gave a promise to a child I couldn't keep, but I made a habit of breaking them to adults. Rex knew exactly what he was doing. I'm not the only survivor still running scenarios through their head. If I'd found the gun and stolen it . . . If I'd checked to see how much he was drinking . . . If I'd listened more closely . . .

Rex wrote some great ghost stories. When it came to haunting his friends, he was a bloody expert. What he'd done to Jenny told me he knew exactly what he was up to. People say all ghost stories are optimistic because they show a belief in life after death. Equally, all artists are optimists because the act of creation is optimistic in itself. Rex's poems and openings are still on our machine. Lu won't erase them. On a bad night I'll pour myself a glass of wine and press the button until I hear his voice. I'll listen to his gentle mockery as he invents an outrageous tale about my getting my toe stuck in the bath's hot tap or being arrested for vagrancy on my way back from a climb. He always gets cut off. If I'm feeling up to it, I'll listen the way you listen to a sweet, familiar tune.

I think that was the real reason why, after Chick's death, Rex never completed anything. There was only one story he really had to tell and from deep habit he had repressed it, choosing suicide rather than write it. 'The Story of Rex and Chick.' Even under such dreadful stress he couldn't let it come out. He had destroyed Chick's journals to ensure it never would be known. And then he had destroyed himself.

Rather than dwell on that I'll listen to his familiar fantasies once again. Then I'll turn off the machine, curse the bastard for a liar and a coward and a calculating fucking sadist, pick up one of his books and head for bed, glad enough, I guess, that I still have a few stories of my own to tell and some rotten bloody friends to remember.

THE MAIDEN FLIGHT OF MCCAULEY'S

BELLEROPHON

Elizabeth Hand

Being assigned to the Head for eight hours was the worst security shift you could pull at the museum. Even now, thirty years later, Robbie had dreams in which he wandered from the Early Flight gallery to Balloons & Airships to Cosmic Soup, where he once again found himself alone in the dark, staring into the bland gaze of the famous scientist as he intoned his endless lecture about the nature of the universe.

'Remember when we thought nothing could be worse than that?' Robbie stared wistfully into his empty glass, then signaled the waiter for another bourbon and Coke. Across the table, his old friend Emery sipped a beer.

'I liked the Head,' said Emery. He cleared his throat and began to recite in the same portentous tone the famous scientist had employed. 'Trillions and trillions of galaxies in which our own is but a mote of cosmic dust. It made you think.'

'It made you think about killing yourself,' said

Robbie. 'Do you want to know how many times I heard that?'

'A trillion?'

'Five thousand.' The waiter handed Robbie a drink, his fourth. 'Twenty-five times an hour, times eight hours a day, times five days a week, times five months.'

'Five thousand, that's not so much. Especially when you think of all those trillions of galleries. I mean galaxies. Only five months? I thought you worked there longer.'

'Just that summer. It only seemed like forever.'

Emery knocked back his beer. 'A long time ago, in a gallery far, far away,' he intoned, not for the first time.

Thirty years before, the Museum of American Aviation and Aerospace had just opened. Robbie was nineteen that summer, a recent dropout from the University of Maryland, living in a group house in Mount Rainier. Employment opportunities were scarce; making $3.40 an hour as a security aide at the Smithsonian's newest museum seemed preferable to bagging groceries at Giant Food. Every morning he'd punch his time card in the guards' locker room and change into his uniform. Then he'd duck outside to smoke a joint before trudging downstairs for the morning meeting and that day's assignments.

Most of the security guards were older than Robbie, with back-grounds in the military and an eye on future careers with the D.C. police department or FBI. Still, they tolerated him with mostly good-natured ribbing about his longish hair and bloodshot eyes. All except for Hedge, the security chief. He was an enormous man with a shaved head who sat, knitting, behind a bank of closed-circuit video monitors, observing tourists and guards with an expression of amused contempt.

'What are you making?' Robbie once asked. Hedge raised his hands to display an intricately patterned baby blanket. 'Hey, that's cool. Where'd you learn to knit?'

'Prison.' Hedge's eyes narrowed. 'You stoned again, Opie? That's it. Gallery Seven. Relieve Jones.'

Robbie's skin went cold, then hot with relief when he realized Hedge wasn't going to fire him. 'Seven? Uh, yeah, sure, sure. For how long?'

'Forever,' said Hedge.

'Oh, man, you got the Head.' Jones clapped his hands gleefully when Robbie arrived. 'Better watch your ass, kids'll throw shit at you,' he said, and sauntered off.

Two projectors at opposite ends of the dark room beamed twin shafts of silvery light onto a head-shaped Styrofoam form. Robbie could never figure out if they'd filmed the famous scientist just once, or if they'd gone to the trouble to shoot him from two different angles.

However they'd done it, the sight of the disembodied Head was surprisingly effective: it looked like a hologram floating amid the hundreds of

270

back-projected twinkly stars that covered the walls and ceiling. The creep factor was intensified by the stilted, slightly puzzled manner in which the Head blinked as it droned on, as though the famous scientist had just realized his body was gone, and was hoping no one else would notice. Once, when he was really stoned, Robbie swore that the Head deviated from its script.

'What'd it say?' asked Emery. At the time he was working in the General Aviation Gallery, operating a flight simulator that tourists clambered into for three-minute rides.

'Something about peaches,' said Robbie. 'I couldn't understand, it sort of mumbled.'

Every morning, Robbie stood outside the entrance to Cosmic Soup and watched as tourists streamed through the main entrance and into the Hall of Flight. Overhead, legendary aircraft hung from the ceiling. The 1903 Wright Flyer with its Orville mannequin; a Lilienthal glider; the Bell X-1 in which Chuck Yeager broke the sound barrier. From a huge pit in the center of the Hall rose a Minuteman III ICBM, rust-colored stains still visible where a protester had tossed a bucket of pig's blood on it a few months earlier. Directly above the entrance to Robbie's gallery dangled the *Spirit of St Louis*. The aides who worked upstairs in the planetarium amused themselves by shooting paper clips onto its wings.

Robbie winced at the memory. He gulped what

was left of his bourbon and sighed. 'That was a long time ago.'

'*Tempus fugit*, baby. Thinking of which—' Emery dug into his pocket for a BlackBerry. 'Check this out. From Leonard.'

Robbie rubbed his eyes blearily, then read.

From: *l.scopes@MAAA.SI.edu*
Subject: Tragic Illness
Date: *April 6, 7:58:22* P.M. EDT
To: *emeryubergeek@gmail.com*

Dear Emery,
I just learned that our Maggie Blevin is very ill. I wrote her at Christmas but never heard back. Fuad El-Hajj says she was diagnosed with advanced breast cancer last fall.
Prognosis is not good. *She is still in the Fayetteville area, and I gather is in a hospice. I want to make a visit though not sure how that will go over. I have something I want to give her but need to talk to you about it.*
L.

'Ahhh.' Robbie sighed. 'God, that's terrible.'

'Yeah. I'm sorry. But I figured you'd want to know.'

Robbie pinched the bridge of his nose. Four years earlier, his wife, Anna, had died of breast cancer, leaving him adrift in a grief so profound it was as though he'd been poisoned, as though

272

his veins had been pumped with the same chemicals that had failed to save her. Anna had been an oncology nurse, a fact that at first afforded some meager black humor, but in the end deprived them of even the faintest of false hopes borne of denial or faith in alternative therapies.

There was no time for any of that. Zach, their son, had just turned twelve. Between his own grief and Zach's subsequent acting out, Robbie got so depressed that he started pouring his first bourbon and Coke before the boy left for school. Two years later, he got fired from his job with the country parks commission.

He now worked in the shipping department at Small's, an off-price store in a desolate shopping mall that resembled the ruins of a regional airport. Robbie found it oddly consoling. It reminded him of the museum. The same generic atriums and industrial carpeting; the same bleak sunlight filtered through clouded glass; the same vacant-faced people trudging from Dollar Store to Sunglass Hut, the way they'd wandered from the General Aviation Gallery to Cosmic Soup.

'Poor Maggie.' Robbie returned the BlackBerry. 'I haven't thought of her in years.'

'I'm going to see Leonard.'

'When? Maybe I'll go with you.'

'Now.' Emery shoved a twenty under his beer bottle and stood. 'You're coming with me.'

'What?'

'You can't drive – you're snackered. Get popped again, you lose your license.'

'Popped? Who's getting popped? And I'm not snackered, I'm—' Robbie thought. 'Snockered. You pronounced it wrong.'

'Whatever.' Emery grabbed Robbie's shoulder and pushed him to the door. 'Let's go.'

Emery drove an expensive hybrid that could get from Rockville to Utica, New York, on a single tank of gas. The vanity plate read MARVO and was flanked by bumper stickers with messages like GUNS DON'T KILL PEOPLE: TYPE 2 PHASERS KILL PEOPLE and FRANK OFF! as well as several slogans that Emery said were in Klingon.

Emery was the only person Robbie knew who was somewhat famous. Back in the early 1980s, he'd created a local-access cable TV show called *Captain Marvo's Secret Spacetime*, taped in his parents' basement and featuring Emery in an aluminum foil costume behind the console of a cardboard spaceship. Captain Marvo watched videotaped episodes of low-budget 1950s science fiction serials with titles like *PAYLOAD: MOONDUST* while bantering with his copilot, a homemade puppet made by Leonard, named Mungbean.

The show was pretty funny if you were stoned. Captain Marvo became a cult hit, and then a real hit when a major network picked it up as a late-night offering. Emery quit his day job at the museum and rented studio time in Baltimore.

He sold the rights after a few years, and was immediately replaced by a flashy actor in Lurex and a glittering robot sidekick. The show limped along for a season then died. Emery's fans claimed this was because their slacker hero had been sidelined.

But maybe it was just that people weren't as stoned as they used to be. These days the program had a surprising afterlife on the Internet, where Robbie's son, Zach, watched it with his friends, and Emery did a brisk business selling memorabilia through his official Captain Marvo Web site.

It took them nearly an hour to get into D.C. and find a parking space near the Mall, by which time Robbie had sobered up enough to wish he'd stayed at the bar.

'Here.' Emery gave him a sugarless breath mint, then plucked at the collar of Robbie's shirt, acid green with SMALLS embroidered in purple. 'Christ, Robbie, you're a freaking mess.'

He reached into the backseat, retrieved a black T-shirt from his gym bag. 'Here, put this on.'

Robbie changed into it and stumbled out onto the sidewalk. It was mid-April but already steamy; the air shimmered above the pavement and smelled sweetly of apple blossom and coolant from innumerable air conditioners. Only as he approached the museum entrance and caught his reflection in a glass wall did Robbie see that his T-shirt was emblazoned with Emery's youthful face and foil helmet above the words O CAPTAIN MY CAPTAIN.

'You wear your own T-shirt?' he asked as he followed Emery through the door.

'Only at the gym. Nothing else was clean.'

They waited at the security desk while a guard checked their IDs, called upstairs to Leonard's office, signed them in and took their pictures before finally issuing each a visitor's pass.

'You'll have to wait for Leonard to escort you upstairs,' the guard said.

'Not like the old days, huh, Robbie?' Emery draped an arm around Robbie and steered him into the Hall of Flight. 'Not a lot of retinal scanning on your watch.'

The museum hadn't changed much. The same aircraft and space capsules gleamed overhead. Tourists clustered around the lucite pyramid that held slivers of moon rock. Sunburned guys sporting military haircuts and tattoos peered at a mockup of an F-15 flight deck. Everything had that old museum smell: soiled carpeting, machine oil, the wet-laundry odor wafting from steam tables in the public cafeteria.

But the Head was long gone. Robbie wondered if anyone even remembered the famous scientist, dead for many years. The General Aviation Gallery, where Emery and Leonard had operated the flight simulators and first met Maggie Blevin, was now devoted to Personal Flight, with models of jet packs worn by alarmingly lifelike mannequins.

'Leonard designed those.' Emery paused to stare

at a child-size figure who seemed to float above a solar-powered skateboard. 'He could have gone to Hollywood.'

'It's not too late.'

Robbie and Emery turned to see their old colleague behind them.

'Leonard,' said Emery.

The two men embraced. Leonard stepped back and tilted his head. 'Robbie. I wasn't expecting you.'

'Surprise,' said Robbie. They shook hands awkwardly. 'Good to see you, man.'

Leonard forced a smile. 'And you.'

They headed toward the staff elevator. Back in the day, Leonard's hair had been long and luxuriantly blond. It fell unbound down the back of the dogshit yellow uniform jacket, designed to evoke an airline pilot's, which he and Emery and the other General Aviation aides wore as they gave their spiel to tourists eager to yank on the controls of their Link Trainers. With his patrician good looks and stern gray eyes, Leonard was the only aide who actually resembled a real pilot.

Now he looked like a cross between Obi-Wan Kenobi and Willie Nelson. His hair was white and hung in two braids that reached almost to his waist. Instead of the crappy polyester uniform, he wore a white linen tunic, a necklace of unpolished turquoise and coral, loose black trousers tucked into scuffed cowboy boots, and a skull earring the size of Robbie's thumb. On his collar gleamed the cheap knockoff pilot's wings that had once adorned his museum uniform jacket. Leonard had always taken his duties very seriously, especially after Margaret Blevin arrived as the museum's first curator of Proto-Flight. Robbie's refusal to do the same, even long after he'd left the museum himself, had resulted in considerable friction between them over the intervening years.

Robbie cleared his throat. 'So, uh. What are you working on these days?' He wished he wasn't wearing Emery's idiotic T-shirt.

'I'll show you,' said Leonard.

Upstairs, they headed for the old photo lab, now an imaging center filled with banks of computers, digital cameras, scanners.

'We still process film there,' Leonard said as they walked down a corridor hung with production photos from *The Day the Earth Stood Still* and *Frau Im Mond*. 'Negatives, old motion picture stock – people still send us things.'

'Any of it interesting?' asked Emery.

Leonard shrugged. 'Sometimes. You never know what you might find. That's part of Maggie's legacy – we're always open to the possibility of discovering something new.'

Robbie shut his eyes. Leonard's voice made his teeth ache. 'Remember how she used to keep a bottle of Scotch in that side drawer, underneath her purse?' he said.

Leonard frowned, but Emery laughed. 'Yeah! And it was good stuff, too.'

'Maggie had a great deal of class,' said Leonard in a somber tone.

You pompous asshole, thought Robbie.

Leonard punched a code into a door and opened it. 'You might remember when this was a storage cupboard.'

They stepped inside. Robbie did remember this place – he'd once had sex here with a General Aviation aide whose name he'd long forgotten. It had been a good-size supply room then, with an odd, sweetish scent from the rolls of film stacked along the shelves.

Now it was a very crowded office. The shelves were crammed with books and curatorial reports dating back to 1981, and archival boxes holding god knows what – Leonard's original government-job application, maybe. A coat had been tossed onto the floor in one corner. There was a large metal desk covered with bottles of nail polish, and an ancient swivel chair that Robbie vaguely remembered having been deployed during his lunch hour tryst.

Mostly, though, the room held Leonard's stuff: tiny cardboard dioramas, mock-ups of space capsules and dirigibles. It smelled overpoweringly of nail polish. It was also extremely cold.

'Man, you must freeze your ass off.' Robbie rubbed his arms.

Emery picked up one of the little bottles. 'You getting a manicurist's license?'

Leonard gestured at the desk. 'I'm painting with nail polish now. You get some very unusual effects.'

'I bet,' said Robbie. 'You're, like, huffing nail polish.' He peered at the shelves, impressed despite himself. 'Jeez, Leonard. You made all these?'

'Damn right I did.'

When Robbie first met Leonard, they were both lowly GS-1s. In those days, Leonard collected paper clips and rode an old Schwinn bicycle to work. He entertained tourists by making balloon animals. In his spare time, he created Mungbean, Captain Marvo's robot friend, out of a busted lamp and some spark plugs.

He also made strange ink drawings, hundreds of them. Montgolfier balloons with sinister faces; B-52s carrying payloads of soap bubbles; caricatures of the museum director and senior curators as greyhounds sniffing each others' nether quarters.

It was this last, drawn on a scrap of legal paper, which Margaret Blevin picked up on her first tour of the General Aviation Gallery. The sketch had fallen out of Leonard's jacket: he watched in horror as the museum's deputy director stooped to retrieve the crumpled page.

'Allow me,' said the woman at the director's side. She was slight, fortyish, with frizzy red hair and enormous hoop earrings, wearing an Indian-print tunic over tight, sky blue trousers and leather clogs. She snatched up the drawing, stuffed it in her pocket, and continued her tour of the gallery. After the deputy director left, the woman walked to where Leonard stood beside his flight simulator, sweating in his polyester jacket as he supervised an overweight kid in a Chewbacca T-shirt. When the kid climbed down, the woman held up the crumpled sheet.

'Who did this?'

The other two aides – one was Emery – shook their heads.

'I did,' said Leonard.

The woman crooked her finger. 'Come with me.'

'Am I fired?' asked Leonard as he followed her out of the gallery.

'Nope. I'm Maggie Blevin. We're shutting down those Link Trainers and making this into a new gallery. I'm in charge. I need someone to start cataloging stuff for me and maybe do some preliminary sketches. You want the job?'

'Yes,' stammered Leonard. 'I mean, sure.'

'Great.' She balled up the sketch and tossed it into a wastebasket. 'Your talents were being wasted. That looks just like the director's butt.'

'If he was a dog,' said Leonard.

'He's a son of a bitch, and that's close enough,' said Maggie. 'Let's go see personnel.'

Leonard's current job description read Museum Effects Specialist, Grade 9, Step 10. For the last two decades, he'd created figurines and models for the museum's exhibits. Not fighter planes or commercial air-craft – there was an entire division of modelers who handled that.

Leonard's work was more rarefied, as evidenced

by the dozens of flying machines perched wherever there was space in the tiny room. Rocket ships, bat-winged aerodromes, biplanes and triplanes and saucers, many of them striped and polka dotted and glazed with, yes, nail polish in circus colors, so that they appeared to be made of ribbon candy.

His specialty was aircraft that had never actually flown; in many instances, aircraft that had never been intended to fly. Crypto-aviation, as some disgruntled curator dubbed it. He worked from plans and photographs, drawings and uncategorizable materials he'd found in the archives Maggie Blevin had been hired to organize. These were housed in a set of oak filing cabinets dating to the 1920s. Officially, the archive was known as the Pre-Langley Collection. But everyone in the museum, including Maggie Blevin, called it the Nut Files.

After Leonard's fateful promotion, Robbie and Emery would sometimes punch out for the day, go upstairs, and stroll to his corner of the library. You could do that then – wander around workrooms and storage areas, the library and archives, without having to check in or get a special pass or security clearance. Robbie just went along for the ride, but Emery was fascinated by the things Leonard found in the Nut Files. Grainy black-and-white photos of purported UFOs; typescripts of encounters with deceased Russian cosmonauts in the Nevada desert; an account of a Raelian wedding ceremony attended by a glowing crimson orb. There was also a large carton donated by the widow of a legendary rocket scientist, which turned out to be filled with 1950s foot-fetish pornography, and sixteen-millimeter film footage of several pioneers of flight doing something unseemly with a spotted pig.

'Whatever happened to that pig movie?' asked Robbie as he admired a biplane with violet-striped ailerons.

'It's been deaccessioned,' said Leonard.

He cleared the swivel chair and motioned for Emery to sit, then perched on the edge of his desk. Robbie looked in vain for another chair, finally settled on the floor beside a wastebasket filled with empty nail polish bottles.

'So I have a plan,' announced Leonard. He stared fixedly at Emery, as though they were alone in the room. 'To help Maggie. Do you remember the *Bellerophon*?'

Emery frowned. 'Vaguely. That old film loop of a plane crash?'

'*Presumed* crash. They never found any wreckage, everyone just assumes it crashed. But yes, that was the *Bellerophon* – it was the clip that played in our gallery. Maggie's gallery.'

'Right – the movie that burned up!' broke in Robbie. 'Yeah, I remember, the film got caught in a sprocket or something. Smoke detectors went off and they evacuated the whole museum. They got all on Maggie's case about it, they thought she'd installed it wrong.'

'She didn't,' Leonard said angrily. 'One of the tech guys screwed up the installation – he told me a few years ago. He didn't vent it properly, the projector bulb overheated and the film caught on fire. He said he always felt bad she got canned.'

'But they didn't fire her for that.' Robbie gave Leonard a sideways look. 'It was the UFO—'

Emery cut him off. 'They were gunning for her,' he said. 'C'mon, Rob, everyone knew – all those old military guys running this place, they couldn't stand a woman getting in their way. Not if she wasn't air force or some shit. Took 'em a few years, that's all. Fucking assholes. I even got a letter-writing campaign going on the show. Didn't help.'

'Nothing would have helped.' Leonard sighed. 'She was a visionary. She *is* a visionary,' he added hastily. 'Which is why I want to do this—'

He hopped from the desk, rooted around in a corner, and pulled out a large cardboard box.

'Move,' he ordered.

Robbie scrambled to his feet. Leonard began to remove things from the carton and set them carefully on his desk. Emery got up to make more room, angling himself beside Robbie. They watched as Leonard arranged piles of paper, curling eight by tens, faded blueprints, and an old 35-millimeter film viewer, along with several large manila envelopes closed with red string. Finally he knelt beside the box and very gingerly reached inside.

284

'I think the Lindbergh baby's in there,' whispered Emery.

Leonard stood, cradling something in his hands, turned and placed it in the middle of the desk.

'Holy shit.' Emery whistled. 'Leonard, you've outdone yourself.'

Robbie crouched so he could view it at eye level: a model of some sort of flying machine, though it seemed impossible that anyone, even Leonard or Maggie Blevin, could ever have dreamed it might fly. It had a zeppelin-shaped body, with a sharp nose like that of a Lockheed Starfighter, slightly uptilted. Suspended beneath this was a basket filled with tiny gears and chains, and beneath that was a contraption with three wheels, like a velocipede, only the wheels were fitted with dozens of stiff flaps, each no bigger than a fingernail, and even tinier propellers.

And everywhere, there were wings, sprouting from every inch of the craft's body in an explosion of canvas and balsa and paper and gauze. Bird-shaped wings, bat-shaped wings; square wings like those of a box kite, elevators and hollow cones of wire; long tubes that, when Robbie peered inside them, were filled with baffles and flaps. Ailerons and struts ran between them to form a dizzying grid, held together with fine gold thread and monofilament and what looked like human hair. Every bit of it was painted in brilliant shades of violet and emerald, scarlet and fuchsia and gold, and here and there shining objects were set into the glossy surface: minute shards of mirror or colored glass; a beetle carapace; flecks of mica.

Above it all, springing from the fuselage like the cap of an immense toadstool, was a feathery parasol made of curved bamboo and multicolored silk.

It was like gazing at the Wright Flyer through a kaleidoscope.

'That's incredible!' Robbie exclaimed. 'How'd you do that?'

'Now we just have to see if it flies,' said Leonard.

Robbie straightened. 'How the hell can that thing fly?'

'The original flew.' Leonard leaned against the wall. 'My theory is, if we can replicate the same conditions – the *exact same* conditions – it will work.'

'But.' Robbie glanced at Emery. 'The original didn't fly. It crashed. I mean, presumably.'

Emery nodded. 'Plus there was a guy in it. McCartney—'

'McCauley,' said Leonard.

'Right, McCauley. And you know, Leonard, no one's gonna fit in that, right?' Emery shot him an alarmed look. 'You're not thinking of making a full-scale model, are you? Because that would be completely insane.'

'No.' Leonard fingered the skull plug in his earlobe. 'I'm going to make another film – I'm going to replicate the original, and I'm going to do it so perfectly that Maggie won't even realize it's *not* the original. I've got it all worked out.' He looked at Emery. 'I can shoot it on digital, if you'll lend me a camera. That way I can edit it on my laptop. And then I'm going to bring it down to Fayetteville so she can see it.'

Robbie and Emery glanced at each other.

'Well, it's not completely insane,' said Robbie.

'But Maggie knows the original was destroyed,' said Emery. 'I mean, I was there, I remember – she saw it. We all saw it. She has cancer, right? Not Alzheimer's or dementia or, I dunno, amnesia.'

'Why don't you just Photoshop something?' asked Robbie. 'You could tell her it was an homage. That way—'

Leonard's glare grew icy. 'It is not an homage. I am going to Cowana Island, just like McCauley did, and I am going to re-create the maiden flight of the *Bellerophon*. I am going to film it, I am going to edit it. And when it's completed, I'm going to tell Maggie that I found a dupe in the archives. Her heart broke when that footage burned up. I'm going to give it back to her.'

Robbie stared at his shoe so Leonard wouldn't see his expression. After a moment he said, 'When Anna was sick, I wanted to do that. Go back to this place by Mount Washington where we stayed before Zach was born. We had all these great photos of us canoeing there, it was so beautiful. But it was winter, and I said we should wait and go in the summer.'

'I'm not waiting.' Leonard sifted through the papers on his desk. 'I have these—'

He opened a manila envelope and withdrew several glassine sleeves. He examined one, then handed it to Emery.

'This is what survived of the original footage, which in fact was *not* the original footage – the original was shot in 1901, on cellulose nitrate film. That's what Maggie and I found when we first started going through the Nut Files. Only of course nitrate stock is like a ticking time bomb. So the Photo Lab duped it onto safety film, which is what you're looking at.'

Emery held the film to the light. Robbie stood beside him, squinting. Five frames, in shades of amber and tortoiseshell, with blurred images that might have been bushes or clouds or smoke damage, for all Robbie could see.

Emery asked, 'How many frames do you have?'

'Total? Seventy-two.'

Emery shook his head. 'Not much, is it? What was it, fifteen seconds?'

'Seventeen seconds.'

'Times twenty-four frames per second – so, out of about four hundred frames, that's all that's left.'

'No. There was actually less than that, because it was silent film, which runs at more like eighteen frames per second, and they corrected the speed. So, about three hundred frames, which means we have about a quarter of the original stock.' Leonard hesitated. He glanced up. 'Lock that door, would you, Robbie?'

Robbie did, looked back to see Leonard crouched in the corner, moving aside his coat to reveal a metal strongbox. He prised the lid from the top.

The box was filled with water – Robbie *hoped* it was water. 'Is that an aquarium?'

Leonard ignored him, tugged up his sleeves, then dipped both hands below the surface. Very, very carefully he removed another metal box. He set it on the floor, grabbed his coat, and meticulously dried the lid, then turned to Robbie.

'You know, maybe you should unlock the door. In case we need to get out fast.'

'Jesus Christ, Leonard, what is it?' exclaimed Emery. 'Snakes?'

'Nope.' Leonard plucked something from the box, and Emery flinched as a serpentine ribbon unfurled in the air. 'It's what's left of the original footage – the 1901 film.'

'That's nitrate?' Emery stared at him, incredulous. 'You *are* insane! How the hell'd you get it?'

'I clipped it before they destroyed the stock. I think it's okay – I take it out every day, so the gases don't build up. And it doesn't seem to interact with the nail polish fumes. It's the part where you can actually see McCauley, where you get the best view of the plane. See?'

He dangled it in front of Emery, who backed toward the door. 'Put it away, put it away!'

'Can I see?' asked Robbie.

Leonard gave him a measuring look, then nodded. 'Hold it by this edge—'

It took a few seconds for Robbie's eyes to focus properly. 'You're right,' he said. 'You can see him – you can see someone, anyway. And you can definitely tell it's an airplane.'

He handed it back to Leonard, who fastidiously replaced it, first in its canister and then the water-filled safe.

'They could really pop you for that.' Emery whistled in disbelief. 'If that stuff blew? This whole place could go up in flames.'

'You say that like it's a bad thing.' Leonard draped his coat over the strongbox, then started to laugh. 'Anyway, I'm done with it. I went into the photo lab one night and duped it myself. So I've got that copy at home. And this one—'

He inclined his head at the corner. 'I'm going to take the nitrate home and give it a Viking funeral in the backyard. You can come if you want.'

'Tonight?' asked Robbie.

'No. I've got to work late tonight, catch up on some stuff before I leave town.'

Emery leaned against the door. 'Where you going?'

'South Carolina. I told you. I'm going to Cowana Island, and . . .' Robbie caught a whiff of acetone as Leonard picked up the *Bellerophon*. 'I am going to make this thing fly.'

'He really is nuts. I mean, when was the last time he even saw Maggie?' Robbie asked as Emery drove him back to the Mall. 'I still don't know what really happened, except for the UFO stuff.'

'She found out he was screwing around with someone else. It was a bad scene. She tried to get him fired; he went to Boynton and told him Maggie was diverting all this time and money to studying UFOs. Which unfortunately was true. They did an audit, she had some kind of nervous breakdown even before they could fire her.'

'What a prick.'

Emery sighed. 'It was horrible. Leonard doesn't talk about it. I don't think he ever got over it. Over her.'

'Yeah, but . . .' Robbie shook his head. 'She must be, what, twenty years older than us? They never would have stayed together. If he feels so bad, he should just go see her. This other stuff is insane.'

'I think maybe those fumes did something to him. Nitrocellulose, it's in nail polish, too. It might have done something to his brain.'

'Is that possible?'

'It's a theory,' said Emery broodingly.

Robbie's house was in a scruffy subdivision on the outskirts of Rockville. The place was small, a bungalow with masonite siding, a cracked cinder-block foundation, and the remains of a garden that Anna had planted. A green GMC pickup with an expired registration was parked in the drive. Robbie peered into the cab. It was filled with empty Bud Light bottles.

Inside, Zach was hunched at a desk beside his

friend Tyler, owner of the pickup. The two of them stared intently at a computer screen.

'What's up?' said Zach without looking away.

'Not much,' said Robbie. 'Eye contact.'

Zach glanced up. He was slight, with Anna's thick blond curls reduced to a buzz cut that Robbie hated. Tyler was tall and gangly, with long black hair and wire-rimmed sunglasses. Both favored tie-dyed T-shirts and madras shorts that made them look as though they were perpetually on vacation.

Robbie went into the kitchen and got a beer. 'You guys eat?'

'We got something on the way home.'

Robbie drank his beer and watched them. The house had a smell that Emery once described as Failed Bachelor. Unwashed clothes, spilled beer, marijuana smoke. Robbie hadn't smoked in years, but Zach and Tyler had taken up the slack. Robbie used to yell at them but eventually gave up. If his own depressing example wasn't enough to straighten them out, what was?

After a minute, Zach looked up again. 'Nice shirt, Dad.'

'Thanks, son.' Robbie sank into a beanbag chair. 'Me and Emery dropped by the museum and saw Leonard.'

'Leonard!' Tyler burst out laughing. 'Leonard is so fucking sweet! He's, like, the craziest guy ever.'

'All Dad's friends are crazy,' said Zach.

'Yeah, but Emery, he's cool. Whereas that guy Leonard is just wack.'

292

Robbie nodded somberly and finished his beer. 'Leonard is indeed wack. He's making a movie.'

'A real movie?' asked Zach.

'More like a home movie. Or, I dunno – he wants to reproduce another movie, one that was already made, do it all the same again. Shot by shot.'

Tyler nodded. 'Like *The Ring* and *Ringu*. What's the movie?'

'Seventeen seconds of a 1901 plane crash. The original footage was destroyed, so he's going to restage the whole thing.'

'A plane crash?' Zach glanced at Tyler. 'Can we watch?'

'Not a real crash – he's doing it with a model. I mean, I think he is.'

'Did they even have planes then?' said Tyler.

'He should put it on YouTube,' said Zach, and turned back to the computer.

'Okay, get out of there.' Robbie rubbed his head wearily. 'I need to go online.'

The boys argued but gave up quickly. Tyler left. Zach grabbed his cell phone and slouched upstairs to his room. Robbie got another beer, sat at the computer, and logged out of whatever they'd been playing, then typed in MCCAULEY BELLEROPHON.

Only a dozen results popped up. He scanned them, then clicked the Wikipedia entry for Ernesto McCauley.

McCauley, Ernesto (18??–1901) American inventor whose eccentric aircraft, the Bellerophon, *allegedly flew for seventeen seconds before it crashed during a 1901 test flight on Cowana Island, South Carolina, killing McCauley. In the 1980s, claims that this flight was successful and predated that of the Wright brothers by two years were made by a Smithsonian expert, based upon archival film footage. The claims have since been disproved and the film record unfortunately lost in a fire. Curiously, no other record of either McCauley or his aircraft has ever been found.*

Robbie took a long pull at his beer, then typed in MARGARET BLEVIN.

Blevin, Margaret (1938–) Influential cultural historian whose groundbreaking work on early flight earned her the nickname 'the Magnificent Blevin.' During her tenure at the Smithsonian's Museum of American Aeronautics and Aerospace, Blevin redesigned the General Aviation Gallery to feature lesser-known pioneers of flight, including Charles Dellschau and Ernesto McCauley, as well as . . .

'"The Magnificent Blevin"?' Robbie snorted. He grabbed another beer and continued reading.

But Blevin's most lasting impact upon the history of aviation was her 1986 best-seller Wings for Humanity!, *in which she presents a dramatic and visionary account of the mystical aspects of flight, from Icarus to the Wright brothers and beyond. Its central premise is that millennia ago a benevolent race seeded the earth, leaving isolated locations with the ability to engender human-powered flight. 'We dream of flight because flight is our birthright,' wrote Blevin, and since its publication* Wings for Humanity! *has never gone out of print.*

'Leonard wrote this frigging thing!'

'What?' Zach came downstairs, yawning.

'This Wikipedia entry!' Robbie jabbed at the screen. 'That book was never a bestseller – she sneaked it into the museum gift shop and no one bought it. The only reason it's still in print is that she published it herself.'

Zach read the entry over his father's shoulder. 'It's sounds cool.'

Robbie shook his head adamantly. 'She was completely nuts. Obsessed with all this New Age crap, aliens and crop circles. She thought that planes could only fly from certain places, and that's why all the early flights crashed. Not because there was something wrong with the aircraft design, but because they were taking off from the wrong spot.'

'Then how come there's airports everywhere?'

'She never worked out that part.'

'"We must embrace our galactic heritage, the spiritual dimension of human flight, lest we forever chain ourselves to earth,"' Zach read from the screen. 'Was she in that plane crash?'

'No, she's still alive. That was just something she had a wild hair about. She thought the guy who invented that plane flew it a few years before the Wright brothers made their flight, but she could never prove it.'

'But it says there was a movie,' said Zach. 'So someone saw it happen.'

'This is Wikipedia.' Robbie stared at the screen in disgust. 'You can say any fucking things you want and people will believe it. Leonard wrote that entry, guarantee you. Probably she faked that whole film loop. That's what Leonard's planning to do now – replicate the footage then pass it off to Maggie as the real thing.'

Zach collapsed into the beanbag chair. 'Why?'

'Because he's crazy, too. He and Maggie had a thing together.'

Zach grimaced. 'Ugh.'

'What, you think we were born old? We were your age, practically. And Maggie was about twenty years older—'

'A cougar!' Zach burst out laughing. 'Why didn't she go for you?'

'Ha ha ha.' Robbie pushed his empty beer bottle against the wall. 'Women liked Leonard. Go

296

figure. Even your mom went out with him for a while. Before she and I got involved, I mean.'

Zach's glassy eyes threatened to roll back in his head. 'Stop.'

'We thought it was pretty strange,' admitted Robbie. 'But Maggie was good-looking for an old hippie.' He glanced at the Wikipedia entry and did the math. 'I guess she's in her seventies now. Leonard's in touch with her. She has cancer. Breast cancer.'

'I heard you,' said Zach. He rolled out of the beanbag chair, flipped open his phone, and began texting. 'I'm going to bed.'

Robbie sat and stared at the computer screen. After a while he shut it down. He shuffled into the kitchen and opened the cabinet where he kept a quart of Jim Beam, hidden behind bottles of vinegar and vegetable oil. He rinsed out the glass he'd used the night before, poured a jolt and downed it, then carried the bourbon with him to bed.

The next day after work, he was on his second drink at the bar when Emery showed up.

'Hey.' Robbie gestured at the stool beside him. 'Have a seat.'

'You okay to drive?'

'Sure.' Robbie scowled. 'What, you keeping an eye on me?'

'No. But I want you to see something. At my house. Leonard's coming over, we're going to meet there at six thirty. I tried calling you but your phone's off.'

'Oh. Right. Sorry.' Robbie signaled the bartender for his tab. 'Yeah, sure. What, is he gonna give us manicures?'

'Nope. I have an idea. I'll tell you when I get there; I'm going to Royal Delhi first to get some takeout. See you—'

Emery lived in a big town house condo that smelled of Moderately Successful Bachelor. The walls held framed photos of Captain Marvo and Mungbean alongside a life-size painting of Leslie Nielsen as Commander J. J. Adams.

But there was also a climate-controlled basement filled with Captain Marvo merchandise and packing material, with another large room stacked with electronics equipment – sound system, video monitors and decks, shelves and files devoted to old Captain Marvo episodes, and dupes of the grade Z movies featured on the show.

This was where Robbie found Leonard, bent over a refurbished Steenbeck editing table.

'Robbie.' Leonard waved, then returned to threading film onto a spindle. 'Emery back with dinner?'

'Uh-uh.' Robbie pulled a chair alongside him. 'What are you doing?'

'Loading up that nitrate I showed you yesterday.'

'It's not going to explode, is it?'

'No, Robbie, it's not going to explode.' Leonard's mouth tightened. 'Did Emery talk to you yet?'

'He just said something about a plan. So what's up?'

'I'll let him tell you.'

Robbie flushed angrily, but before he could retort there was a knock behind them.

'Chow time, campers.' Emery held up two steaming paper bags. 'Can you leave that for a few minutes, Leonard?'

They ate on the couch in the next room. Emery talked about a pitch he'd made to revive Captain Marvo in cell-phone format. 'It'd be freaking perfect, if I could figure out a way to make any money from it.'

Leonard said nothing. Robbie noted that the cuffs of his white tunic were stained with flecks of orange pigment, as were his fingernails. He looked tired, his face lined and his eyes sunken.

'You getting enough sleep?' Emery asked.

Leonard smiled wanly. 'Enough.'

Finally the food was gone, and the beer. Emery clapped his hands on his knees, pushed aside the empty plates, then leaned forward.

'Okay. So here's the plan. I rented a house on Cowana for a week, starting this Saturday. I mapped it online and it's about ten hours. If we leave right after you guys get off work on Friday and drive all night, we'll get there early Saturday morning. Leonard, you said you've got everything pretty much assembled, so all you need to do is pack it up. I've got everything else here. Be a tight fit in the Prius, though, so we'll have to take two cars.

We'll bring everything we need with us, we'll have a week to shoot and edit or whatever, then on the way back we swing through Fayetteville and show the finished product to Maggie. What do you think?'

'That's not a lot of time,' said Leonard. 'But we could do it.'

Emery turned to Robbie. 'Is your car roadworthy? It's about twelve hundred miles round-trip.'

Robbie stared at him. 'What the hell are you talking about?'

'The *Bellerophon*. Leonard's got storyboards and all kinds of drawings and still frames, enough to work from. The Realtor's in Charleston; she said there wouldn't be many people this early in the season. Plus there was a hurricane a couple years ago; I gather the island got hammered and no one's had money to rebuild. So we'll have it all to ourselves, pretty much.'

'Are you high?' Robbie laughed. 'I can't just take off. I have a job.'

'You get vacation time, right? You can take a week. It'll be great, man. The Realtor says it's already in the eighties down there. Warm water, a beach – what more you want?'

'Uh, maybe a beach with people besides you and Leonard?' Robbie searched in vain for another beer. 'I couldn't go anyway – next week's Zach's spring break.'

'Yeah?' Emery shook his head. 'So, you're going to be at the store all day, and he'll be home getting stoned. Bring him. We'll put him to work.'

Leonard frowned, but Robbie looked thoughful. 'Yeah, you're right. I hadn't thought of that. I can't really leave him alone. I guess I'll think about it.'

'Don't think, just do it. It's Wednesday, tell 'em you're taking off next week. They gonna fire you?'

'Maybe.'

'I'm not babysitting some—' Leonard started.

Emery cut him off. 'You got that nitrate loaded? Let's see it.'

They filed into the workroom. Leonard sat at the Steenbeck. The others watched as he adjusted the film on its sprockets. He turned to Robbie, then indicated the black projection box in the center of the deck.

'Emery knows all this, so I'm just telling you. That's a quartz halogen lamp. I haven't turned it on yet, because if the frame was just sitting there it might incinerate the film, and us. But there's only about four seconds of footage, so we're going to take our chances and watch it, once. Maybe you remember it from the gallery?'

Robbie nodded. 'Yeah, I saw it a bunch of times. Not as much as the Head, but enough.'

'Good. Hit that light, would you, Emery? Everyone ready? Blink and you'll miss it.'

Robbie craned his neck, staring at a blank white screen. There was a whir, the stutter of film running through a projector.

At the bottom of the frame the horizon lurched, bright flickers that might be an expanse of water. Then a blurred image, faded sepia and amber, etched with blotches and something resembling a beetle leg: the absurd contraption Robbie recognized as the original *Bellerophon*. Only it was moving – it was flying – its countless gears and propellers and wings spinning and whirring and flapping all at once, so it seemed the entire thing would vibrate into a thousand pieces. Beneath the fuselage, a dark figure perched precariously atop the velocipede, legs like black scissors slicing at the air. From the left corner of the frame leaped a flare of light, like a shooting star or burning firecracker tossed at the pedaling figure. The pilot listed to one side, and—

Nothing. The film ended as abruptly as it had begun. Leonard quickly reached to turn off the lamp, and immediately removed the film from the take-up drive.

Robbie felt his neck prickle – he'd forgotten how weird, uncanny even, the footage was.

'Jesus, that's some bizarre shit,' said Emery.

'It doesn't even look real.' Robbie watched as Leonard coiled the film and slid it in a canister. 'I mean, the guy, he looks fake.'

Emery nodded. 'Yeah, I know. It looks like one of those old silents, *The Lost World* or something. But it's not. I used to watch it back when it ran a hundred times a day in our gallery, the way you used to watch the Head. And it's definitely real. At least the pilot, McCauley – that's a real guy. I got a big magnifier once and just stood there and watched it over and over again. He was breathing,

I could see it. And the plane, it's real too, far as I could tell. The thing I can't figure is, who the hell shot that footage? And what was the angle?'

Robbie stared at the empty screen, then shut his eyes. He tried to recall the rest of the film from when it played in the General Aviation gallery: the swift, jerky trajectory of that eerie little vehicle with its bizarre pilot, a man in a black suit and bowler hat; then the flash from the corner of the screen, and the man toppling from his perch into the white and empty air. The last thing you saw was a tiny hand at the bottom of the frame, then some blank leader, followed by the words 'The Maiden Flight of McCauley's *Bellerophon* (1901).' And the whole thing began again.

'It was like someone was in the air next to him,' said Robbie. 'Unless he got only six feet off the ground. I always assumed it was faked.'

'It wasn't faked,' said Leonard. 'The cameraman was on the beach filming. It was a windy day, they were hoping that would help give the plane some lift but there must have been a sudden gust. When the *Bellerophon* went into the ocean, the cameraman dove in to save McCauley. They both drowned. They never found the bodies, or the wreckage. Only the camera with the film.'

'Who found it?' asked Robbie.

'We don't know.' Leonard sighed, his shoulders slumping. 'We don't know anything. Not the name of the cameraman, nothing. When Maggie and I ran the original footage, the leader said

303

"Maiden Flight of McCauley's *Bellerophon*." The can had the date and "Cowana Island" written on it. So Maggie and I went down there to research it. A weird place. Hardly any people, and this was in the summer. There's a tiny historical society on the island, but we couldn't find anything about McCauley or the aircraft. No newspaper accounts, no gravestones. The only thing we did find was in a diary kept by the guy who delivered the mail back then. On May 13, 1901, he wrote that it was a very windy day and two men had drowned while attempting to launch a flying machine on the beach. Someone must have found the camera afterward. Somebody processed the film, and somehow it found its way to the museum.'

Robbie followed Leonard into the next room. 'What was that weird flash of light?'

'I don't know.' Leonard stared out a glass door into the parking lot. 'But it's not overexposure or lens flare or anything like that. It's something the cameraman actually filmed. Water, maybe – if it was a windy day, a big wave might have come up onto the beach or something.'

'I always thought it was fire. Like a rocket or some kind of flare.'

Leonard nodded. 'That's what Maggie thought, too. The mailman – mostly all he wrote about was the weather. Which if you were relying on a horse-drawn cart, makes sense. About two weeks before he mentioned the flying machine, he described something that sounds like a major meteor shower.'

'And Maggie thought it was hit by a meteor?'

'No.' Leonard sighed. 'She thought it was something else. The weird thing is, a few years ago I checked online, and it turns out there was an unusual amount of meteor activity in 1901.'

Robbie raised an eyebrow. 'Meaning?'

Leonard said nothing. Finally he opened the door and walked outside. The others trailed after him.

They reached the edge of the parking lot, where cracked tarmac gave way to stony ground. Leonard glanced back, then stooped. He brushed away a few stray leaves and tufts of dead grass, set the film canister down and unscrewed the metal lid. He picked up one end of the coil of film, gently tugging until it trailed a few inches across the ground. Then he withdrew a lighter, flicked it, and held the flame to the tail of film.

'What the—' began Robbie.

There was a dull *whoosh*, like the sound of a gas burner igniting. A plume of crimson and gold leaped from the canister, writhing in the air within a ball of black smoke. Leonard staggered to his feet, covering his head as he backed away.

'Leonard!' Emery grabbed him roughly, then turned and raced to the house.

Before Robbie could move, a strong chemical stink surrounded him. The flames shrank to a

305

shining thread that lashed at the smoke then faded into flecks of ash. Robbie ducked his head, coughing. He grasped Leonard's arm and tried to drag him away, glanced up to see Emery running toward them with a fire extinguisher.

'Sorry,' gasped Leonard. He made a slashing motion through the smoke, which dispersed. The flames were gone. Leonard's face was black with ash. Robbie touched his own cheek gingerly, looked at his fingers, and saw they were coated with something dark and oily.

Emery halted, panting, and stared at the twisted remains of the film can. On the ground beside it, a glowing thread wormed toward a dead leaf, then expired in a gray wisp. Emery raised the fire extinguisher threateningly, set it down, and stomped on the canister.

'Good thing you didn't do that in the museum,' said Robbie. He let go of Leonard's arm.

'Don't think it didn't cross my mind,' said Leonard, and walked back inside.

They left Friday evening. Robbie got the week off, after giving his dubious boss a long story about a dying relative down South. Zach shouted and broke a lamp when informed he would be accompanying his father on a trip during his spring vacation.

'With Emery and *Leonard?* Are you fucking *insane?*'

Robbie was too exhausted to fight: he quickly

offered to let Tyler come with them. Tyler, surprisingly, agreed, and even showed up on Friday afternoon to help load the car. Robbie made a pointed effort not to inspect the various backpacks and duffel bags the boys threw into the trunk of the battered Taurus. Alcohol, drugs, firearms: he no longer cared.

Instead he focused on the online weather report for Cowana Island. Eighty degrees and sunshine, photographs of blue water, white sand, a skein of pelicans skimming above the waves. Ten hours, that wasn't so bad. In another weak moment, he told Zach he could drive part of the way, so Robbie could sleep.

'What about me?' asked Tyler. 'Can I drive?'

'Only if I never wake up,' said Robbie.

Around six Emery pulled into the driveway, honking. The boys were already slumped in Robbie's Taurus, Zach in front with earbuds dangling around his face and a knit cap pulled down over his eyes, Tyler in the back, staring blankly, as though they were already on I-95.

'You ready?' Emery rolled down his window. He wore a blue flannel shirt and a gimme cap that read STARFLEET ACADEMY. In the hybrid's passenger seat, Leonard perused a road atlas. He looked up and shot Robbie a smile.

'Hey, a road trip.'

'Yeah.' Robbie smiled back and patted the hybrid's roof. 'See you.'

It took almost two hours just to get beyond the

gravitational pull of the Washington Beltway. Farms and forest had long ago disappeared beneath an endless grid of malls and housing developments, many of them vacant. Every time Robbie turned up the radio for a song he liked, the boys complained that they could hear it through their earphones.

Only as the sky darkened and Virginia gave way to North Carolina did the world take on a faint fairy glow, distant green and yellow lights reflecting the first stars and a shining cusp of moon. Sprawl gave way to pine forest. The boys had been asleep for hours, in that amazing, self-willed hibernation they summoned whenever in the presence of adults for more than fifteen minutes. Robbie put the radio on, low, searched until he caught the echo of a melody he knew, and then another. He thought of driving with Anna beside him, a restive Zach behind them in his car seat; the aimless trips they'd make until the toddler fell asleep and they could talk or, once, park in a vacant lot and make out.

How long had it been since he'd remembered that? Years, maybe. He fought against thinking of Anna; sometimes it felt as though he fought Anna herself, her hands pummeling him as he poured another drink or staggered up to bed.

Now, though, the darkness soothed him the way those long-ago drives had lulled Zach to sleep. He felt an ache lift from his breast, as though a splinter had been dislodged; blinked and in the rearview mirror glimpsed Anna's face, slightly turned from him as she gazed out at the passing sky.

He started, realized he'd begun to nod off. On the dashboard his fuel indicator glowed red. He called Emery, and at the next exit pulled off 95, the Prius behind him.

After a few minutes they found a gas station set back from the road in a pine grove, with an old-fashioned pump out front and yellow light streaming through a screen door. The boys blinked awake.

'Where are we?' asked Zach.

'No idea.' Robbie got out of the car. 'North Carolina.'

It was like stepping into a twilight garden, or some hidden biosphere at the zoo. Warmth flowed around him, violet and rustling green, scented overpoweringly of honeysuckle and wet stone. He could hear rushing water, the stirring of wind in the leaves, and countless small things – frogs peeping, insects he couldn't identify. A nightbird that made a burbling song. In the shadows behind the building, fireflies floated between kudzu-choked trees, like tiny glowing fish.

For an instant he felt himself suspended in that enveloping darkness. The warm air moved through him, sweetly fragrant, pulsing with life he could neither see nor touch. He tasted something honeyed and faintly astringent in the back of his throat, and drew his breath in sharply.

'What?' demanded Zach.

'Nothing.' Robbie shook his head and turned to the pump. 'Just – isn't this great?'

He filled the tank. Zach and Tyler went in search of food, and Emery strolled over.

'How you holding up?'

'I'm good. Probably let Zach drive for a while so I can catch some z's.'

He moved the car, then went inside to pay. He found Leonard buying a pack of cigarettes as the boys headed out, laden with energy drinks and bags of chips. Robbie slid his credit card across the counter to a woman wearing a tank top that set off a tattoo that looked like the face of Marilyn Manson, or maybe it was Jesus.

'Do you have a restroom?'

The woman handed him a key. 'Round back.'

'Bathroom's here,' Robbie yelled at the boys. 'We're not stopping again.'

They trailed him into a dank room with gray walls. A fluorescent light buzzed overhead. After Tyler left, Robbie and Zach stood side by side at the sink, trying to coax water from a rusted spigot to wash their hands.

'The hell with it,' said Robbie. 'Let's hit the road. You want to drive?'

'Dad.' Zach pointed at the ceiling. 'Dad, look.'

Robbie glanced up. A screen bulged from a small window above the sink. Something had blown against the wire mesh, a leaf or scrap of paper.

But then the leaf moved, and he saw that it wasn't a leaf at all but a butterfly.

No, not a butterfly – a moth. The biggest he'd ever seen, bigger than his hand. Its fan-shaped upper wings opened, revealing vivid golden eyespots; its trailing lower wings formed two perfect arabesques, all a milky, luminous green.

'A luna moth,' breathed Robbie. 'I've never seen one.'

Zach clambered onto the sink. 'It wants to get out—'

'Hang on.' Robbie boosted him, bracing himself so the boy's weight wouldn't yank the sink from the wall. 'Be careful! Don't hurt it—'

The moth remained where it was. Robbie grunted – Zach weighed as much as he did – felt his legs trembling as the boy prised the screen from the wall then struggled to pull it free.

'It's stuck,' he said. 'I can't get it—'

The moth fluttered weakly. One wing tip looked ragged, as though it had been singed.

'Tear it!' Robbie cried. 'Just tear the screen.'

Zach wedged his fingers beneath a corner of the window frame and yanked, hard enough that he fell. Robbie caught him as the screen tore away to dangle above the sink. The luna moth crawled onto the sill.

'Go!' Zach banged on the wall. 'Go on, fly!'

Like a kite catching the wind, the moth lifted. Its trailing lower wings quivered and the eyespots seemed to blink, a pallid face gazing at them from the darkness. Then it was gone.

'That was cool.' For an instant, Zach's arm

draped across his father's shoulder, so fleetingly Robbie might have imagined it. 'I'm going to the car.'

When the boy was gone, Robbie tried to push the screen back into place. He returned the key and went to join Leonard, smoking a cigarette at the edge of the woods. Behind them a car horn blared.

'Come on!' shouted Zach. 'I'm leaving!'

'Happy trails,' said Leonard.

Robbie slept fitfully in back as Zach drove, the two boys arguing about music and a girl named Eileen. After an hour he took over again.

The night ground on. The boys fell back asleep. Robbie drank one of their Red Bulls and thought of the glimmering wonder that had been the luna moth. A thin rind of emerald appeared on the horizon, deepening to copper then gold as it overtook the sky. He began to see palmettos among the loblolly pines and pin oaks, and spiky plants he didn't recognize. When he opened the window, the air smelled of roses, and the sea.

'Hey.' He poked Zach, breathing heavily in the seat beside him. 'Hey, we're almost there.'

He glanced at the directions, looked up to see the hybrid passing him and Emery gesturing at a sandy track that veered to the left. It was bounded by barbed-wire fences and clumps of cactus thick with blossoms the color of lemon cream. The pines surrendered to palmettos and prehistoric-looking trees with gnarled roots that thrust up from pools where egrets and herons stabbed at frogs.

'Look,' said Robbie.

Ahead of them the road narrowed to a path barely wide enough for a single vehicle, built up with shells and chunks of concrete. On one side stretched a blur of cypress and long-legged birds; on the other, an aquamarine estuary that gave way to the sea and rolling white dunes.

Robbie slowed the car to a crawl, humping across mounds of shells and doing his best to avoid sinkholes. After a quarter mile, the make-shift causeway ended. An old metal gate lay in a twisted heap on the ground, covered by creeping vines. Above it a weathered sign clung to a cypress.

WELCOME TO COWANA ISLAND
NO DUNE BUGGIES

They drove past the ruins of a mobile home. Emery's car was out of sight. Robbie looked at his cell phone and saw there was no signal. In the back, Tyler stirred.

'Hey, Rob, where are we?'

'We're here. Wherever here is. The island.'

'Sweet.' Tyler leaned over the seat to jostle Zach awake. 'Hey, get up.'

Robbie peered through the overgrown greenery, looking for something resembling a beach house. He tried to remember which hurricane had pounded this part of the coast, and how long ago. Two years? Five?

The place looked as though it had been abandoned for decades. Fallen palmettos were everywhere, their leaves stiff and reddish-brown, like rusted blades. Some remained upright, their crowns lopped off. Acid-green lizards sunned themselves in driveways where ferns poked through the blacktop. The remains of carports and decks dangled above piles of timber and mold-blackened Sheetrock. Now and then an intact house appeared within the jungle of flowering vines.

But no people, no cars except for an SUV crushed beneath a toppled utility pole. The only store was a modest grocery with a brick facade and shattered windows, through which the ghostly outlines of aisles and displays could still be glimpsed.

'It's like 28 *Days*,' said Zach, and shot a baleful look at his father.

Robbie shrugged. 'Talk to the man from the Starfleet Academy.'

He pulled down a rutted drive to where the hybrid sat beneath a thriving palmetto. Driftwood edged a path that led to an old wood-frame house raised on stiltlike pilings. Stands of blooming cactus surrounded it, and trees choked with honeysuckle. The patchy lawn was covered with hundreds of conch shells arranged in concentric circles and spirals. On the deck a tattered red whirligig spun in the breeze, and rope hammocks hung like flaccid cocoons.

'I'm sleeping there,' said Tyler.

Leonard gazed at the house with an unreadable expression. Emery had already sprinted up the uneven steps to what Robbie assumed was the front door. When he reached the top, he bent to pick up a square of coconut matting, retrieved something from beneath it, then straightened, grinning.

'Come on!' he shouted, turning to unlock the door; and the others raced to join him.

The house had linoleum floors, sifted with a fine layer of sand, and mismatched furniture – rattan chairs, couches covered with faded bark-cloth cushions, a canvas seat that hung from the ceiling by a chain and groaned alarmingly whenever the boys sat in it. The sea breeze stirred dusty white curtains at the windows. Anoles skittered across the floor, and Tyler fled shouting from the outdoor shower, where he'd seen a black widow spider. The electricity worked, but there was no air-conditioning and no television, no Internet.

'This is what you get for three hundred bucks in the off season,' said Emery when Tyler complained.

'I don't get it.' Robbie stood on the deck, staring across the empty road to where the dunes stretched, tufted with thorny greenery. 'Even if there was a hurricane – this is practically ocean-front, all of it. Where is everybody?'

'Who can afford to build anything?' said Leonard. 'Come on, I want to get my stuff inside before it heats up.'

Leonard commandeered the master bedroom. He installed his laptop, Emery's camera equipment, piles of storyboards, the box that contained the miniature *Bellerophon*. This formidable array took up every inch of floor space, as well as the surface of a Ping-Pong table.

'Why is there a Ping-Pong table in the bedroom?' asked Robbie as he set down a tripod.

Emery shrugged. 'You might ask, why is there not a Ping-Pong table in all bedrooms?'

'We're going to the beach,' announced Zach.

Robbie kicked off his shoes and followed them, across the deserted road and down a path that wound through a miniature wilderness of cactus and bristly vines. He felt light-headed from lack of sleep, and also from the beer he'd snagged from one of the cases Emery had brought. The sand was already hot; twice he had to stop and pluck sharp spurs from his bare feet. A horned toad darted across the path, and a skink with a blue tongue. His son's voice came to him, laughing, and the sound of waves on the shore.

Atop the last dune small yellow roses grew in a thick carpet, their soapy fragrance mingling with the salt breeze. Robbie bent to pluck a handful of petals and tossed them into the air.

'It's not a bad place to fly, is it?'

He turned and saw Emery, shirtless. He handed Robbie a bottle of Tecate with a slice of lime jammed in its neck, raised his own beer and took a sip.

'It's beautiful.' Robbie squeezed the lime into his beer, then drank. 'But that model. It won't fly.'

'I know.' Emery stared at where Zach and Tyler leaped in the shallow water, sending up rainbow spray as they splashed each other. 'But it's a good excuse for a vacation, isn't it?'

'It is,' replied Robbie, and slid down the dune to join the boys.

Over the next few days, they fell into an odd, almost sleepless rhythm, staying up till two or three A.M., drinking and talking. The adults pretended not to notice when the boys slipped a Tecate from the fridge, and ignored the incense-scented smoke that drifted from the deck after they stumbled off to bed. Everyone woke shortly after dawn, even the boys. Blinding sunlight slanted through the worn curtains. On the deck where Zach and Tyler huddled inside their hammocks, a tree frog made a sound like rusty hinges. No one slept enough, everyone drank too much.

For once it didn't matter. Robbie's hangovers dissolved as he waded into water as warm as blood, then floated on his back and watched pelicans skim above him. Afterward he'd carry equipment from the house to the dunes, where Emery had created a shelter from old canvas deck chairs and bedsheets. The boys helped him, the three of them lugging tripods and digital cameras, the box that contained Leonard's model of the *Bellerophon*, a cooler filled with beer and Red Bull.

That left Emery in charge of household duties. He'd found an ancient red wagon half buried in the dunes, and used this to transport bags of tortilla chips and a cooler filled with Tecate and limes. There was no store on the island save the abandoned wreck they'd passed when they first arrived. No gas station, and the historical society building appeared to be long gone.

But while driving around, Emery discovered a roadside stand that sold homemade salsa in mason jars and sage-green eggs in recycled cardboard cartons. The drive beside it was blocked with a barbed-wire fence and a sign that said BEWARE OF TWO-HEADED DOG.

'You ever see it?' asked Tyler.

'Nope. I never saw anyone except an alligator.' Emery opened a beer. 'And it was big enough to eat a two-headed dog.'

By Thursday morning, they'd carted everything from one end of the island to the other, waiting with increasing impatience as Leonard climbed up and down dunes and stared broodingly at the blue horizon.

'How will you know which is the right one?' asked Robbie.

Leonard shook his head. 'I don't know. Maggie said she thought it would be around here—'

He swept his arm out, encompassing a high ridge of sand that crested above the beach like a frozen wave. Below, Tyler and Zach argued over whose turn it was to haul everything uphill again. Robbie shoved his sunglasses against his nose.

'This beach has probably been washed away a hundred times since McCauley was here. Maybe we should just choose a place at random. Pick the highest dune or something.'

'Yeah, I know.' Leonard sighed. 'This is probably our best choice, here.'

He stood and for a long time gazed at the sky. Finally he turned and walked down to join the boys.

'We'll do it here,' he said brusquely, and headed back to the house.

Late that afternoon they made a bonfire on the beach. The day had ended gray and much cooler than it had been, the sun swallowed in a haze of bruise-tinged cloud. Robbie waded into the shallow water, feeling with his toes for conch shells. Beside the fire, Zach came across a shark's tooth the size of a guitar pick.

'That's probably a million years old,' said Tyler enviously.

'Almost as old as Dad,' said Zach.

Robbie flopped down beside Leonard. 'It's so weird,' he said, shaking sand from a conch. 'There's a whole string of these islands, but I haven't seen a boat the entire time we've been here.'

'Are you complaining?' said Leonard.

'No. Just, don't you think it's weird?'

'Maybe.' Leonard tossed his cigarette into the fire.

'I want to stay.' Zach rolled onto his back and watched as sparks flew among the first stars. 'Dad? Why can't we just stay here?'

Robbie took a long pull from his beer. 'I have to get back to work. And you guys have school.'

'Fuck school,' said Zach and Tyler.

'Listen.' The boys fell silent as Leonard glared at them. 'Tomorrow morning I want to set everything up. We'll shoot before the wind picks up too much. I'll have the rest of the day to edit. Then we pack and head to Fayetteville on Saturday. We'll find some cheap place to stay, and drive home on Sunday.'

The boys groaned. Emery sighed. 'Back to the salt mines. I gotta call that guy about the show.'

'I want to have a few hours with Maggie.' Leonard pulled at the silver skull in his ear. 'I told the nurse I'd be there Saturday before noon.'

'We'll have to leave pretty early,' said Emery.

For a few minutes nobody spoke. Wind rattled brush in the dunes behind them. The bonfire leaped then subsided, and Zach fed it a knot of driftwood. An unseen bird gave a piping cry that was joined by another, then another, until their plaintive voices momentarily drowned out the soft rush of waves.

Robbie gazed into the darkening water. In his hand, the conch shell felt warm and as silken as skin.

'Look, Dad,' said Zach. 'Bats.'

Robbie leaned back to see black shapes dodging sparks above their heads.

'Nice,' he said, his voice thick from drink.

'Well.' Leonard stood and lit another cigarette. 'I'm going to bed.'

'Me, too,' said Zach.

Robbie watched with mild surprise as the boys clambered to their feet, yawning. Emery removed a beer from the cooler, handed it to Robbie.

'Keep an eye on the fire, compadre,' he said, and followed the others.

Robbie turned to study the dying blaze. Ghostly runnels of green and blue ran along the driftwood branch. Salt, Leonard had explained to the boys, though Robbie wondered if that was true. How did Leonard know all this stuff? He frowned, picked up a handful of sand and tossed it at the feeble blaze, which promptly sank into sullen embers.

Robbie swore under his breath. He finished his beer, stood, and walked unsteadily toward the water. The clouds obscured the moon, though there was a faint umber glow reflected in the distant waves. He stared at the horizon, searching in vain for some sign of life, lights from a cruise ship or plane; turned and gazed up and down the length of the beach.

Nothing. Even the bonfire had died. He stood on tiptoe and tried to peer past the high dune, to where the beach house stood within the grove of palmettos. Night swallowed everything,

He turned back to the waves licking at his bare feet. Something stung his face, blown sand or maybe a gnat. He waved to disperse it, then froze.

In the water, plumes of light coiled and unfolded, dazzling him. Deepest violet, a fiery emerald that stabbed his eyes; cobalt and a pure blaze of scarlet. He shook his head, edging backward; caught himself and looked around.

He was alone. He turned back, and the lights were still there, just below the surface, furling and unfurling to some secret rhythm.

Like a machine, he thought; some kind of underwater wind farm. A wave farm?

But no, that was crazy. He rubbed his cheeks, trying to sober up. He'd seen something like this in Ocean City late one night – it was something alive, Leonard had explained, plankton or jellyfish, one of those things that glowed. They'd gotten high and raced into the Atlantic to watch pale green streamers trail them as they body-surfed.

Now he took a deep breath and waded in, kicking at the waves, then halted to see if he'd churned up a luminous cloud.

Darkness lapped almost to his knees: there was no telltale glow where he'd stirred the water. But a few yards away, the lights continued to turn in upon themselves beneath the surface: scores of fist-size nebulae, as soundless and steady as his own pulse.

He stared until his head ached, trying to get a fix on them. The lights weren't diffuse, like phosphorescence. And they didn't float like jellyfish. They seemed to be rooted in place, near enough for him to touch.

Yet his eyes couldn't focus: the harder he tried, the more the lights seemed to shift, like an optical illusion or some dizzying computer game.

He stood there for five minutes, maybe longer. Nothing changed. He started to back away, slowly, finally turned and stumbled across the sand, stopping every few steps to glance over his shoulder. The lights were still there, though now he saw them only as a soft yellowish glow.

He ran the rest of the way to the house. There were no lights on, no music or laughter.

But he could smell cigarette smoke, and traced it to the deck, where Leonard stood beside the rail.

'Leonard!' Robbie drew alongside him, then glanced around for the boys.

'They slept inside,' said Leonard. 'Too cold.'

'Listen, you have to see something. On the beach – these lights. Not on the beach, in the water.' He grabbed Leonard's arm. 'Like – just come on.'

Leonard shook him off angrily. 'You're drunk.'

'I'm not drunk! Or, okay, maybe I am, a little. But I'm not kidding. Look—'

He pointed past the sea of palmettos, past the dunes, toward the dark line of waves. The yellow glow was now spangled with silver. It spread across the water, narrowing as it faded toward the horizon, like a wavering path.

Leonard stared, then turned to Robbie in disbelief. 'You idiot. It's the fucking moon.'

Robbie looked up. And yes, there was the quarter moon, a blaze of gold between gaps in the cloud.

'That's not it.' He knew he sounded not just drunk but desperate. 'It was *in* the water—'

'Bioluminescence.' Leonard sighed and tossed his cigarette, then headed for the door. 'Go to bed, Robbie.'

Robbie started to yell after him, but caught himself and leaned against the rail. His head throbbed. Phantom blots of light swam across his vision. He felt dizzy, and on the verge of tears.

He closed his eyes; forced himself to breathe slowly, to channel the pulsing in his head into the memory of spectral whirlpools, a miniature galaxy blossoming beneath the water. After a minute he looked out again, but saw nothing save the blades of palmetto leaves etched against the moonlit sky.

He woke several hours later on the couch, feeling as though an ax were embedded in his forehead. Gray light washed across the floor. It was cold;

he reached fruitlessly for a blanket, groaned, and sat up.

Emery was in the open kitchen, washing something in the sink. He glanced at Robbie, then hefted a coffeepot. 'Ready for this?'

Robbie nodded, and Emery handed him a steaming mug. 'What time is it?'

'Eight, a little after. The boys are with Leonard – they went out about an hour ago. It looks like rain, which kind of throws a monkey wrench into everything. Maybe it'll hold off long enough to get that thing off the ground.'

Robbie sipped his coffee. 'Seventeen seconds. He could just throw it into the air.'

'Yeah, I thought of that, too. So what happened to you last night?'

'Nothing. Too much Tecate.'

'Leonard said you were raving drunk.'

'Leonard sets the bar pretty low. I was – relaxed.'

'Well, time to unrelax. I told him I'd get you up and we'd be at the beach by eight.'

'I don't even know what I'm doing. Am I a cameraman?'

'Uh-uh. That's me. You don't know how to work it, plus it's my camera. The boys are in charge of the windbreak and, I dunno, props. They hand things to Leonard.'

'Things? What things?' Robbie scowled. 'It's a fucking model airplane. It doesn't have a remote, does it? Because that would have been a *good* idea.'

Emery picked up his camera bag. 'Come on. You

can carry the tripod, how's that? Maybe the boys will hand you things, and you can hand them to Leonard.'

'I'll be there in a minute. Tell Leonard he can start without me.'

After Emery left he finished his coffee and went into his room. He rummaged through his clothes until he found a bottle of ibuprofen, downed six, then pulled on a hooded sweatshirt and sat on the edge of his bed, staring at the wall.

He'd obviously had some kind of blackout, the first since he'd been fired from the parks commission. Somewhere between his seventh beer and this morning's hangover was the blurred image of Crayola-colored pinwheels turning beneath dark water, his stumbling flight from the beach, and Leonard's disgusted voice: *You idiot. It's the fucking moon.*

Robbie grimaced. He *had* seen something, he knew that.

But he could no longer recall it clearly, and what he could remember made no sense. It was like a movie he'd watched half awake, or an accident he'd glimpsed from the corner of his eye from a moving car. Maybe it had been the moonlight, or some kind of fluorescent seaweed.

Or maybe he'd just been totally wasted.

Robbie sighed. He put on his sneakers, grabbed Emery's tripod, and headed out.

A scattering of cold rain met him as he hit the beach. It was windy. The sea glinted gray and silver, like crumpled tinfoil. Clumps of seaweed covered the sand, and small round disks that resembled pieces of clouded glass: jellyfish, hundreds of them. Robbie prodded one with his foot, then continued down the shore.

The dune was on the north side of the island, where it rose steeply a good fifteen feet above the sand. Now, a few hours before low tide, the water was about thirty feet away. It was exactly the kind of place you might choose to launch a human-powered craft, if you knew little about aerodynamics. Robbie didn't know much, but he was fairly certain you needed to be higher to get any kind of lift.

Still, that would be for a full-size craft. For a scale model you could hold in your two cupped hands, maybe it would be high enough. He saw Emery pacing along the water's edge, vid cam slung around his neck. The only sign of the others was a trail of footsteps leading to the dune. Robbie clambered up, using the tripod to keep from slipping on sand the color and texture of damp cornmeal. He was panting when he reached the top.

'Hey, Dad. Where were you?'

Robbie smiled weakly as Zach peered out from the windbreak. 'I have a sinus infection.'

Zach motioned him inside. 'Come on, I can't leave this open.'

Robbie set down the tripod, then crouched to enter the makeshift tent. Inside, bedsheet walls billowed in the wind, straining at an elaborate scaffold of broom handles, driftwood, the remains of wooden deck chairs. Tyler and Zach sat cross-legged on a blanket and stared at their cell phones.

'You can get a strong signal here,' said Tyler. 'Nope, it's gone again.'

Next to them, Leonard knelt beside a cardboard box. Instead of his customary white tunic, he wore one that was sky blue, embroidered with yellow birds. He glanced at Robbie, his gray eyes cold and dismissive. 'There's only room for three people in here.'

'That's okay – I'm going out,' said Zach, and crawled through the gap in the sheets. Tyler followed him. Robbie jammed his hands into his pockets and forced a smile.

'So,' he said. 'Did you see all those jellyfish?'

Leonard nodded without looking at him. Very carefully he removed the *Bellerophon* and set it on a neatly folded towel. He reached into the box again and withdrew something else. A doll no bigger than his hand, dressed in a black frock coat and trousers, with a bowler hat so small that Robbie could have swallowed it.

'Voilà,' said Leonard.

'Jesus, Leonard.' Robbie hesitated, then asked, 'Can I look at it?'

To his surprise, Leonard nodded. Robbie picked it up. The little figure was so light he wondered if there was anything inside the tiny suit.

But as he turned it gently, he could feel slender joints under its clothing, a miniature torso. Tiny

328

hands protruded from the sleeves, and it wore minute, highly polished shoes that appeared to be made of black leather. Under the frock coat was a waistcoat, with a watch chain of gold thread that dangled from a nearly invisible pocket. From beneath the bowler hat peeked a fringe of red hair as fine as milk-weed down. The cameo-size face that stared up at Robbie was Maggie Blevin's, painted in hairline strokes so that he could see every eyelash, every freckle on her rounded cheeks.

He looked at Leonard in amazement. 'How did you do this?'

'It took a long time.' He held out his hand, and Robbie returned the doll. 'The hardest part was making sure the *Bellerophon* could carry her weight. And that she fit into the bicycle seat and could pedal it. You wouldn't think that would be difficult, but it was.'

'It – it looks just like her.' Robbie glanced at the doll again, then said, 'I thought you wanted to make everything look like the original film. You know, with McCauley – I thought that was the point.'

'The point is for it to fly.'

'But—'

'You don't need to understand,' said Leonard. 'Maggie will.'

He bent over the little aircraft, its multicolored wings and silken parasol as bright as a toy carousel, and tenderly began to fit the doll-size pilot into its seat.

Robbie shivered. He'd seen Leonard's handiwork before, mannequins so realistic that tourists constantly poked them to see if they were alive.

But those were life-size, and they weren't designed to resemble someone he *knew*. The sight of Leonard holding a tiny Maggie Blevin tenderly, as though she were a captive bird, made Robbie feel light-headed and slightly sick. He turned toward the tent opening. 'I'll see if I can help Emery set up.'

Leonard's gaze remained fixed on the tiny figure. 'I'll be right there,' he said at last.

At the foot of the dune, the boys were trying to talk Emery into letting them use the camera.

'No way.' He waved as Robbie scrambled down. 'See, I'm not even letting your dad do it.'

'That's because Dad would suck,' Zach said as Emery grabbed Robbie and steered him toward the water. 'Come on, just for a minute.'

'Trouble with the crew?' asked Robbie.

'Nah. They're just getting bored.'

'Did you see that doll?'

'The Incredible Shrinking Maggie?' Emery stopped to stare at the dune. 'The thing about Leonard is, I can never figure out if he's brilliant or potentially dangerous. The fact that he'll be able to retire with a full government pension suggests he's normal. The Maggie voodoo doll, though . . .'

He shook his head and began to pace again. Robbie walked beside him, kicking at wet sand

and staring curiously at the sky. The air smelled odd, of ozone or hot metal. But it felt too chilly for a thunderstorm, and the dark ridge that hung above the palmettos and live oaks looked more like encroaching fog than cumulus clouds.

'Well, at least the wind's from the right direction,' said Robbie.

Emery nodded. 'Yeah. I was starting to think we'd have to throw it from the roof.'

A few minutes later, Leonard's voice rang out above the wind. 'Okay, everyone over here.'

They gathered at the base of the dune and stared up at him, his tunic an azure rent in the ominous sky. Between Leonard's feet was a cardboard box. He glanced at it and went on.

'I'm going to wait till the wind seems right, and then I'll yell, "*Now!*" Emery, you'll just have to watch me and see where she goes, then do your best. Zach and Tyler – you guys fan out and be ready to catch her if she starts to fall. Catch her *gently*,' he added.

'What about me?' called Robbie.

'You stay with Emery in case he needs backup.'

'Backup?' Robbie frowned.

'You know,' said Emery in a low voice. 'In case I need help getting Leonard back to the rubber room.'

The boys began to walk toward the water. Tyler had his cell phone out. He looked at Zach, who dug his phone from his pocket.

'Are they *texting* each other?' asked Emery in disbelief. 'They're ten feet apart.'

331

'Ready?' Leonard shouted.

'Ready,' the boys yelled back.

Robbie turned to Emery. 'What about you, Captain Marvo?'

Emery grinned and held up the camera. 'I have never been readier.'

Atop the dune, Leonard stooped to retrieve the *Bellerophon* from its box. As he straightened, its propellers began turning madly. Candy-striped rotators spun like pinwheels as he cradled it against his chest, his long white braids threatening to tangle with the parasol.

The wind gusted suddenly: Robbie's throat tightened as he watched the tiny black figure beneath the fuselage swing wildly back and forth, like an accelerated pendulum. Leonard slipped in the sand and fought to regain his balance.

'Uh-oh,' said Emery.

The wind died, and Leonard righted himself. Even from the beach, Robbie could see how his face had gone white.

'Are you okay?' yelled Zach.

'I'm okay,' Leonard yelled back.

He gave them a shaky smile, then stared intently at the horizon. After a minute his head tilted, as though listening to something. Abruptly he straightened and raised the *Bellerophon* in both hands. Behind him, palmettos thrashed as the wind gusted.

'*Now!*' he shouted.

Leonard opened his hands. As though it were a

butterfly, the *Bellerophon* lifted into the air. Its feathery parasol billowed. Fan-shaped wings rose and fell; ailerons flapped and gears whirled like pinwheels. There was a sound like a train rushing through a tunnel, and Robbie stared open-mouthed as the *Bellerophon* skimmed the air above his head, its pilot pedaling furiously as it headed toward the sea.

Robbie gasped. The boys raced after it, yelling. Emery followed, camera clamped to his face and Robbie at his heels.

'This is fucking incredible!' Emery shouted. 'Look at that thing go!'

They drew up a few yards from the water. The *Bellerophon* whirred past, barely an arm's length above them. Robbie's eyes blurred as he stared after that brilliant whirl of color and motion, a child's dream of flight soaring just out of reach. Emery waded into the shallows with his camera. The boys followed, splashing and waving at the little plane. From the dune behind them echoed Leonard's voice.

'*Godspeed.*'

Robbie gazed silently at the horizon as the *Bellerophon* continued on, its pilot silhouetted black against the sky, wings opened like sails. Its sound grew fainter, a soft whirring that might have been a flock of birds. Soon it would be gone. Robbie stepped to the water's edge and cranced his neck to keep it in sight.

Without warning a green flare erupted from the waves and streamed toward the little aircraft. Like

333

a meteor shooting *upward*, emerald blossomed into a blinding raidance that engulfed the *Bellerophon*. For an instant Robbie saw the flying machine, a golden wheel spinning within a comet's heart.

Then the blazing light was gone, and with it the *Bellerophon*.

Robbie gazed, stunned, at the empty air. After an endless moment he became aware of something – someone – near him. He turned to see Emery stagger from the water, soaking wet, the camera held uselessly at his side.

'I dropped it,' he gasped. 'When that – whatever the fuck it was, when it came, I dropped the camera.'

Robbie helped him onto the sand.

'I felt it.' Emery shuddered, his hand tight around Robbie's arm. 'Like a riptide. I thought I'd go under.'

Robbie pulled away from him. 'Zach?' he shouted, panicked. 'Tyler, Zach, are you—'

Emery pointed at the water, and Robbie saw them, heron-stepping through the waves and whooping in triumph as they hurried back to shore.

'What happened?' Leonard ran up alongside Robbie and grabbed him. 'Did you see that?'

Robbie nodded. Leonard turned to Emery, his eyes wild. 'Did you get it? The *Bellerophon*? And that flare? Like the original film! The same thing, the exact same thing!'

Emery reached for Robbie's sweatshirt. 'Give me that, I'll see if I can dry the camera.'

Leonard stared blankly at Emery's soaked clothes, the water dripping from the vid cam.

'Oh no.' He covered his face with his hands. 'Oh no . . .'

'We got it!' Zach pushed between the grown-ups. 'We got it, we got it!' Tyler ran up beside him, waving his cell phone. 'Look!'

Everyone crowded together, the boys tilting their phones until the screens showed black.

'Okay,' said Tyler. 'Watch this.'

Robbie shaded his eyes, squinting.

And there it was, a bright mote bobbing across a formless gray field, growing bigger and bigger until he could see it clearly – the whirl of wings and gears, the ballooning peacock-feather parasol and steadfast pilot on the velocipede; the swift, silent flare that lashed from the water then disappeared in an eyeblink.

'Now watch mine,' said Zach, and the same scene played again from a different angle. 'Eighteen seconds.'

'Mine says twenty,' said Tyler.

Robbie glanced uneasily at the water. 'Maybe we should head back to the house,' he said.

Leonard seized Zach's shoulder. 'Can you get me that? Both of you? E-mail it or something?'

'Sure. But we'll need to go where we can get a signal.'

'I'll drive you,' said Emery. 'Let me get into some dry clothes.'

He turned and trudged up the beach, the boys laughing and running behind him.

Leonard walked the last few steps to the water's edge, spray staining the tip of one cowboy boot. He stared at the horizon, his expression puzzled yet oddly expectant.

Robbie hesitated, then joined him. The sea appeared calm, green-glass waves rolling in long swells beneath parchment-colored sky. Through a gap in the clouds he could make out a glint of blue, like a noonday star. He gazed at it in silence, and after a minute asked, 'Did you know that was going to happen?'

Leonard shook his head. 'No. How could I?'

'Then – what was it?' Robbie looked at him helplessly. 'Do you have any idea?'

Leonard said nothing. Finally he turned to Robbie. Unexpectedly, he smiled.

'I have no clue. But you saw it, right?' Robbie nodded. 'And you saw her fly. The *Bellerophon*.'

Leonard took another step, heedless of the waves at his feet. 'She flew.' His voice was barely a whisper. 'She really flew.'

That night nobody slept. Emery drove Zach, Tyler, and Leonard to a Dunkin' Donuts where the boys got a cell-phone signal and sent their movie footage to Leonard's laptop. Back at the house, he disappeared while the others sat on the deck and discussed, over and over again, what they had seen. The boys wanted to return to the beach, but Robbie refused to let them go. As a peace offering, he gave them each a beer. By the time Leonard emerged from his room with the laptop, it was after three A.M.

He set the computer on a table in the living room. 'See what you think.' When the others had assembled, he hit Play.

Blotched letters filled the screen: 'The Maiden Flight of McCauley's *Bellerophon*.' The familiar tipsy horizon appeared, sepia and amber, silvery flashes from the sea below. Robbie held his breath.

And there was the *Bellerophon* with its flickering wheels and wings propelled by a steadfast pilot, until the brilliant light struck from below and the clip abruptly ended, at exactly seventeen seconds. Nothing betrayed the figure as Maggie rather than McCauley; nothing seemed any different at all, no matter how many times Leonard played it back.

'So that's it,' he said at last, and closed his laptop.

'Are you going to put it on YouTube?' asked Zach.

'No,' he replied wearily. The boys exchanged a look, but for once remained silent.

'Well.' Emery stood and stretched his arms, yawning. 'Time to pack.'

Two hours later they were on the road.

The hospice was a few miles outside town, a rambling old white house surrounded by neatly kept azaleas and rhododendrons. The boys were turned loose to wander the neighborhood. The others walked up to the veranda, Leonard carrying his laptop. He looked terrible, his gray eyes bloodshot and his face unshaven. Emery put an arm over his shoulder and Leonard nodded stiffly.

A nurse met them at the door, a trim blond woman in chinos and a yellow blouse.

'I told her you were coming,' she said as she showed them into a sunlit room with wicker furniture and a low table covered with books and magazines. 'She's the only one here now, though we expect someone tomorrow.'

'How is she?' asked Leonard.

'She sleeps most of the time. And she's on morphine for the pain, so she's not very lucid. Her body's shutting down. But she's conscious.'

'Has she had many visitors?' asked Emery.

'Not since she's been here. In the hospital a few neighbors dropped by. I gather there's no family. It's a shame.' She shook her head sadly. 'She's a lovely woman.'

'Can I see her?' Leonard glanced at a closed door at the end of the bright room.

'Of course.'

Robbie and Emery watched them go, then settled into the wicker chairs.

'God, this is depressing,' said Emery.

'It's better than a hospital,' said Robbie. 'Anna was going to go into a hospice, but she died before she could.'

Emery winced. 'Sorry. Of course, I wasn't thinking.'

'It's okay.'

Robbie leaned back and shut his eyes. He saw Anna sitting on the grass with azaleas all around her, bees in the flowers and Zach laughing as he opened his hands to release a green moth that lit momentarily upon her head, then drifted into the sky.

'Robbie.' He started awake. Emery sat beside him, shaking him gently. 'Hey – I'm going in now. Go back to sleep if you want, I'll wake you when I come out.'

Robbie looked around blearily. 'Where's Leonard?'

'He went for a walk. He's pretty broken up. He wanted to be alone for a while.'

'Sure, sure.' Robbie rubbed his eyes. 'I'll just wait.'

When Emery was gone he stood and paced the room. After a few minutes he sighed and sank back into his chair, then idly flipped through the magazines and books on the table. *Tricycle*, *Newsweek*, the *Utne Reader*; some pamphlets on end-of-life issues; works by Viktor Frankl and Elisabeth Kübler-Ross.

And, underneath yesterday's newspaper, a familiar sky blue dust jacket emblazoned with the garish image of a naked man and woman, hands linked as they floated above a vast abyss, surrounded by a glowing purple sphere. Beneath them the title appeared in embossed green letters.

Wings for Humanity!
The Next Step is OURS!
by Margaret S. Blevin, PhD

Robbie picked it up. On the back was a photograph of the younger Maggie in a white, embroidered tunic, her hair a bright corona around her piquant face. She stood in the Hall of Flight beside a mock-up of the *Apollo* lunar module, the Wright Flyer high above her head. She was laughing, her hands raised in welcome. He opened it to a random page.

> *. . . that time has come: with the dawn of the Golden Millennium we will welcome their return, meeting them at last as equals to share in the glory that is the birthright of our species.*

He glanced at the frontispiece and title page, and then the dedication.
For Leonard, who never doubted
'Isn't that an amazing book?'
Robbie looked up to see the nurse smiling down at him.
'Uh, yeah,' he said, and set it on the table.
'It's incredible she predicted so much stuff.' The nurse shook her head. 'Like the Hubble telescope, and that caveman they found in the glacier, the guy with the lens? And those turbines that can make energy in the jet stream? I never even heard of that, but my husband said they're

real. Everything she says, it's all so hopeful. You know?'

Robbie stared at her, then quickly nodded. Behind her the door opened. Emery stepped out.

'She's kind of drifting,' he said.

'Morning's her good time. She usually fades around now.' The nurse glanced at her watch, then at Robbie. 'You go ahead. Don't be surprised if she nods off.'

He stood. 'Sure. Thanks.'

The room was small, its walls painted a soft lavender-gray. The bed faced a large window overlooking a garden. Goldfinches and tiny green wrens darted between a bird feeder and a small pool lined with flat white stones. For a moment Robbie thought the bed was empty. Then he saw that an emaciated figure had slipped down between the white sheets, dwarfed by pillows and a bolster.

'Maggie?'

The figure turned its head. Hairless, skin white as paper, mottled with bruises like spilled ink. Her lips and fingernails were violet, her face so pale and lined it was like gazing at a cracked egg. Only the eyes were recognizably Maggie's, huge, the deep slatey blue of an infant's. As she stared at him, she drew her wizened arms up, slowly, until her fingers grazed her shoulders. She reminded Robbie disturbingly of a praying mantis.

'I don't know if you remember me.' He sat in a chair beside the bed. 'I'm Robbie. I worked with Leonard. At the museum.'

341

'He told me.' Her voice was so soft he had to lean close to hear her. 'I'm glad they got here. I expected them yesterday, when it was still snowing.'

Robbie recalled Anna in her hospital bed, doped to the gills and talking to herself. 'Sure,' he said.

Maggie shot him a glance that might have held annoyance, then gazed past him into the garden. Her eyes widened as she struggled to lift her hand, fingers twitching. Robbie realized she was waving. He turned to stare out the window, but there was no one there. Maggie looked at him, then gestured at the door.

'You can go now,' she said. 'I have guests.'

'Oh. Yeah, sorry.'

He stood awkwardly, then leaned down to kiss the top of her head. Her skin was as smooth and cold as metal. ''Bye, Maggie.'

At the door he looked back, and saw her gazing with a rapt expression at the window, head cocked slightly and her hands open, as though to catch the sunlight.

Two days after they got home, Robbie received an e-mail from Leonard.

Dear Robbie,
Maggie died this morning. The nurse said she became unconscious early yesterday, seemed to be in pain but at least it didn't last long. She had arranged to be cremated. No memorial

service or anything like that. I will do some-
thing, probably not till the fall, and let you
know.
Yours,
Leonard

Robbie sighed. Already the week on Cowana seemed long ago and faintly dreamlike, like the memory of a childhood vacation. He wrote Leonard a note of condolence, then left for work.

Weeks passed. Zach and Tyler posted their clips of the *Bellerophon* online. Robbie met Emery for drinks every week or two, and saw Leonard once, at Emery's Fourth of July barbecue. By the end of summer, Tyler's footage had been viewed 347,623 times, and Zach's 347,401. Both provided a link to the Captain Marvo site, where Emery had a free download of the entire text of *Wings for Humanity!* There were now over a thousand Google hits for Margaret Blevin, and Emery added a *Bellerophon* T-shirt to his merchandise: organic cotton with a silk-screened image of the baroque aircraft and its bowler-hatted pilot.

Early in September, Leonard called Robbie.

'Can you meet me at the museum tomorrow, around eight thirty? I'm having a memorial for Maggie, just you and me and Emery. After hours, I'll sign you in.'

'Sure,' said Robbie. 'Can I bring something?'

'Just yourself. See you then.'

He drove in with Emery. They walked across the

twilit Mall, the museum a white cube that glowed against a sky swiftly darkening to indigo. Leonard waited for them by the side door. He wore an embroidered tunic, sky blue, his white hair loose upon his shoulders, and held a cardboard box with a small printed label.

'Come on,' he said. The museum had been closed since five, but a guard opened the door for them. 'We don't have a lot of time.'

Hedges sat at the security desk, bald and even more imposing than when Robbie last saw him, decades ago. He signed them in, eyeing Robbie curiously then grinning when he read his signature.

'I remember you – Opie, right?'

Robbie winced at the nickname, then nodded. Hedges handed Leonard a slip of paper. 'Be quick.'

'Thanks. I will.'

They walked to the staff elevator, the empty museum eerie and blue lit. High above them the silent aircraft seemed smaller than they had been in the past, battered and oddly toylike. Robbie noticed a crack in the *Gemini VII* space capsule, and strands of dust clinging to the Wright Flyer. When they reached the third floor, Leonard led them down the corridor, past the photo lab, past the staff cafeteria, past the library where the Nut Files used to be. Finally he stopped at a door near some open ductwork. He looked at the slip of paper Hedges had given him, punched a series of numbers into the lock, opened it then reached in to switch on the light. Inside was a narrow room with a metal ladder fixed to one wall.

'Where are we going?' asked Robbie.

'The roof,' said Leonard. 'If we get caught, Hedges and I are screwed. Actually, we're all screwed. So we have to make this fast.'

He tucked the cardboard box against his chest, then began to climb the ladder. Emery and Robbie followed him, to a small metal platform and another door. Leonard punched in another code and pushed it open. They stepped out into the night.

It was like being atop an ocean liner. The museum's roof was flat, nearly a block long. Hot air blasted from huge exhaust vents, and Leonard motioned the others to move away, toward the far end of the building.

The air was cooler here, a breeze that smelled sweet and rain-washed, despite the cloudless sky. Beneath them stretched the Mall, a vast green game board, with the other museums and monuments huge game pieces, ivory and onyx and glass. The spire of the Washington Monument rose in the distance, and beyond that the glittering reaches of Roslyn and Crystal City.

'I've never been here,' said Robbie, stepping beside Leonard.

Emery shook his head. 'Me neither.'

'I have,' said Leonard, and smiled. 'Just once, with Maggie.'

Above the Capitol's dome hung the full moon,

so bright against the starless sky that Robbie could read what was printed on Leonard's box.

MARGARET BLEVIN

'These are her ashes.' Leonard set the box down and removed the top, revealing a ziplocked bag. He opened the bag, picked up the box again, and stood. 'She wanted me to scatter them here. I wanted both of you to be with me.'

He dipped his hand into the bag and withdrew a clenched fist; held the box out to Emery, who nodded silently and did the same; then turned to Robbie.

'You too,' he said.

Robbie hesitated, then put his hand into the box. What was inside felt gritty, more like sand than ash. When he looked up, he saw that Leonard had stepped forward, head thrown back so that he gazed at the moon. He drew his arm back, flung the ashes into the sky, and stooped to grab more.

Emery glanced at Robbie, and the two of them opened their hands.

Robbie watched the ashes stream from between his fingers, like a flight of tiny moths. Then he turned and gathered more, the three of them tossing handful after handful into the sky.

When the box was finally empty, Robbie straightened, breathing hard, and ran a hand across his eyes. He didn't know if it was some trick of the moonlight or the freshening wind, but everywhere around them, everywhere he looked, the air was filled with wings.

The
Devil on
the Staircase
by
Joe
Hill

I was
born in
Sulle Scale
the child of a
common bricklayer.

The
village
of my birth
nested in the
highest sharpest
ridges, high above
Positano, and in the
cold spring the clouds
crawled along the streets
like a procession of ghosts.
It was eight hundred and twenty
steps from Sulle Scale to the world
below. I know. I walked them again and
again with my father, following his tread,
from our home in the sky, and then back again.
After his death I walked them often enough alone.

Up
  and   each
    down   with   step
      carrying   until   it
          freight   seemed as
if the bones
in my knees were
being ground up into
sharp white splinters.

The
cliffs
were mazed
with crooked
staircases, made
from brick in some
places, granite in others.
Marble here, limestone there,
clay tiles, or beams of lumber.
When there were stairs to build my
father built them. When the steps were
washed out by spring rains it fell to him
to repair them. For years he had a donkey to
carry his stone. After it fell dead, he had me.

                                                    I
                                                hated
                                              him of
                                             course.
                                          He had his
                                        cats and he
                                       sang to them
                                     and poured them
                                   saucers of milk and
                                 told them foolish stories
                               and stroked them in his lap
                             and when one time I kicked one –
                          I do not remember why – he kicked me to
                             the floor and said not to touch his babies.

So I
carried
his rocks
when I should
have been carrying
schoolbooks, but I cannot
pretend I hated him for that.
I had no use for school, hated to
study, hated to read, felt acutely the
stifling heat of the single room schoolhouse,

the only good thing in it my cousin, Lithodora, who read
to the little children, sitting on a stool with her back erect,
chin lifted high, and her white throat showing.

                                                I
                                           often
                                       imagined
                                     her throat
                                was as cool as
                            the marble altar
                         in our church and I
                   I wanted to rest my brow
               upon it as I had the altar.
        How she read in her low steady
         voice, the very voice you dream of
         calling to you when you're sick, saying
       you will be healthy again and know only the
      sweet fever of her body. I could've loved books
  if I had her to read them to me, beside me in my bed.
I
knew
every
step of
the stairs
between Sulle
Scale and Positano,
long flights that dropped
through canyons and descended
into tunnels bored in the limestone,
past orchards and the ruins of derelict
paper mills, past waterfalls and green pools.
I walked those stairs when I slept, in my dreams.

                                              The
                                            trail
                                    my father
                               and I walked
                           most often led
                        past a painted red
                    gate, barring the way
                 to a crooked staircase.

I thought those steps led to
a private villa and paid the gate
no mind until the day I paused on the
way down with a load of marble and leaned
on it to rest and it swung open to my touch.

My
father,
he lagged
thirty or so
stairs behind me.
I stepped through the
gate onto the landing to
see where these stairs led.
I saw no villa or vineyard below,
only the staircase falling away from
me down among the sheerest of sheer cliffs.

'Father,'
I called out
as he came near,
the slap of his feet
echoing off the rocks and
his breath whistling out of him.
'Have you ever taken these stairs?'

When
he saw
me standing
inside the gate
he paled and had my
shoulder in an instant
was hauling me back onto
the main staircase. He said,
'How did you open the red gate?'

'It was
open when
I got here,'
I said. 'Don't
they lead all the
way down to the sea?'

'No.'
'But it

looks as if
they go all the
way to the bottom.'
                                                'They go
                                            farther than
                                          that,' my father
                                      said and he crossed
                                    himself. Then he said
                                 again, 'The gate is always
                              locked.' And he stared at me,
                        the whites of his eyes showing. I
                    had never seen him look at me so, had
              never thought I would see him afraid of me.

Lithodora
laughed when
I told her and
said my father was
old and superstitious.
She told me that there was
a tale that the stairs beyond
the painted gate led down to hell.
I had walked the mountain a thousand
times more than Lithodora and wanted to
know how she could know such a story when
I myself had never heard any mention of it.

                                              She said
                                      the old folks
                                   never spoke of it,
                               but had put the story
                             down in a history of the
                           region, which I would know
                          if I had ever read any of the
                        teacher's assignments. I told her
                 I could never concentrate on books when
            she was in the same room with me. She laughed.
           But when I tried to touch her throat she flinched.

My
fingers
brushed her

breast instead
and she was angry
and she told me that
I needed to wash my hands.

> After
> my father
> died – he was
> walking down the
> stairs with a load
> of tiles when a stray
> cat shot out in front of
> him and rather than step on
> it, he stepped into space and
> fell fifty feet to be impaled upon
> a tree – I found a more lucrative use
> for my donkey legs and yardarm shoulders.
> I entered the employ of Don Carlotta who kept
> a terraced vineyard in the steeps of Sulle Scale.

I hauled
his wine down
the eight hundred
odd steps to Positano,
where it was sold to a rich
Saracen, a prince it was told,
dark and slender and more fluent
in my language than myself, a clever
young man who knew how to read things:
musical notes, the stars, a map, a sextant.

> Once I
> stumbled
> on a flight
> of brick steps
> as I was making my
> way down with the Don's
> wine and a strap slipped and
> the crate on my back struck the
> cliff wall and a bottle was smashed.
> I brought it to the Saracen on the quay.
> He said either I drank it or I should have,

for that bottle was worth all I made in a month.
He told me I could consider myself paid and paid well.
He laughed and his white teeth flashed in his black face.
I was
sober when
he laughed at
me but soon enough
had a head full of wine.
Not Don Carlotta's smooth and
peppery red mountain wine but the
cheapest Chianti in the Taverna, which
I drank with a passel of unemployed friends.

Lithodora
found me after
it was dark and she
stood over me, her dark
hair framing her cool, white
beautiful, disgusted, loving face.
She said she had the silver I was owed.
She had told her friend Ahmed that he had
insulted an honest man, that my family traded
in hard labor, not lies and he was lucky I had not –
' – did
you call
him friend?'
I said. 'A monkey
of the desert who knows
nothing of Christ the lord?'

The way that
she looked at me
then made me ashamed.
The way she put the money in
front of me made me more ashamed.
'I see you have more use for this than
you have for me,' she said before she went.
I almost
got up to go
after her. Almost.
One of my friends asked,

'Have you heard the Saracen
gave your cousin a slave bracelet,
a loop of silver bells, to wear around
her ankle? I suppose in the Arab lands, such
gifts are made to every new whore in the harem.'
I came
to my feet
so quickly my
chair fell over.
I grabbed his throat
in both hands and said,
'You lie. Her father would
never allow her to accept such
a gift from a godless blackamoor.'
But
another
friend said
the Arab trader
was godless no more.
Lithodora had taught Ahmed
to read Latin, using the Bible
as his grammar, and he claimed now
to have entered into the light of Christ,
and he gave the bracelet to her with the full
knowledge of her parents, as a way to show thanks
for introducing him to the grace of our Father who art.
When
my first
friend had
recovered his
breath, he told
me Lithodora climbed
the stairs every night
to meet with him secretly
in empty shepherds' huts or in
the caves, or among the ruins of
the paper mills, by the roar of the
waterfall, as it leapt like liquid silver
in the moonlight, and in such places she was
his pupil and he a firm and most demanding tutor.

He
always
went ahead
and then she
would ascend the
stairs in the dark
wearing the bracelet.
When he heard the bells he would light a candle to show her
where he waited to begin the lesson.

                                                    I
                                                 was
                                           so drunk.

I set
out for
Lithodora's
house, with no
idea what I meant
to do when I got there.
I came up behind the cottage
where she lived with her parents
thinking I would throw a few stones
to wake her and bring her to her window.
But as I stole toward the back of the house
I heard a silvery tinkling somewhere above me.

                                         She was
                                      already on
                                   the stairs and
                                 climbing into the
                              stars with her white
                           dress swinging from her
                        hips and the bracelet around
                     her ankle so bright in the gloom.

My
heart.
thudded,
a cask flung
down a staircase:
doom doom doom doom.
I knew the hills better
than anyone and I ran another

way, making a steep climb up crude
steps of mud to get ahead of her, then
rejoining the main path up to Sulle Scale.
I still had the silver coin the Saracen prince
had given her, when she went to him and dishonored
me by begging him to pay me the wage I was properly
owed.

> I put
> his silver
> in a tin cup
> I had and slowed
> to a walk and went
> along shaking his Judas
> coin in my old battered mug.
> Such a pretty ringing, It made in
> the echoing canyons, on the stairs;
> in the night, high above Positano and the
> crash and sigh of the sea, as the tide consummated
> the desire of water to pound the earth into submission.

At
last,
pausing
to catch my
breath, I saw
a candleflame leap
up off in the darkness.
It was in a handsome ruin,
a place of high granite walls
matted with wildflowers and ivy.
A vast entryway looked into a room
with a grass floor and a roof of stars,
as if the place had been built, not to give shelter from the
natural world, but to protect a virgin corner of wildness
from the violation of man.

> Then
> again it
> seemed a pagan
> place, the natural
> setting for an orgy hosted

by fauns with their goaty hooves,
their flutes and their furred cocks.
So the archway into that private courtyard
of weeds and summer green seemed the entrance
to a hall awaiting revelers for a private bacchanal.
He
waited
on spread
blanket, with
a bottle of the
Don's wine and some
books and he smiled at
the tinkling sound of my
approach but stopped when I
came into the light, a block of
rough stone already in my free hand.

I
killed
him there.

I did
not kill
him out of
family honor
or jealousy, did
not hit him with the
stone because he had laid
claim to Lithodora's cool white
body, which she would never offer me.

I
hit
him with
the block of
stone because I
hated his black face.

After
I stopped
hitting him,
I sat with him.
I think I took his

wrist to see if he had
a pulse, but after I knew
he was dead, I went on holding
his hand listening to the hum of the
crickets in the grass, as if he were a
small child, *my* child, who had only drifted
off after fighting sleep for a very long time.

What
brought
me out of
my stupor was
the sweet music
of bells coming up
the stairs toward us.

I leapt
up and ran
but Dora was
already there,
coming through the
doorway, and I nearly
struck her on my way by.
She reached out for me with
one of her delicate white hands
and said my name but I did not stop.
I took the stairs three at a time, running
without thought, but I was not fast enough and
I heard her when she shouted *his* name, once and again.

I
don't
know where
I was running.
Sulle Scale, maybe,
though I knew they would
look for me there first once
Lithodora went down the steps and
told them what I had done to the Arab.
I did not slow down until I was gulping for
air and my chest was filled with fire and then
I leaned against a gate at the side of the path –

you know
what gate –

                          and it
                    swung open
                at first touch.
        I went through the
      gate and started down
    the steep staircase beyond.
  I thought no one will look for
me here and I can hide a while and –

No.

                            I
                     thought,
                 these stairs
             will lead to the
         road and I will head
      north to Napoli and buy
    a ticket for a ship to the U.S.
  and take a new name, start a new –

No.
Enough.
The truth:

                            I
                   believed
               the stairs
           led down into
       hell and hell was
    where I wanted to go.

The
steps
at first
were of old
white stone, but
as I continued along
they grew sooty and dark.
Other staircases merged with
them here and there, descending
from other points on the mountain.
I couldn't see how that was possible.

I thought I had walked all the flights of
stairs in the hills, except for the steps I
was on and I couldn't think for the life of me
where those other staircases might be coming from.
The
forest
around me
had been purged
by fire at some time
in the not so far-off past,
and I made my descent through
stands of scorched, shattered pines,
the hillside all blackened and charred.
Only there had been no fire on that part of
the hill, not for as long as I could remember.
The breeze carried on it an unmistakable warmth.
I began to feel unpleasantly overheated in my clothes.
I
followed
the staircase
round a switchback
and saw below me a boy
sitting on a stone landing.

He
had a
collection
of curious wares
spread on a blanket.
There was a wind-up tin
bird in a cage, a basket of
white apples, a dented gold lighter.
There was a jar and in the jar was light.
This light would increase in brightness until
the landing was lit as if by the rising sun, and
then it would collapse into darkness, shrinking to a
single point like some impossibly brilliant lightning bug.
He
smiled
to see me.

He had golden
hair and the most
beautiful smile I have
ever seen on a child's face
and I was afraid of him – even
before he called out to me by name.
I pretended I didn't hear him, pretended
he wasn't there, that I didn't see him, walked
right past him. He laughed to see me hurrying by.

                                                    The
                                                farther
                                            I went the
                                        steeper it got.
                                There seemed to be
                            a light below, as if
                    somewhere beyond a ledge,
                through the trees, there was
            a great city, on the scale of Roma,
        a bowl of lights like a bed of embers.
    I could smell food cooking on the breeze.

If
it was
food – that
hungry-making
perfume of meat
charring over flame.

                                                    Voices
                                            ahead of me:
                                        a man speaking
                                    wearily, perhaps
                                to himself, a long
                            and joyless discourse;
                    someone else laughing, bad
                laughter, unhinged and angry.
        A third man was asking questions.

'Is
a plum
sweeter after
it has been pushed

in the mouth of a virgin
to silence her as she is taken?
And who will claim the baby child
sleeping in the cradle made from the
rotten carcass of the lamb that laid with
the lion only to be eviscerated?' And so on.

                                          At
                                         the
                                        next
                                     turn in
                                   the steps
                                 they finally
                              came into sight.
                          They lined the stairs:
                       half a dozen men nailed on
                        to crosses of blackened pine.
                       I couldn't go on and for a time
                       I couldn't go back; it was the cats.
                   One of the men had a wound in his side,
                a red seeping would that made a puddle on
                    the stairs, and kittens lapped at it as if it
           were cream and he was talking to them in his tired
           voice, telling all the good kitties to drink their fill.

I
did
not go
close enough
to see his face.

                                          At
                                        last
                                   I returned
                                 the way I had
                              come on shaky legs.
                        The boy awaited me with
                           his collection of oddities.

'Why
not sit
and rest your
sore feet, Quirinus

Calvino?' he asked me.
And I sat down across from
him, not because I wanted to but
because that was where my legs gave out.

Neither of us spoke at first. He smiled across the blanket spread with his goods, and I pretended an interest in the stone wall that overhung the landing there. That light in the jar built and built until our shadows lunged against the rock like deformed giants, before the brightness winked out and plunged us back into our shared darkness. He offered me a skin of water but I knew better than to take anything from that child. Or thought I knew better. The light in the jar began to grow again, a single floating point of perfect whiteness, swelling like a balloon. I tried to look at it, but felt a pinch of pain in the back of my eye-balls and glanced away.

'What is that? It burns my eyes,' I asked.

'A little spark stolen from the sun. You can do all sorts of wonderful things with it. You could make a furnace with it, a giant furnace, powerful enough to warm a whole city, and light a thousand Edison lights. Look how bright it gets. You have to be careful though. If you were to smash this jar and let the spark escape, that same city would disappear in a clap of brightness. You can have it if you want.'

'No, I don't want it,' I said.

'No. Of course not. That isn't your sort of thing.

No matter. Someone will be along later for this. But take something. Anything you want,' he said.

'Are you Lucifer?' I asked in a rough voice.

'Lucifer is an awful old goat who has a pitchfork and hooves and makes people suffer. I hate suffering. I only want to help people. I give gifts. That's why I'm here. Everyone who walks these stairs before their time gets a gift to welcome them. You look thirsty. Would you like an apple?' Holding up the basket of white apples as he spoke.

I was thirsty – my throat felt not just sore, but singed, as if I had inhaled smoke recently, and I began to reach for the offered fruit, almost reflexively, but then drew my hand back for I knew the lessons of at least one book. He grinned at me.

'Are those—' I asked.

'They're from a very old and honorable tree,' he said. 'You will never taste a sweeter fruit. And when you eat of it, you will be filled with ideas. Yes, even one such as you, Quirinus Calvino, who barely learned to read.'

'I don't want it,' I said, when what I really wanted to tell him was not to call me by name. I could not bear that he knew my name.

He said, 'Everyone will want it. They will eat and eat and be filled with understanding. Why, learning how to speak another language will be as simple as, oh, learning to build a bomb. Just one bite of the apple away. What about the lighter? You can light anything with this lighter. A cigarette. A pipe. A campfire. Imaginations. Revolutions. Books. Rivers.

The sky. Another man's soul. Even the human soul has a temperature at which it becomes flammable. The lighter has an enchantment on it, is tapped into the deepest wells of oil on the planet, and will set fire to things for as long as the oil lasts, which I am sure will be forever.'

'You have nothing I want,' I said.

'I have something for everyone,' he said.

I rose to my feet, ready to leave, although I had nowhere to go. I couldn't walk back down the stairs. The thought made me dizzy. Neither could I go back up. Lithodora would have returned to the village by now. They would be searching the stairs for me with torches. I was surprised I hadn't heard them already.

The tin bird turned its head to look at me as I swayed on my heels, and blinked, the metal shutters of its eyes snapping closed, then popping open again. It let out a rusty cheep. So did I, startled by its sudden movement. I had thought it a toy, inanimate. It watched me steadily and I stared back. I had, as a child, always had an interest in ingenious mechanical objects, clockwork people who ran out of their hiding places at the stroke of noon, the woodcutter to chop wood, the maiden to dance a round. The boy followed my gaze, and smiled, then opened the cage and reached in for it. The bird leaped lightly onto his finger.

'It sings the most beautiful song,' he said. 'It finds a master, a shoulder it likes to perch on, and it sings for this person all the rest of its days. The trick to making it sing for you is to tell a lie. The bigger the better. Feed it a lie, and it will sing you the most marvelous little tune. People love to hear its song. They love it so much, they don't even care they're being lied to. He's yours if you want him.'

'I don't want anything from you,' I said, but when I said it, the bird began to whistle: the sweetest, softest melody, as good a sound as the laughter of a pretty girl, or your mother calling you to dinner. The song sounded a bit like something played on a music box, and I imagined a studded cylinder turning inside it, banging the teeth of a silver comb. I shivered to hear it. In this place, on these stairs, I had never imagined I could hear something so right.

He laughed and waved his hand at me. The bird's wings snapped from the side of its body, like knives leaping from sheaths, and it glided up and lit on my shoulder.

'You see,' said the boy on the stairs. 'It likes you.'

'I can't pay,' I said, my voice rough and strange.

'You've already paid,' said the boy.

Then he turned his head and looked down the stairs and seemed to listen. I heard a wind rising. It made a low, soughing moan as it came up through the channel of the staircase, a deep and lonely and restless cry. The boy looked back at me. 'Now go. I hear my father coming. The awful old goat.'

I backed away and my heels struck the stair
behind me. I was in such a hurry to get away I
fell sprawling across the granite steps. The bird
on my shoulder took off, rising in widening circles
through the air, but when I found my feet it glided
down to where it had rested before on my
shoulder
and I began
to run back up
the way I had come.

                                                                                    I
                                                            climbed
                                                        in haste for
                                                    a time but soon
                                                was tired again and
                                            had to slow to a walk.
                                    I began to think about what
                                I would say when I reached the
                            main staircase and was discovered.
                            'I will confess everything and accept
                        my punishment, whatever that is,' I said.
            The tin bird sang a gay and humorous ditty.

It
fell
silent
though as
I reached the
gate, quieted by
a different song not
far off: a girl's sobs.
I listened, confused, and
crept uncertainly back to where
I had murdered Lithodora's beloved.
I heard no sound except for Dora's cries.
No men shouting, no feet running on the steps.
I had been gone half the night, it seemed to me but
when I reached the ruins where I had left the Saracen
and looked upon Dora it was as if only minutes had passed.

I
came
toward
her and
whispered
to her, afraid
almost to be heard.
The second time I spoke
her name she turned her head
and looked at me with red-rimmed
hating eyes and screamed to get away.
I wanted to comfort her, to tell her I was
sorry, but when I came close she sprang to her
feet and ran at me, striking me and flaying at my
face with her fingernails while she cursed my name.
I meant
to put my
hands on her
shoulders to hold
her still but when I
reached for her they found
her smooth white neck instead.

Her
father
and his
fellows and
my unemployed
friends discovered
me weeping over her.
Running my fingers through
the silk of her long black hair.
Her father fell to his knees and took
her in his arms and for a while the hills
rang with her name repeated over and over again.
Another
man, who held
a rifle, asked me
what had happened and
I told him – I told him –

the Arab, that monkey from the
desert, had lured her here and when
he couldn't force her innocence from her
he throttled her in the grass and I found them
and we fought and I killed him with a block of stone.
                                                And
                                              as I
                                          told it
                                  the tin bird
                          began to whistle
                      and sing, the most
                  mournful and sweetest
              melody I had ever heard
          and the men listened until
      the sad song was sung complete.
I
held
Lithodora
in my arms as
we walked back down.
And as we went on our way
the bird began to sing again as
I told them the Saracen had planned
to take the sweetest and most beautiful
girls and auction their white flesh in Araby –
a more profitable line of trade than selling wine.
The bird was by now whistling a marching song and the
faces of the men who walked with me were rigid and dark.
                                            Ahmed's
                                      men burned
                                  along with the
                              Arab's ship, and
                          sank in the harbor.
                      His goods, stored in a
                  warehouse by the quay, were
              seized and his money box fell
          to me as a reward for my heroism.
No
one

ever
would've
imagined when
I was a boy that
one day I would be
the wealthiest trader
on the whole Amalfi coast,
or that I would come to own the
prized vineyards of Don Carlotta, I
who once worked like a mule for his coin.

No
one
would've
guessed that
one day I would
be the beloved mayor
of Sulle Scale, or a man
of such renown that I would be
invited to a personal audience with
his holiness the pope himself, who thanked
me for my many well-noted acts of generosity.

The
springs
inside the
pretty tin bird
wore down, in time,
and it ceased to sing,
but by then it did not matter
if anyone believed my lies or not
such was my wealth and power and fame.

However.
Several years
before the tin bird
fell silent, I woke one
morning in my manor to find
it had constructed a nest of wire
on my windowsill, and filled it with
fragile eggs made of bright silver foil.
I regarded these eggs with unease but when I

reached to touch them, their mechanical mother
nipped at me with her needle-sharp beak and I did
not after that time make any attempt to disturb them.
Months
later the
nest was filled
with foil tatters.
The young of this new
species, creatures of a new
age, had fluttered on their way.

                                                                    I
                                                             cannot
                                                          tell you
                                              how many birds
                                            of tin and wire and
                                        electric current there
                                  are in the world now – but I
                            have, this very month, heard speak
                        our newest prime minister, Mr Mussolini.
            When he sings of the greatness of the Italian
      people and our kinship with our German neighbors,
   I am quite sure I can hear a tin bird singing with him.
Its tune plays especially well amplified over modern radio.
I don't
live in the
hills anymore.
It has been years
since I saw Sulle Scale.
I discovered, as I descended
at last into my senior years, that
I could no longer attempt the staircases.
I told people it was my poor sore old knees.
                              But in truth I
                              developed a
                                 fear of
                                  heights.

ABOUT THE CONTRIBUTORS

Chuck Palahniuk is the author of *Fight Club* and numerous other novels, including the recent novel *Pygmy*. He is the recipient of many awards, among them the Pacific Northwest Bookseller Association Award. He lives in Washington State.

Diana Wynne Jones has written many fantasy novels for adults and children, among them the Chrestomanci series, which won the 1977 Guardian Award for children's books. Her *Howl's Moving Castle* was made into a notable film by Japanese director Havai Miazaki. She lives in Great Britain.

Pittsburgh native **Stewart O'Nan** is the author of numerous novels, such as *Songs for the Missing* and *The Good Wife*. His first short story collection, *In the Walled City*, was awarded the Drue Heinz Literature Prize in 1933.

Multiple award-winning science fiction and fantasy writter **Gene Wolf** is perhaps best known for *The Book of the New Sun*, which comprises four volumes. He lives in Illinois.

Carolyn Parkhurst is the bestselling author of *The Dogs of Babel* (which was also a *New York Times* notable book in 2003) and *Lost and Found*. She lives in Washington, D.C.

Kat Howard currently lives in Minneapolis. She earned a law degree, then acquired a Ph.D. in English literature, both from the University of Minnesota. She is a 2008 graduate of the Clarion Writers' Workshop. 'A Life in Fictions' is her first published story.

Jonathan Carroll, generally considered a magic realist, is the author of the novel *The Land of the Laughs* and many others. He has won the Bram Stoker, World Fantasy, and British Fantasy awards.

International number one bestselling author **Jeffery Deaver's** books are sold in 150 countries and have been translated into 25 languages. He is the winner of numerous awards. His most recent books are *The Bodies Left Behind* and *More Twisted: Collected Stories, Volume II*.

Tim Powers, another magic realist, has won the World Fantasy Award two times, for his novels *Last Call* and *Declare*. Born in Buffalo, New York, he grew up in California, where he still lives.

Kurt Andersen is a novelist and host of the public radio program *Studio 360*. A cofounder of *Spy* magazine and former editor in chief of *New York* magazine, he has also written for *Vanity Fair, Time*, the *New York Times*, and the *New Yorker*.

Michael Moorcock has published science fiction and fantasy novels, as well as more overtly literary works. As editor of *New Worlds* magazine, he helped foster the new wave movement in science fiction, which helped bring it into the literary mainstream.

Elizabeth Hand grew up in New York and currently lives in Maine. She is the winner of the World Fantasy, Shirley Jackson, and International Horror Guild awards. Among her novels are *Illyria* and *Generation Loss*.

New England native **Joe Hill**'s first novel, *Heart-Shaped Box*, was a best-seller. He has won many awards. His first short-story collection, *20th Century Ghosts*, was published in 2005, and his most recent novel is *Horns*.